Unattainable

Leslie P. García

CRIMSON
ROMANCE

F+W Media, Inc.

This edition published by
Crimson Romance
an imprint of F+W Media, Inc.
10151 Carver Road, Suite 200
Blue Ash, Ohio 45242

www.crimsonromance.com

ISBN 10: 1-4405-6553-8
ISBN 13: 978-1-4405-6553-3
eISBN 10: 1-4405-6554-6
eISBN 13: 978-1-4405-6554-0

DEDICATION

Many people support us through our lives, and garner our love, devotion, and gratitude. My life has been touched by so many of you along the way, and I thank you all.

Cruzito, Jamie, Greg, and Lee—thank you for what I know were sacrifices along this road, and I dedicate *Unattainable* to each of you. You've provided love, support, inspiration, and the occasional headache—in other words, the substance of any worthwhile life. No mother could be prouder of her children than I am of you. No one can love you more.

And Stephanie and Vicky—you've shared a lifetime getting here with me, and are part of everything I've done. It seems to me that sisters share a very special love, and for that and all the rest— I'm grateful beyond words. If anyone knows how much it means to me dedicate this book to you, the two of you do. Love always.

ACKNOWLEDGMENTS

To my brother-in-law Daniel Ortiz—thanks for sharing your criminal justice background and years of dealing with troubled teens to help me understand issues, risks, and how committed individuals like you can provide solutions and hope.

To friend and U.S. Customs and Border Protection agent, Vessel Commander Lázaro Pérez, Jr., thanks for real insight into the day to day details of your job. First responders are the backbone of any community, but those who protect the nation's borders assume responsibility for the safety of an entire country.

Finally, I want to thank my editors Jennifer Lawler, Katriena Knights and Jess Verdi for their enthusiasm and professionalism in welcoming me to Crimson Romance. And for finally giving me reason to leave work on time shouting, "I have to go check my e-mail! Have to go do revisions!" I probably still should have signed out, but . . .

CHAPTER ONE

Jovani Treviño slipped from the pickup, his boots thudding dully on the dry soil as he looked around carefully but not with particular unease. A crescent moon climbed up over the far side of the interstate, but here darkness allowed considerable isolation. Cars speeding by on the freeway wouldn't notice him, and if they did, hopefully they'd avert their eyes, assuming someone needed to take a leak.

Only moments passed before a second, dark vehicle pulled in behind him. The driver switched off the headlights but left the parking lights on. Jovi reached into the cab and pulled the lever to open the hood then moved to the front of the truck. Seconds later the newcomer joined him, extending his hand briefly.

"Jovi."

"Hey, Rick." Almost immediately, both turned their attention to the engine.

"So—you gonna apply for the job at *Nueva Brisa*?" the newcomer asked.

"Tomorrow," Jovi agreed, turning at a slight rustle in the weeds that framed the roadside clearing, then relaxing when he realized the noise couldn't have come from anything large.

"Still jumping at shadows?" Rick shook his head. "We leave the job, but the edge never leaves."

"You don't let anyone leave," Jovi retorted, slapping a mosquito seconds too late, and rubbing his arm. "Tell me why I said yes again."

"Cause you're one of the good guys, we pay well, and you get to be close to your mom while she gets back on her feet. It's win-win, Jovi."

"Cut the bull, friend. I left DEA because no one wins—the work's important, but the war's unwinnable, Rick."

Rick Ortega shrugged his thin shoulders. "Maybe."

"And this one smells."

"Why?" He nudged Jovi with an elbow. "'Cause we're looking at some honey the locals call untouchable?"

"Unattainable." Jovi motioned Ortega back and slammed the hood. "Your reasons for looking at this woman are shaky at best, and if I'm investigating her, I damn sure won't be thinking about her looks."

"Touchier than ever," the DEA agent muttered.

"And in a week or two, when my plane lands in Florida—I'm done, Rick. No more arm-twisting, no favors. I'm serious."

"Look, I know you mostly came until your mom beats her pneumonia—not so much to help us. But you're perfect, Jovi—the border's home to you, but you've been gone long enough you're an outsider now."

"Hell, I was always an outsider. Everywhere."

"Whining isn't your style, *amigo*," Ortega chided. "You know how things are. No trust left—our side or theirs. The cartels are winning. For Christ's sake, they're slaughtering innocents on the streets a mile from here." He jerked his head toward the tree-framed skyline. Behind those trees, the Rio Grande whispered its newly violent song to the night. "Check her out, that's all. She worked for a major importer, but quit suddenly. Her father left her some money, but—" He shook his head. "Something's not right, buddy."

Jovi glanced at him. "Because her father left money?"

"No. Because insurance aside, her father shouldn't have had money to leave. The ranch is a joke—big property value, but no livestock except horses. On paper, he sold horses—horses we're not real sure existed. Horses! No market for horses right now, going on back even before his death. The man went through a bitter divorce from the wife, yet got big bucks from the ex father-in-law, Lionel De Cordova."

"De Cordova? Man!" The name surprised him. "But for all his sins, I never heard he trafficked."

"We know some of the younger cousins do. Nobody's tagged him, true. But the foreman you're replacing? Arrested in Sinaloa several weeks ago. Arranging to drive a load to El Paso."

"So she has to know?"

Ortega shrugged. "Hard to say. The man's a Mexican national, and the story wasn't broadcast here. We only found out through our sources. But if he worked out of her barn . . . "

"She either knows or she's stupid?" he suggested.

Again, Ortega made a slight gesture of denial. "She'd been in New York and Houston more than home until recently. She worked for an import firm with headquarters in Houston and branches all over Mexico, as well as in several border towns. The horses were more or less at the mercy of the foreman and the two grooms."

"Sketchy at best," Jovi pointed out again. "This is my last call, though," he repeated, walking to the driver's side and pulling the door open. "This job's too hard on the soul, Rick. Too much lying and too many half-truths—and to save what? "

Ortega paused by the open door as his friend climbed back in. "Did I tell you that little four-year old girl—Lisa, remember her? She turned seven yesterday. They put her photo on one of those news lead-ins."

"Damn you," Jovi snarled, thinking of the child he, Ortega, and others had found cowering in the corner of a crack house after a deal turned particularly violent. And her brothers, 5 and 8, lying broken on the floor in their own blood. His last official case—the last case he'd tried to stomach.

"Sometimes we win," Rick insisted, and slapped his arm. "*Suerte*," he ended, walking away.

Luck. Jovi shook his head, turned on the truck, and poked the radio button. He wouldn't need luck if he kept his mind on work and on the stable full of thoroughbreds waiting for him in Florida. As he eased back onto the access road, blessed darkness and George Strait's melodious voice surrounded him.

CHAPTER TWO

Dell Rosales tossed the sheaf of bank statements aside and stood up, agitated. Numbers should make sense, but the disorganized financial records her father left behind meant nothing. Once again she kicked herself for staying away from the ranch for so long. She had loved her father, loved him still, even after his unexpected death. But the pain of this place had been too great; her mother's absence—and worse, memories of her mother's presence—overwhelmed. She sucked in her breath, a sharp sound not unlike the snorts and soft snuffles from some of the horses in the aisle outside. *To hell with it.* Her father's records were disorganized, not wrong. She wouldn't believe anything else. She clenched her fists and closed her eyes momentarily, wishing she hadn't touched any of his money before she'd unscrambled the paper mess he'd left; that would have been smarter. She should have gone back to the import business immediately, instead of deciding to help a friend out while she licked her wounds—that would have been smarter, too.

Like smart was ever your thing. Angrily, she cast the self-accusation away. She'd been stupid hurting over her mother's abandonment. She'd been stupid in love. But she damn well had learned not to be stupid when it counted.

A flash of movement outside, unexpected at this mid-afternoon hour, snared her attention. Her stomach knotted momentarily as she wondered what emergency dragged her housekeeper down to the stable in the heat. Tempted to cross her fingers, or cross herself, she hurried out to meet the older woman.

"Rosa, what's wrong?" she asked. "Major or minor?"

Rosa drew in a breath that shook her ample frame and wiped a hand across her forehead, then glowered at Dell. "You're not sweating?"

Dell shrugged, glanced briefly at the cloudless sky. The South Texas sun was a nuclear blast of heat and light, so intense that nothing moved around them. The oleander and bougainvillea bordering the drive were motionless, testimony to the complete absence of circulating air.

"The heat doesn't bother me. You know that, Rosa." She ran a hand over her crisp, white blouse. "Besides, I just came from the office."

"Did you ride at all?" Rosa asked, and Dell shook her head, her ponytail flopping heavily against her neck.

Dell started toward the house, Rosa huffing alongside. "No. I spend most of my time just keeping up with the girls and their paperwork, then when I get to the barn—with no foreman, I'm ordering feed and paying vet bills. I did pet a couple of them, though." She glanced at the older woman. "Think I'd even recognize a saddle anymore?"

They reached the back porch, and Rosa pulled a key from her pocket. "Karla was upstairs with *la princesa*," she explained, "but—"

"Better safe than sorry," the two finished in unison.

"So what happened, anyway?" Dell asked, motioning Rosa into the kitchen first.

"*Nada*."

Dell cast a sideways glance. "Nothing? Rosa, you practically ran down to the barn."

"Well, you know I don't like using that fancy phone you put in. The intercom thing."

Dell waited as Rosa offered her usual, detailed explanation. "Don't understand it. Had to get you."

Dell still wasn't sure what the problem was. "And?" she prompted, shifting the vase of silk flowers on the kitchen table.

Rosa's jaw dropped. "Oh—forgot the important part, huh? Gettin' old, I guess. There's a man here."

"A man?" Dell looked down at Rosa blankly.

"*Tu sabes,*" Rosa replied, "a man. About the job."

"Already?" Dell arched an eyebrow. "That was fast." Then she frowned. "You do mean the foreman's job? Not just someone looking for work?"

"The foreman's job," Rosa confirmed. "He's in the den." She drew in a breath, sagging a little as the cool air surrounded her, then looked up at Dell, her eyes concerned. "I didn't like him."

Rosa's blunt statement triggered an immediate reaction. There were few people whose judgment Dell relied on; she trusted her own opinions about people—and Rosa's. "What's wrong with him?"

Rosa shrugged. "I don't know, exactly. He's local—how many young Laredoans have experience with horses?"

"Well, the Asmussens—"

Rosa's plump hand brushed aside the renowned family, whose sons made racing headlines internationally. "Besides them. This man—I don't know. He's arrogant. *Chocante.* He's—he's—" Her hand traced a circle in the air as she searched for the words to finish her description.

Dell laughed. "He's a man. Reason enough to be suspicious, *¿verdad?* But I'll be careful." Her good humor faded. "I have reason to be careful, don't I? But we need someone so badly, Rosa. I don't want to give up the horses. They're all I have left from before."

"I know." Rosa reached a hand up to touch her cheek. "You'll manage, *chiquita.* You always do."

Dell looked around the house—comfortable, affluent, so tidy—and so empty.

"Where are the girls?" she asked.

"You worry too much. Pete took Michelle, Selina, and Amy into Laredo with him for groceries. They'll be okay. And *la princesa* is upstairs, asleep."

"All right." Dell drew a deep breath and squared her shoulders. "Do I look like a brisk, efficient, professional employer should?"

"No." Rosa grinned, her eyes sweeping over Dell. "You look like some spoiled and sexy *Cosmo* cover girl. But like you tell those mule-headed girls—looks aren't everything!"

"Thanks!" Dell retorted, pulling her blouse down lower over her hips. "Make me feel vulnerable, why don't you?"

"You?" Rosa snorted disdainfully. "Not any danger of that. They don't call you '*la inalcanzable*' for nothing, you know!"

"Don't bring that up again," Dell protested, frowning a little at the nickname she had earned among some of her acquaintances. Literally, the word meant unreachable. Someone distant and untouchable.

She supposed being a little distant wasn't a bad idea if she were going to interview some macho-man jerk for the position she had in mind. Resolutely she walked through the house, her boots clicking on tile, then muffled on carpet as she stepped into the den. The man staring out the window at the green expanse of lawn turned as she came into the room.

"*Buenas tardes*," she greeted him, as he nodded at her.

"*Buenas*," he replied, his voice deep and throaty as he drawled the abbreviated greeting.

He was an immensely tall man, square-shouldered and bronzed. His dark eyes appraised her, and she was not surprised that a mustache framed sensual lips or that he held a Stetson against his leg. She *was* looking for someone to manage her horses, after all.

"A. Rosales?"

"Dell Rosales," she answered, walking over to shake his hand. "And you are—

"J. Treviño." He clasped her hand briefly. His hands were well groomed, Dell noted. She wondered just how much experience this man really had with horses. He looked more like an office worker. Or would, except that the creamy knit shirt he wore did nothing to hide well-sculpted muscles. Moving hay bales could do that.

"Please, sit down." She waved at a chair near her desk.

He sat down, placed the Stetson on the corner of her desk, and pulled a newspaper clipping out of his pocket. There was a splash of yellow highlighter on the crumpled ad she recognized as her own. "You're the person I'm supposed to see?"

"I'm Adela Rosales, Mr. Treviño, but I prefer Dell. So, is 'J' really your first name?"

"No," he admitted, smiling for the first time, and his eyes danced a little. She could see instantly that Rosa was right to dislike him—men with killer good looks generally knew exactly how to use them on susceptible women. Not that she was at all susceptible. Not anymore. *La inalcanzable*, she reminded herself sternly. *Unreachable. Untouchable. Unattainable.*

"It's Jovani."

"Jovani," she repeated thoughtfully, her forehead wrinkling a little. "Like the musical group?"

His grin widened. "You must not be into rock. That's Bon Jovi, not Jovani."

"Oh, that's right. So what do *you* go by, Mr. Treviño?"

He laughed. "Jovi. Mom says she named me Giovani—just couldn't spell it."

"I see. How did you become interested in horses, Mr. Treviño? You do have experience?"

"Yes. I'll fax my resume to you later today, if you'd like. I was driving in from San Antonio and decided to stop by. I'd seen your ad. Several days ago already." He fluttered the clipping. "I didn't want to wait too long." His sincerity bordered on intense. Somehow not the tone she expected from an applicant. "I'm interested in your job, Ms. Rosales."

"Why?" she asked, her tone as frank as his own.

He shrugged one shoulder, picked the hat up, and placed it idly on a jeans-clad thigh. "There aren't a lot of jobs in the area that let you concentrate on breeding quality horses. Most ranches are cattle—or cattle and oil." He paused, frowned a little. "I don't want an indoor job."

"Where had you been working?"

"Do you know Heaven's Thunder Farms in Florida?"

"Ocala, right? Of course. Everyone does—well, everyone in horses, anyway," Dell amended, thinking how few of her acquaintances would recognize the name. The racing stable had come out of the blue like the lightning bolt that graced their jockeys' silks. At a time when the thoroughbred industry was depressed, especially in central Florida, Heaven's Thunder Farms had sprung up and immediately become a force.

"I'm impressed," Dell added truthfully. "Their horses took everything last year—the Derby, the Belmont—even the Breeder's Cup Classic." She tilted her head, studying him. "You couldn't have been there long, though—they just got started what, four years ago? They were racing their own colts for the first time last year."

"I was there when Dave and Griselda bought the farm, and I chose their broodmares. Love the place," he said.

Dell leaned back a little in her chair, regarding him thoughtfully. He met her eyes evenly.

"You're going to ask why I left, right?"

"I have to."

"Yes." He stood up, flipping the hat into the empty chair. Her question had agitated him, though she didn't understand why. She watched through narrowed eyes as he walked back to the window and looked out for a minute or two before turning back.

"I had to," he said. "I was afraid."

"Afraid of what?" she asked, surprised this tough-looking man would admit fear so easily.

"Of doing something stupid." He sighed, then came back across, reclaimed the hat, and sat down. "I fell for Griselda Cooper." He looked down at the hat and brushed his fingers over the smooth, clean felt. Finally he looked back at her, his dark eyes grim. "Falling in love with the boss's wife *is* stupid. Especially when the boss is a friend."

Dell tapped a polished nail on the smooth surface of the desk. "Mr. Treviño, I'm sorry if I seem insensitive in an uncomfortable situation," she said after a minute. "But I need references. Would that be a problem?"

"No." He shook his head. "The Coopers will give me good references. My mother lives in Laredo. She's been sick." A muscle twitched in his jaw. "They think that's why I left."

Dell pursed her lips thoughtfully. "So Mrs. Cooper didn't know about your feelings? There were no problems?"

"No problems that had anything to do with my job," he replied brusquely. "The rest is none of your business."

"Actually, Mr. Treviño, what happened between you and Mrs. Cooper *is* my business." Dell pulled open a desk drawer and dug out a folded newspaper. A group of teenaged girls sat on horses, and Dell stood next to one of them, a hand resting on the pinto's neck. "I have some projects I'm trying to get off the ground. That's why I need help. I intended to raise the horses alone, and when my last foreman just disappeared, I thought I'd hire another groom and run things alone. But I don't have time to bring the breeding program back, because—well, I'm providing a temporary home for some troubled girls." She tapped a finger again, this time on the photo. "I'll be blunt, Mr. Treviño. I have to be careful about whom I hire. I'd actually prefer a woman for the position, but I need someone right away. The girls who stay here have problems— and I have to be sure that anyone I hire would be . . . safe."

"Look, *Ms.* Rosales," he said, his expression shuttered, "if you're interested, I'll send you my resume today. Check my references.

Call me if you need me." He stood, visibly irritated. "And don't worry. I'm no threat to teenagers—or anyone else. Like I said, I recognize stupidity. Especially my own."

CHAPTER THREE

Dell glanced at the girl sitting next to her desk then down at the papers in front of her. "Well, Maribel," she offered, "Welcome to *Nueva Brisa*."

The girl ignored her, looked at her blue-enameled nails, and then methodically began to chip the polish off one of them.

Dell bit back her frown. The girl had chopped her hair off, and makeup that could have made her attractive coarsened her appearance. The girl's skimpy tube top bared virtually everything, including a cobra tattoo that slithered across her bosom and onto her left arm, and she wondered which overtaxed social worker had let her walk out the door in that attire.

The girl continued to ignore her, and Dell counted silently to ten then stood and walked to the front of the desk. She leaned against the edge, hoping either her height or proximity might intimidate the girl, who stubbornly kept her head down, working on the nail with detached determination.

"Maribel, this isn't getting us anywhere. The judge sent you here—"

The girl's head came up then, and she fixed Dell with a remorseless, dark stare. "Don't give me no shit about sending me back to juvenile. Just do it."

Dell smiled. "You'd like the center, wouldn't you? No, Maribel, you didn't let me finish. She thought I could help you."

"Should have left me alone. I wasn't hurtin' no one."

"Except yourself." Dell fought the urge to tell the sixteen-year-old just how badly she was hurting herself. Lecturing wouldn't work.

"You get paid a lot?" Maribel looked around the study, taking in the shelves of books, the richly upholstered furniture, and the

Amado Peña prints on the paneled walls. "Guess if you send me back, you lose money, huh?"

Dell didn't argue the girl's mistaken ideas. There was no point in describing how or why she had become involved in this project, not yet. Not to Maribel.

"Bet it ain't the place the judge thinks," the teenager went on, apparently annoyed Dell hadn't refuted her suspicions. She ran her eyes over Dell insultingly. "Think you're hot, huh? Maybe this is just like where I was, no? Your *vatos* come over for a good time, too?" Maribel's eyes glittered dangerously. "I don't mind doin' it for money—you know that. But I choose who I work for."

Dell shook her head. "No, you don't. You gave up your choices the first time you slept with someone just to prove you could. You're just too young and stupid to see it."

"You—you can't call me stupid—" Maribel sputtered, flustered. "Who the hell you think you are, talking to me like—like—"

"Like someone who just called me a ho?" Dell suggested blandly. "Look, Maribel, insults aren't going to get either of us anywhere. You made stupid choices. Change them if you're smart enough." She shrugged. "Up to you, either way. Let's get you settled so you can do other things."

"What other things?" Maribel asked suspiciously.

Dell grinned. "You'll see," she said, picturing the defiant girl mucking stalls. "Let's show you your room."

*

A few minutes later, blowing out her frustration in a couple of short puffs, Dell walked back down to the den, idly straightening a picture on the hall wall as she went before slumping into the chair behind her desk. *What have I put my foot in?* she asked herself. Selina, Amy, and Michelle were girls with temporary problems— too little parenting, mostly. She'd been there, but her path had been different than theirs—she'd had a father who loved her and money to pave her way. Those girls had so little, and when her high school friend, now family judge, Patricia Ovalle, asked for her help—she'd agreed without hesitation.

But Maribel. Dell's lips twisted. The girl was a piece of work. She picked up the unfamiliar papers with their legalese. Being asked to keep a high-school dropout who'd been working the streets was new. The other girls were part of a pilot project to get them away from family discord, substance abuse, truancy—light stuff. But being asked to keep a street kid who'd been turning tricks—that was new. And scary, in a way, though Judge Ovalle assured her this placement would be brief. The detention center was overfilled, and arrangements were in the works to move the girl out of the county.

Still . . . she drummed a finger on the polished desktop. Did she want someone like that around Becky, even for a few days? As if she'd heard her name cross Dell's mind, the toddler appeared in the door with Rosa right behind her.

"Go spend time with Dell," Rosa ordered, bussing the little girl's dark head before heading off down the hall.

"Hi, gorgeous!" Dell went across the room, picking the child up and hugging her. "How's my princess?"

"Fi," the child answered, squeezing Dell's neck and kissing her wetly on the cheek before struggling to be put down.

Reluctantly Dell put her back on the carpet. The little girl needed to be active and explore—she'd lost months of stimulation to an environment of neglect, unloved by a mother addicted to drugs and alcohol. She rubbed her arms as the memory of the child she'd first seen made her shiver.

"You angel," she murmured, but Becky plucked a magazine off a coffee table and trundled over to the loveseat, oblivious to anything Dell said. She made a half-hearted attempt to climb up before sliding down and turning a page. Careful not to disturb

Becky, Dell pulled her cell phone out of her pocket and snapped a picture of the toddler "reading" the magazine. Someone should have memories of Becky later, she thought. And wondered, as she occasionally did, if there were pictures of a baby Adela anywhere. Real pictures, not the formal sittings at yearly intervals that graced her childhood room.

The desk phone shrilled, distracting her. She glanced around to be sure nothing dangerous was within the child's reach and lifted the receiver.

"*Nueva Brisa*," she said into the phone, a little breathlessly. "Dell Rosales speaking."

"Oh, good!" a woman's voice said pleasantly. "Griselda Cooper at Heaven's Thunder Farms, Ms. Rosales. I'm returning your call—how can I help you today? We have some excellent two year olds—"

Dell laughed. "Slow down, Mrs. Cooper! I'm not buying thoroughbreds—at least, not right now."

"Sorry," the voice said unrepentantly. Dell thought back to the races she'd watched last year, trying to remember what the woman had looked like there in the winner's circle. A calm woman, Dell recalled, married to a man delightfully ignorant of how to behave around the Kentucky blue bloods when his Gladiator's Rose became only the fourth filly in history to win the legendary Kentucky Derby. He managed to carry a bucket of some icy liquid to the winner's circle and dumped it over his trainer's head, football style. Gladiator's Rose shied, ditching the blanket of roses and her jockey and knocking down a cameraman. Griselda Cooper had laughed, kissed her husband on the cheek, quieted the nervous filly.

"So, what can I do for you, then?" Griselda asked, calling her back to her purpose. Dell found herself unusually reluctant to broach a difficult subject.

"I'm calling about an employee of yours," she admitted. "He applied for a job, and—"

"Oh, Jovi!" Griselda said instantly. "Worked for us until his mother got sick. He chose our broodmares, you know. If you have horses, hire him!"

"Is he reliable? Were there ever any problems?"

"Dave and I really should have given him a letter of reference. Would you like us to fax you something? He's absolutely trustworthy," she assured Dell, as enthusiastically as she had tried to sell horses moments before.

Dell toyed with a pen, then picked it up and began an abstract doodle. "I have Western stock, primarily. A couple of thoroughbreds and some Arabians, but mostly quarter horses and Appaloosas. Could he manage the switch?"

"Absolutely," the voice on the other end affirmed. "He's knowledgeable already, and a fast learner to boot. Dedicated, too. Dave and I are Texas stock ourselves. Dave's dad owned quarter horses, and he lived with us 'til his death. You know they talked shop."

Dell hesitated, frowning. According to his ex-employer, the man had no faults. "Mrs. Cooper—"

"Griselda," the woman insisted cheerfully.

"Griselda, were there ever any personal problems with Jovi?" She hesitated, not sure how deeply she should delve.

"Personal problems? I'm not sure what you mean. Look, Jovi's a hard worker, and he's honest and reliable. Nobody's better with horses."

Clearly the other woman either didn't know about or wouldn't admit to the feelings Jovi claimed he'd developed for her. Dell thanked her and hung up, then walked over to sit on the floor with the toddler. Becky clutched the magazine to her tummy like a blanket, crooning to herself in a strange, low monotone. Another mark, her case worker explained, of growing up without normal communication with people who cared for her.

Dell sighed. She needed someone to take care of the horses.

That had been her father's one passion, raising and selling quality horses. Quarter horses, Appaloosas, Arabians—even the thoroughbreds he'd belittled as being too delicate for the south Texas climate. She'd tried to walk away, but horses must be in her blood . . . and Becky's, she thought, smiling at the little girl who was now trying to tear a page out of the glossy journal.

She wouldn't give up the horses, even if it meant hiring the first applicant for the vacant foreman's position.

She stood up and hoisted Becky into her arms then paced around the room, reviewing her options. Jovi's resume had been neat and concise. He'd worked in the military and for DEA. Griselda gave him glowing references, and Rosa disliked him. She nudged Becky's head, blowing into the dark hair and letting the child's giggle soothe her. She needed a foreman, and he was available. For the moment, she'd go with that. Decided, she walked over to dial his number.

CHAPTER FOUR

Jovi stood at the window in the office, looking out at the girls cantering around the nearby training ring. Selina, the tall, quiet one, was sitting easily on the leopard Appaloosa, laughing and looking happy. Michelle and Amy were riding with confidence, though neither seemed particularly outgoing or cheerful. But Dell told him they tended to be quiet and serious, still troubled by the problems that had brought them here. He'd been surprised the three girls were on the ranch on a judge's informal agreement with their mothers and were participating in what amounted to a summer camp for troubled teens.

His mouth twisted as his gaze turned to Maribel. She sat rigidly on the big, gentle bay she rode, and unlike the others, her face was etched into hard, unfeeling lines, her mouth tightly compressed. He didn't know her story, he realized; he'd barely seen Dell since he started, and she'd said nothing about this bitter young woman who showed up one afternoon using a vocabulary that made Pete, the elderly groom, shake his head and mutter "*perdida*" whenever he saw her.

Jovi grimaced. Pete was from a time of manners and respect, in spite of his job or circumstance. The man was probably right, too—he suspected Maribel truly was a lost cause. He squinted back in the direction of the ring, watching the players moving unknowingly across their stage. Not for the first time, he felt a small prick of guilt over being here to find evidence of Dell's innocence—or guilt—in drug running.

Maribel's horse was trailing the others, and he frowned as she suddenly slashed the bay with her reins, making him lunge forward to overtake Amy and Michelle. She turned her head and said something, and he saw Michelle pull her horse in, ducking her head. Amy instantly reined her horse around, coming back and putting her hand on her friend's arm in a comforting way. He bit back an expletive as he headed for the door, but saw Dell walking into the corral, holding up her hand for the girls to pull up their horses. He narrowed his eyes again, and his lips tightened involuntarily.

Dell didn't look like a criminal, he thought again. She looked . . . gorgeous. She was tall, slender, and graceful, with lively dark eyes and dark, glossy hair that fell to her shoulders when she didn't tie it up out of her way. He thought of the little he'd learned about her since he started working for her just a week ago. Not much. Apparently she hadn't lied when she said that managing her other affairs didn't leave her time for the horses, though he could tell she loved them—and the girls she was trying to help.

Would a drug smuggler help girls like these? Girls who might well have been referred here for problems with substance abuse? He sighed. That would be ugly, if the judge were unwittingly sending troubled youngsters right into something worse. Out in the ring, Dell had taken the horse away from Maribel. The girl shrugged her shoulders insolently and turned away from whatever she was being told. The other three girls were clustered together, seemingly finding comfort in each other.

The riding session was over; the girls loosened the girths on their sweaty horses and began walking them around the ring. Maribel took the bay's reins back unwillingly and began to circle alongside the fence, lagging behind and aiming occasional kicks at the thick sand under her feet.

Dell turned and headed toward the barn, and he left the window and went to the desk, hurriedly pulling a sheaf of papers he'd been working on from a desk drawer and picking up his pen.

He was bent over his work, pretending to be engrossed with the papers, when Dell came through the open door. He looked up, and she greeted him with a slight smile and nod. He remembered the sketchy preliminary report he'd received on her had said they called her *la inalcanzable*. Unattainable. He wasn't sure how she'd received the nickname, or how many used it, but it fit. There was a remoteness about her, a distance, as if she were holding herself away from something she didn't want to touch. He realized he must have frowned when she shook her head and sank into the chair in front of the desk.

"Are things that bad?"

"No." Her perfume teased him, light and intriguing, a pleasant change from the mustiness of straw and the pungent odor occasionally drifting in from the stalls. She glanced at the papers he had out. He smiled easily, trying not to breathe her scent in too deeply, and handed the papers across the desk. "My mom always said I was *un enojon*. Easily angered. I deny it, but . . ." He shrugged. "As you can see, I've been trying to analyze what you have in the way of stock."

"And?" She leaned back in her chair, studying him. She wondered how he'd been received in Florida and Kentucky, with his South Texas habit of throwing Spanish words into a perfectly good English conversation. The habit gave purists fits—and she'd suffered herself, at college in New York. Here, though, it made him seem genuine and unaffected. She wondered, too, how easily angered he actually was—how much of "*un enojon*"—he'd seemed rather unruffled since his show of temper during that initial interview.

He gestured at the papers he'd turned over to her. "How do you feel about selling everything and starting over?"

Dell blanched. "Selling? Everything?" she asked, and he could hear pain in her voice. "The horses—which horses? I can't sell the horses—"

He ran a hand over his forehead, rearranging his hair, then rubbed his chin. "Ms. Rosales—"

"Call me Dell, Jovi. I can't talk to some stranger about my horses. Why do I need to sell them? My father had excellent stock—some of the horses I trained myself, some of them before I left home for college. Before—" She stopped, then gave her head a decided shake. "I don't think I want to sell any of them," she finished.

"Dell, this is a horse farm," he said. "You have too many horses. Some of them are too old to be productive. Why do you need"—he pointed at a highlighted item—"Fourteen quarter horse mares if you intend to raise primarily Appaloosas and Arabians?"

"My father liked quarter horses best. They're his horses. And they're all really good horses. Besides, we use some of them with the girls."

"He's not here any longer, Dell," Jovi said gently but matter-of-factly. "So they're not his—they're yours. And they haven't produced colts in several years."

"We don't have a quarter horse stallion, and I haven't had time to have them bred." She frowned across the desk at Jovi. "That's where you come in, remember?"

"But fourteen?" He shook his head slowly. "Dell, I don't know your financial condition. But most people can't afford twenty-nine horses and two ponies—old ponies—even in good times. How can you justify all these mouths to feed when they're not bringing in a single penny?" Pain touched her eyes, but he pushed on. "I have to call it like I see it. You're spending a fortune—feed, insurance, vet bills, help. Your father had excellent horses, true enough. I noticed the trophy case, and I've looked at some of the past books—the ranch used to sell almost all the two-year-olds for top-dollar prices. But not recently. And with economic conditions—you may struggle to sell stock even when you have the mares bred."

Dell stood up and walked over to the window, looking out for a few, silent moments. Finally she sighed heavily and turned back around. "I suppose we need to talk about a sale, then. But not today." Her lips twisted in a wry smile. "I have to make peace with the idea first, I guess." She came back again and sat down. "Tell me something, Jovi . . . how big a stickler are you for job descriptions and doing only what you were hired to do?"

He arched an eyebrow. "I don't know. Why?"

"How are you at *carne asada*?"

He blinked, then grinned. "The best, naturally. I wasn't away that long!"

"Good." She plucked absently at the eyelet blouse she was wearing, removing invisible lint. He couldn't look away.

"These girls have lost so much—all of them have either left or been taken away from their families." Emotion came and went in her eyes as she spoke. "Amy was telling me the other day that the thing she missed most was the Sunday *carne asada*—the family getting together—even the smell of the smoke, she said. I can't give it all back, but I thought we might try to reproduce some of it."

"Fine with me." He leaned back a little and idly tapped the desk.

"I could do it," she continued seriously. But Jovi, you remember *carne asadas* in these parts, right?"

He nodded. "Alcohol, music, and fighting, too often."

"I want something better than that for the girls. A good time without the bad thrown in."

"So I come in because . . . ?"

"You can cook the meat," she said immediately, "while I chaperone."

Jovi gazed across the desk at her, straightening in his chair. This was an unwelcome situation. There was an intimacy about a *carne asada*—friends had *carne asadas*. And families. He was the last person she could trust, even if she didn't know that. Yet. He couldn't have hidden his irritation. She looked startled by his abrupt change in demeanor, and then the impenetrable air of calm and distance settled back around her. "Is something wrong?" she asked. "If you'd rather not, don't feel obligated—"

"There's no problem," he answered. "Just don't expect miracles, Dell. Those girls are tough cookies, deep down."

Dell stood, her own annoyance undisguised. "I don't expect miracles, Jovani," she retorted. "I'm not that naïve. But the girls aren't nearly as tough as you think." She cast a quick glance at the clock on the office wall. "I thought we'd start around five." She turned toward the door then stopped to look back over her shoulder. "I'll let you know about the horses within the week." Her tone was dismissive, boss to employee.

Good. Better that way, he reminded himself brusquely. Because at best, Dell was just his boss. And at worst . . . at worst, she was the woman he'd destroy. Soon.

The lights in the side yard glowed, scattered around the large expanse with tasteful flare. Tejano music played softly, and roses and honeysuckle sweetened the night air, although the smell of fajitas sizzling on the grill overpowered the lighter floral scents at the moment. Jovi propped a shoulder against the brick wall of the grill and glanced around the patio again, relishing the abrupt quiet.

Minutes ago, the girls chattered and argued by the pool, but Rosa had herded them off to change out of their bathing suits.

He reached over and poked at a piece of fajita, lifting it up and flipping it over. Laughter announced the return of the girls, and he frowned. Had Dell noticed when Maribel approached him, flirting with a determination that should have been beyond her years? He hoped she knew what she'd gotten into with the teenager. Bad, bad news.

Then again . . . His mouth tightened, and he speared another piece of meat. There was a real possibility Dell's main concern wasn't the girls' welfare, anyhow, however unlikely that seemed when he watched them together.

The girls were loaded down with trays of dishes, glasses, and condiments, and Rosa came behind them, carrying a steaming *jarro* of beans. The earthenware pitcher and the aroma of the bacon and cilantro-spiced beans filled him with nostalgia.

There had been days, many, many years ago, when the beans cooking slowly on his mother's stove had been the day's food. He'd worked hard to overcome that—and she could afford what she chose, now—but the beans were still a constant in her kitchen. It was who they were, she would tell him, clucking at his insistence that she go out with him to eat in some new restaurant or other.

Selina unloaded her tray on the table, and she ran across the lawn toward him, her long, unruly hair flying with abandon. "We're starving, Jovi," she announced. "Need help?"

"Nope. Got it under control." He held out a tray of cooked meat for inspection. "How does that look?"

"Perfect!" She took the tray from him. "Give it. Are you gonna eat with us?"

"Sure." He looked at the last of the meat, just beginning to cook. "This can take care of itself for a while." He walked across the lawn with her, and Rosa, Michelle, and Amy all greeted him with smiles. Maribel frowned.

"Bet you didn't even use beer on it," she sniffed. "*Carne asada* with no beer sucks."

"Smells pretty good to me," Dell said, her voice floating melodically on the hot summer air. He turned, his indrawn breath of surprise not quite audible over the girls' conversation. Dell had abandoned her usual slim-fitting pants and skirts for a loose dress. Its scooped neck was embroidered with flowers, and the gauzy material draped her body enticingly. The yard lights glinted on the silver earrings exposed by her upswept hair and the matching necklace around her slender throat. As stunned as he was by her appearance, though, his eyes widened involuntarily when he took in the toddler at her side. The little girl appeared to be two or three.

Her huge, black eyes took in everything with infinite interest, and a mass of curly black hair tumbled around her tiny, pale face.

So, he thought, and was abruptly annoyed with himself. There were hundreds—thousands—of single mothers. It meant nothing. Nothing about morals, or lack of them. Nothing about whether or not this woman might be engaged in illegal activity. Surprising no one had mentioned the girl, but oh, well. He masked his surprise, and when Dell came over to him, the child in tow, he smiled at the little girl with genuine warmth. It was impossible not to—she was irrepressible.

"Jovi, this is Becky." Dell stooped, lifting the child with tenderness and holding her up for him to meet. "Becky, this is Mr. Treviño."

"Hi." The girl pressed her face into Dell's shoulder briefly, then shot him a slight smile before giggling and burying her face against Dell again.

"She's shy," Dell explained, "but she's getting better."

"She's precious," he murmured, reaching out a hand to touch the girl's hair. Dell's face softened at the gesture, and she smiled.

"Afraid of giving her *ojo*?" she asked.

He seemed a little embarrassed, but nodded. "Our old superstitions die hard, don't they?"

"You probably got some glares in Florida," she said, still grinning. "Even more up there in Kentucky during Derby week. In New York there were people who thought they should report me." The custom of touching something you admired—or envied—to prevent harming it was largely unknown outside of the Mexican-American culture that embraced the practice. Many mothers who were unaware of the benevolent intent of warding off *ojo* were offended—or frightened—when strangers touched their child's cheek or head in passing.

"Some," he admitted, his eyes dancing. "Guess I can see why strangers might freak out just a little in this day and age."

Dell put Becky down, and the child toddled over and climbed up on the bench with Michelle's help. "Looks like someone's hungry."

"She always is." Dell smiled, inhaling deeply. "Shall we eat?" She waved a hand at the girls clustered around the end of the table filling glasses with tea.

Everyone claimed a place at the table, with Jovi sitting near the end so he could keep an eye on the meat still cooking over the dying coals. Rosa sat with the girls, ignoring Maribel's hostile looks and the endless chatter of the other three. Dell walked over to re-light a citron light meant to discourage mosquitoes, and returned to find most of the bench occupied. She glanced at the others, then pulled her skirt up slightly and maneuvered herself onto the bench between Becky and Jovi.

"I hate this attached seating," she grumbled. "There's no way to get in and out gracefully."

"You did pretty well," he said mildly, and she shot him a sideways glance. He smiled. Next to her, Becky babbled happily. The girls were rolling pieces of the spicy meat into Rosa's homemade flour tortillas, and Dell reached for a basket and passed it to him.

"Get 'em 'fore they're gone," she warned.

"Gone!" Amy snorted. "After the hours it took to make the damn-darn things—"

"Mamá always said they invented stores so women could quit making tortillas," Selina interjected. "But *¿sabes?* Rosa's tortillas are kickass."

"*Riquisimas,*" Jovi agreed.

Rosa beamed across the table, basking in the praise. "*Gracias, gracias.*"

She reached over and patted Selina's cheek, then smiled across the table at Dell, ignoring Jovi altogether. "These *niñitas* can cook up a storm, now."

The girls exchanged a look and Amy giggled. "Lying's a sin, Rosa. We burned half your *masa* and rolled the other into cardboard."

"And still we have enough," Rosa retorted gently.

"I'm impressed you girls even tried," Dell admitted. "I never quite got it, did I, Rosa?" She passed the *pico de gallo* to Jovi, and he spooned the chili-tomato salsa over his meat with a flourish.

"Beats store-bought food all to hel—heck," he said, choking a little on the last word as he remembered his audience, and everyone laughed. Everyone except Maribel.

"*Santito!*" she muttered sarcastically. "Afraid to let the boss hear you curse? 'Fraid she'll find out you're not really a saint, *papacito*?"

The girls shifted nervously and exchanged worried glances. Dell set her glass of tea down carefully. "Maribel, it's not fair to embarrass Jovi like that. Don't ruin the evening for everyone just because you're out of sorts."

"I'm not out of sorts. I just hate all this—this crap." She waved a hand at the assembled group. "Tortillas—shit! I was turnin' tricks and them—" She waved a hand at the other three. "Them, I don't know about. Probably doing it for free, huh, Selina? So your mom shipped you out? But at least you're good in the kitchen, according to Rosa." Then she turned derisive eyes on Dell. "Maybe you're not happy to hear, that, huh, *jefa*? Beneath us women to be in the kitchen, huh?"

Jovi stood, unsure whether or not Dell would appreciate him sticking his nose in. Dell wiped her mouth on a napkin, seemingly unperturbed, before responding to Maribel in her usual, level tone. "Maribel, quit trying to pick fights. No one's going to let you ruin their evening."

The girls were watching Dell and Maribel silently, their eyes apprehensive, as she continued. "I don't know what tore your life apart. But I think the real deal here is you can't handle how your choices turned out—and you need to." She picked up her tea and took another sip. "This isn't an appropriate conversation around Becky, though. Or the other girls, if you're using it to shock or belittle them. Finish dinner."

Maribel started to say something, but her eyes fell momentarily on Becky, and she clamped her lips shut. For a moment, softness came and went across her face. "My sister's about three," she said, then seemed startled and embarrassed at the proclamation. She pushed aside her plate and went over to the pool, and Dell let her go. Almost immediately, Amy and Selina were giggling over something, and after a minute, Michelle chimed in, making faces at Becky while she cut up another piece of meat for the child.

Jovi went over to check on the remaining meat, turning it over with pursed lips. He had come to find out if Dell's apparently ample income was honestly come by; he had more or less expected his suspicions would have been clearly confirmed by now. Instead, he found himself struggling to remain objective and detached from this woman they called "*la inalcanzable.*" Her concern for the girls, the apparent distaste she had for impropriety—nothing tagged her as a calculating woman who helped funnel illegal drugs across the Rio Grande and onto highways heading north. He swatted at a solitary mosquito, frowning. She was a mother, too, one who clearly doted on her child. Yet he had been told she might be letting traffickers move freely across her ranch. And profiting from it?

He stood in the shadows by the grill, watching her thoughtfully. On the tiled patio near the house, the girls were dancing, except for Amy, who was standing shyly to one side, watching. Even Maribel was moving across the large, flat slabs with the music, spinning around and seeming, for once, her age. Becky clambered off the bench and trundled over to join the fun, and Rosa began carrying things in from the table. Dell sat alone at the table, her features in profile, the light falling around her as she watched over them, her slender fingers tapping out music on the table.

Sighing, he forked the last of the meat onto a tray and carried it into the kitchen. He put the tray down and was turning to go when the phone shrilled. "Can someone get that?" Rosa called from the pantry. "I'm on a stool."

He picked up the receiver. "Hello?" There was a long pause on the other end, and his instincts told them someone was debating whether or not to answer. He tried again in, in Spanish. "*Bueno? Quién es?*" He could sense the other party still on the other end, but no one answered. Then, after a moment, the line clicked as the caller hung up.

"Was it for Dell?" Rosa asked, coming out of the pantry, still breathless from her climbing and storing.

He shrugged. "I don't know. No one answered." He looked at Rosa consideringly. "She doesn't have caller ID?"

The older woman frowned at his question. "I think she does, in her office—but it's not much your business, is it?"

"No, but it might make sense with the girls here and all. Do their families call? Wouldn't it be a problem if strangers—or friends of theirs, even—called at all hours?"

Rosa's frown faded into an expression of concern. "Don't suppose Dell's ever thought about the kitchen phone needing all that modern stuff—she knows I don't like it. Probably was just some wrong number, or someone playing with the phone. Nothing to fuss over."

"I'm sure it wasn't," he agreed quickly. Rosa didn't like him, and he couldn't increase her agitation—or suspicions. "I suppose I was out of line." He hesitated, trying to come up with something to smooth over his insistent questions. "Guess I'm borrowing trouble. Maribel's attitude bothers me. I just don't want her to cause problems for Dell."

Rosa's frown deepened. "Well, amen to that! I tried to talk Dell out of opening her home to these—these delinquents, but she just wouldn't listen. She's too softhearted to say no, even when she should. Just hope she doesn't come to grief!" The woman shook her head. "I'll tell you what, her grandfather would disown her all over again if he knew what she was up to."

"Disowned?" Jovi cocked his head a little, kept his tone light. "What, she's an heiress or something?"

"Again, no business of yours, and no, she's not. The only ones who could leave her a dime wouldn't. Not that she'd take it if they did."

Rosa turned to the counter full of leftovers and began straightening up, effectively dismissing him.

"Everything was delicious," he offered, turning toward the door.

She gave him a brief nod and a forced smile. "Thanks. You did all right with the meat, yourself."

He nodded politely and went back outside.

The girls seemed to have called it a night; they had disappeared. Dell was fiddling with the dials on the boom box, and after a moment, Jose Luis Perales's mellow voice drifted out, singing a song Jovi hadn't heard in ages, *¿Cómo es él?* She looked embarrassed when Jovi stopped and smiled at her. "I may be the only person in the world whose favorite singer is Diego Verdaguer," she admitted. "I can't help it. I like these songs." Her smile widened. "My friends call them my grandmotherly songs. The only thing is, *their* grandmothers are into Ricky Martin."

He laughed. "There are people our age who discover Sinatra. What can I say?" He sat down on the bench, leaning back against the table. "So, was the evening a success, overall?" He glanced at the empty patio. "The girls disappeared pretty quick."

"Hmmm. Some to-die for group on the tube. I would have preferred they stay here where I can keep an eye on them, but . . . " She shrugged. "I don't want to be unreasonable. I avoid most censorship."

They sat a few minutes in silence, the sultry summer night blanketing them. In the rosebushes along the patio fence, a lone firefly flickered through the foliage, only visible when it delved into the shadows, away from the artificial lights. Far, far off, a faint howl echoed; Dell and Jovi both cocked their heads, listening.

"Coyote," Dell said eventually. "There are undoubtedly some on the ranch. But that one was pretty far off."

"I couldn't have told the difference between a coyote and a dog," Jovi admitted. "In Florida, we didn't have coyotes, not as far as I know. When I was here, I was a city kid."

"It sounds funny to hear someone call Laredo a city," she noted. "I'm so used to thinking of it just as home—the town I drive into for supplies, that kind of thing."

"And yet they say it's the fastest growing city in the country, with the trade going through here all the time." He grinned. "It's nothing like when I was growing up, that's for sure. You know, all my cousins would go out to their families' *ranchitos*—they knew coyotes, I guess. I just heard dogs barking."

She turned to regard him thoughtfully. "Why not you?"

He shrugged, fighting down the faint resurgence of old anger and bitterness. "My mom married against her family's wishes, and then my dad left her when I was five. We were the poor relatives— the church mice. They never forgave her for not doing what she was told, and then, when they might have . . ." He sighed. "She has her pride. She wasn't willing to be 'forgiven.'" After a moment, he forced a smile. "So I never heard coyotes, except in movies. And of course, I read about them almost daily since I came back to Laredo. The rabid kind, on ranches, and the human kind, too."

She was silent, ignoring his mention of the smugglers, or *coyotes*, who brought illegal aliens across the Rio Grande, and she seemed lost in distant thought. The lights overhead fell softly on her face, highlighting her wistful expression. Not wistful, he decided. Pained. He hesitated, torn between speaking and leaving, when abruptly she made a visible effort to refocus her thoughts on him. "Coyotes are a real problem. Webb County has been fighting the rabid coyote population for years. I think there's some headway—but they're the only animals I've ever shot at. The four-legged kind. The two-legged kind *should* be shot. They rape and kill the people who pay them for protection for a chance at a new life . . . I don't think very much of alien smugglers."

"You weren't thinking about *coyotes*, though," he said, and saw surprise come and go in her eyes.

"No," she admitted, "I wasn't." She looked off into the darkness. "I was thinking about family." She didn't look at him. "My mother married someone against her family's wishes, too. It cost her more than weekends at family ranches, though." Color swept through her cheeks when she realized what she'd said, and she turned back to him with embarrassment. "I'm sorry—that sounds so conceited," she apologized. "I didn't mean to be condescending about what happened to your mother. It's just—" She stopped. He wanted to tell her he hadn't even thought about her words, but didn't, hoping she would say more.

"My mother is a De Cordova."

Jovi stared at her, feigning surprise. "*The* De Cordovas? The Monterrey De Cordovas?"

"My grandfather is Lionel De Cordova Estrada," she said, her words matter-of-fact but her tone icy. "Or was." She gave him a tight-lipped smile. "I'm disinherited—not that I give a damn. I take no pride in claiming that particular part of my heritage."

"Your mother—"

"My mother is Lionel's baby—Erika Claudia De Cordova. She took her name back legally after the divorce from my father—it was the only way he'd take her back, I guess." Dell's face was hard, her expression grim. "I haven't seen my mother since my father's funeral, nine years ago. Not that she came for that. She came for me. To take me home, she said."

"To Monterrey?"

"To Monterrey. She suggested if I was really attached to this place"—Dell looked around the patio again—"that I keep it. Land's always an asset, she said, especially this land, since it's on the river."

"But you didn't go back?"

Dell shrugged, shivering a little with anger. "I was twenty-two. I didn't have to. I couldn't believe her nerve—she divorced my father when I was fifteen. She'd been away seven years—then she decided my place was with her!" Dell's fingers tapped nervously on the table for a moment, her long, slender fingers showing the agitation she was fighting to conceal. When she looked across the table again, the grimness had gone.

"When I said I'd lost more than you, Jovi, I didn't mean the money," she explained quietly. "You have a mother. I can't imagine what it would have been . . . having a mother. A real mother. When I was little, before my mother decided she was a De Cordova, not a Rosales, and for the year or two when my grandparents played along with her marriage, I'd see friends of mine with their mothers. Real mothers, who'd make tacos and comb their kids' hair instead of having someone else do it." Agitated, she slid off the bench and stood, crossing her arms over her chest. "Even in Monterrey, where all the families who visited us had maids and chauffeurs, the mothers were there. They cared. You could tell. For some reason my mother never did." She blinked once, and the faint sheen of tears glistened across her dark eyes. "That's why I said I lost more—but excuse me for how it must have sounded."

He stood too, surprising himself, and laid a hand against her cheek. "No one should lose a mother," he said. "I'm sorry."

For a brief second, she leaned into the caress, drawing comfort from the warm, strong fingers cupping her face. Just as abruptly she straightened, drawing away from him, drawing her aloofness around her like a cloak.

"Thanks. But it's late, and I didn't mean to bore you with old history. If you have time tomorrow morning, I'd like to meet with you about the horses."

She was back to being unreachable again, moving back at the precise instance tenderness had jolted into sexual awareness.

Not the best time, he decided, to ask anything else about the De Cordovas. "You're the boss," he drawled. "Good night, Dell."

He walked into the darkness away from the patio, unsettled and annoyed. He'd worked undercover before, successfully and not much bothered by lies or half-truths. Truth be known, Dell's distance and remoteness provided protection—against him, and the danger he represented. Truth be known—that was the hell of it. The truth couldn't be known until much too late to matter.

CHAPTER FIVE

Dell stood at the bedroom window watching rain slash against the pane. The storm had come as a shock—there was virtually no mid-summer rain in this arid part of the country. Clouds threatened regularly, and occasionally lightning could be seen in the distance, but storms usually poured out their fury trying to get over the mountains that all but encircled Monterrey, 150 miles to the south. *Well, this time, we're getting the rain*, she thought. The conversation with Jovi last night must really have brought back the old hostility, she mused. Here she was, dutifully dredging up every old anti-Monterrey sentiment she'd ever heard expressed, just as if she hadn't once moved among Monterrey's elite. Besides it really wasn't the city that sapped resources from the surrounding areas—the city was blameless.

The culprits were the Lionel De Cordovas, Mexico's version of the robber barons, the expansionists. They couldn't move west physically, so they just enriched themselves by every means possible within the limits of their own territory. She walked over to her desk and picked up her brush, dragging it through her hair, wishing away all the errant thoughts. The brush caught momentarily, and she breathed an oath as she jerked it free.

Her fiancé Jeremy had hated the way she'd brushed her hair. She shuddered, remembering his hands on her hair, smoothing the dark length with such care. Except it hadn't been love at all. Just need. Need for the money she always provided. Need for the safety net when no one else would let him back in. She'd never seen him with drugs, made it clear it was her or the drugs. But she always thought he'd choose her. That he loved her. And in the end . . . The end didn't matter. Not any more, she reminded herself angrily. There'd been too many ends in her life, but she could start over. Would. She just needed to focus on changing her immediate world. She reached across the dresser to pick up the heavy, silver-framed photo of her father, holding her and beaming with pride as she reached up to pet his favorite mare on the forehead. Idly she ran a finger over the cold glass.

She loved the horses, but horse ranching was expensive—not really something she could afford anymore. Her father had kept this property in the divorce settlement, although taking anything from the woman who had spurned him had galled him. He had lived his last years in bitterness, seeking some way to win back the woman he never really could have. Dell wondered if he'd ever accepted that her mother no longer loved him. If she ever had. She herself suspected Erika Claudia De Cordova was incapable of love. Her father Samuel had been a summer fling—a rebellious moment in a rich girl's life. They had married, Dell suspected, because Samuel was in love, and a devout Catholic, and because Erika felt like it—for a few months.

In any event, they were both gone now, and she had herself and the girls to think about. Keeping the horses—at least raising horses—might not be in her best interests. She'd always planned on coming back to the ranch to do that, but with her father. And now that she was providing shelter to girls with family problems, largely at her own expense, she needed time to devote to them. She needed to be home.

Her training in international trade, though, made staying home inconvenient. Out of college, she'd worked as an independent advisor to companies seeking input into trade matters involving Mexican companies. She'd made good money helping American and Canadian companies set up ventures in Mexico—especially Monterrey. That option was out there, but the waters were muddied by the drug wars and her reluctance to leave the ranch again. With so much violence seizing virtually all of Mexico, could she risk her own safety at the girls' expense? Surely she could find a way to earn a decent income without constant travel . . .

Thinking about money always dragged her back to her father's unexpected legacy. How on earth had he accumulated the amount of money he'd left her?

She slapped the photo back in its place. Damn the horses! If they weren't so tied to everything good in her childhood, she'd sell the whole lot and be done with them. That way she could fire Jovani Treviño and be done with him, too. She paced around the room, still irritated that this morning she'd gone down to the stable to talk to him, only to find out he'd gone into Laredo on business and would call her when he got back and had time. The nerve of the man. She was in charge here, wasn't she? Hadn't she made an appointment with him to discuss the horses? The abrupt thought of his hand on her face stopped her in mid-step, and she lifted a hand to touch her own cheek. She was in charge—and she'd better be very certain Jovi Treviño kept his distance.

The absence of rain beating on the window slowly penetrated her consciousness. The storm had pounded itself out and gone, and sun was thrusting through the remaining clouds. She glanced at the clock. Becky probably was waking from her nap right about now. She'd take the toddler down to the stable with her. The little girl loved going, and she was good company. Dell didn't get quite as much done when the toddler was around, but it was still a good trade-off. Humming to herself, she hurried down the hall.

The door to the girls' room was open. Selina, Michelle, and Amy all stayed together, although she had offered Amy, who had come after Selina and Michelle, a room of her own. Amy had refused, wanting to stay with the other two. They seemed to draw strength from each other, and Dell was glad they got along so well.

She glanced again at her watch. The four girls should be downstairs now, with the retired teacher who drove out three times a week to give them classes. The door to Maribel's room was closed, and she knocked once, then pushed the door open. The room was a shambles—the bed linens on a heap in the floor, clothes on the floor, one of the dresser drawers pulled out crookedly. She fought the urge to walk around tidying the room—Maribel needed to do it herself. She sniffed, frowning. There was a faint but undeniable smoke smell in the room. She wondered how the sixteen-year-old had come by cigarettes, which she had been told not to bring. Again she wondered if she should send Maribel back to the juvenile detention center—this had just started as a favor to a friend, after all. She really couldn't jeopardize everyone's health for one bull-headed little . . .

"Dell!" Becky came out of her room, rubbing still-sleepy eyes, and held her arms out to be picked up. Dell laughed and hugged her close, wondering how anyone could have abandoned this sweet-tempered bundle of happiness. Becky was here at the moment as a foster child, but her mother had little interest in reclaiming her. Dell pressed another kiss against her head, breathing her daily prayer to win permanent custody.

"Do you want to help me work?" she asked, and Becky nodded, her curls bouncing.

"Me hep."

"You're a sweetheart," Dell told her. "But you're also getting so big. Would you like to walk now? All the way to the barn?"

"*Yo camino*," the girl said immediately and slid from Dell's arms. The quick, Spanish reply was a relief. Becky's mother spoke only Spanish. Sending Becky home—if, God forbid, that was ever home again—with no ability to communicate would be unfair to everyone.

"Everything's so complicated," Dell muttered, sighing, and then she laughed out loud when Becky mimicked her with an exaggerated sigh of her own.

Dell stopped by the kitchen, telling Rosa where they'd be and double-checking that the girls were in fact with their teacher. All the girls had spotty attendance during the regular school year, and wouldn't catch up without help.

On the way, Becky delighted in jumping into every puddle along the drive. Dell cringed each time the water splashed up, covering those little legs and spotting the pastel plaid playsuit, but she bit back any scolding words. She vividly remembered being forced to be constantly clean and neat as a child, always dressed in frilly, light-colored clothes except when her father smuggled her out of the house to ride. She didn't want to impose her own abhorrence of mud-spattered clothes on the child. Still, by the time they made it to the barn, she was glad to see Karla Gonzalez walking toward them, leading her daughter Allison on the spotted Shetland pony she boarded here at the ranch.

Becky immediately ran up to her, arms outstretched, and the woman laughed and swept her up, unmindful of the mud as she clasped her close.

"Hi, *princesa*," she greeted the little one. She smiled at Dell. "I see Becky discovered mud puddles. Can she come ride with Allison?"

Allison Gonzalez smiled shyly, clinging apprehensively to the saddle horn in front of her. Dell smiled back at the older child and nodded. "Sure. Do you want to borrow *Carbón*?"

"That poor old pony wouldn't know what to do with a saddle on his back," Karla said, shaking her head. "No, the girls can share." She cast a meaningful glance at her five-year-old. "Everyone needs to share sometimes."

Dell grinned and walked with them to the corral. Karla was as close to being a friend as anyone. Karla was strong, and Dell admired her ability to make painful decisions and move on them. The woman had recently divorced her husband when she discovered another woman in the picture, and struck out on her own despite her family's objections. Unwilling to leave Allison in day care centers, she'd originally come to the ranch to apply for a day job. Rosa had been indignant that Dell had given Karla part-time work in the house, but helping with the teenagers had become a convenient excuse, and as their friendship had grown, Karla had become something of a fixture on the ranch, working or not.

Karla was in her usual high spirits, chatting lightly as they walked together. When they reached the corral gate, though, she paused a moment, looking up at Dell with curiosity in her eyes.

"So . . . where is he?"

"He?" Dell repeated, and Karla laughed.

"Ay, *niña*!—Jovi. Who else?"

Dell looked at her with some surprise. "You've met Jovani?"

"Met him? Dear girl, I propositioned him. I devoured him with my eyes. I asked him to marry me!" She laughed. "Unfortunately, he said no, and I haven't seen him since. Where in the world did you find that gorgeous man?"

Karla's enthusiasm surprised her—hadn't this very same woman told her just two weeks ago that she had decided against joining an online dating service? That she'd decided she liked her independence, at least for the moment? And that if her resolve didn't fail, she intended to die a "later-life virgin," as she had put it?

When Dell didn't immediately respond, the laughter faded from the other woman's eyes. "You're not pissed, are you?" she asked, setting Becky down in front of her. "I mean, I am mostly kidding." Then she smiled again. "Except about the gorgeous part. And asking him out."

Dell shook her head. "I'm not angry. Just a little startled. I thought you swore off men, Karla?"

"Oh, come on, Dell. We all claim to, but none of us do."

"I have," she retorted instantly, stubbornly, and was relieved Karla didn't laugh at her cool pronouncement.

The woman merely shrugged. "I know you think you have, Dell. And Lord knows you've kept your vows longer than I'm likely to keep mine. But sooner or later you'll meet a man." She bent to pick Becky back up, settling her in the saddle in front of Allison and patting the pony's neck then turning back to Dell. *The man—the one you want. It won't matter if he doesn't want you."* Her teasing tone turned serious. "It won't even matter if you can't have him—if he's married, or a sleazeball or a jerk—there'll be a man even *you'll* want." She pushed the gate open and led the pony in, then paused and said over her shoulder, "Wouldn't it be funny if that man were Jovani Treviño?"

*

A few minutes later, unsmiling and unamused by Karla's parting words, Dell walked into the office and sat down at the desk. Somehow, knowing someone else used this office now made her feel awkward. Reminding herself she was the employer, she jerked the desk drawer open. A folded piece of yellow legal paper caught her eye, and she pulled it out, looking at it curiously. There was a scribbled name and a phone number with a Houston area code. One of the advantages to her old job—and her excellent memory—was that she rarely needed to look up an area code for any major center of commerce. The name beneath the phone number, in Jovi's casual scrawl, meant nothing to her, nor did the words "not entirely sure." But the hairs on her neck and arms bristled when her eyes moved to the Spanish words written just under that in the same, dark ink: *la inalcanzable.*

"*Buenas tardes,*" Jovi said from the doorway, and she started, dropping the paper and flushing guiltily. He lounged comfortably against the doorjamb, tall and imposing, his dark eyes unreadable as he watched her. She wasn't sure how long he'd been there, either; in spite of his size and his worn leather boots, she hadn't heard him until he spoke.

"Hello." She stood, waving at the chair across from her. "Have a seat. I was just going to see what needed doing."

She didn't realize she'd left the paper on the desk until he settled into his seat and saw it. He picked the yellow scrap of paper up without comment, folding it and sticking it in a pocket, and gave her a guarded smile.

"I see Mrs. Gonzalez came. She seems to enjoy bringing her daughter over."

She fought the urge to tell him *why* she enjoyed bringing Allison, aware it would sound petty and controlling. But she frowned, nevertheless. "I thought we decided we'd get together this morning?" she ventured, after a moment. "I came down around eight-thirty, and you were gone."

"Yep. Drove in to Laredo unexpectedly." He didn't seem at all repentant as he watched her from across the desk. "I assume that's not a problem—we didn't really discuss issues like sick leave or emergency time off."

"It doesn't matter," Dell said. "Is it your mother? If she needs you—"

Jovi waved it off. "Everything's taken care of."

"We need to talk about the horses, then." She leaned back in her chair, trying to put some distance between them. Even across the desk, his presence was distracting. His eyes glinted, and sun touched his hair, his mustache, creating tiny, fiery sparks mingled in with the darker browns. Damn Karla! Dell hadn't needed anyone to call attention to Jovani's good looks. Across from her, Jovi shifted slightly in his chair, then raised his arms and crossed them behind his head. His white shirt, partially unbuttoned, gaped a little, showing a patch of bronzed skin.

"I hope you don't mind that I was at your desk," she said after a moment. "It seems strange, sharing the office with someone else."

"I can use the other desk," he offered, waving a hand at the room's second desk, unused in years except to hold an unorganized collection of old magazines and clutter. "And there's no need to feel uncomfortable in your own office." She regarded him thoughtfully. What he said was perfectly reasonable, but there had been something in his voice, some shadow of . . . something. Impatient with herself, she decided she was imagining it, due, no doubt, to Karla's unexpected confidences. Stalling, she stretched—and knew she wasn't imagining the way his eyes swept across the thin, blue fabric of the knit top she was wearing. She ignored the unspoken interest in his eyes and went on.

"I'm hardly ever here. It would be silly, really—although it would look better." She hesitated, trying to find a way to ask about the words on the yellow paper without seeming nosy. "Do we have business contacts in Houston already?" she asked after a moment.

His lips twitched. "*I* do," he answered, and then laughed out loud. "Why do the words 'control freak' suddenly come to mind, Ms. Rosales?"

"What do you mean?" she asked indignantly, flushing a little, because she realized her annoyance must have shown in her eyes in spite of her determination to mask it.

"You need to delegate, but you don't like turning anything loose. You still want to be in charge." He shook his head at her. "Maybe we can't deny our heritage, Dell. I don't know old *Don* Lionel, but you probably just did him proud." Ignoring the anger replacing her annoyance, he pulled the scrap out of his pocket and waved it between them like a flag. "This actually is a business acquaintance of mine—nothing about the work I do here. Well, except that I had a job offer with a Houston company. I turned it down."

"Hmmm." Dell tapped a finger on her knee, leaning forward a little. "And just out of curiosity, since we've established that I'm nosy and controlling, what does *la inalcanzable* mean?" She held up a hand as Jovi started to answer. "Don't tell me what it means—we both speak Spanish. Tell me why it's written here on this paper."

Jovi straightened in his chair, and his eyes bored into hers. For a moment, she thought he wasn't going to answer. "*La inalcanzable.*" He hesitated, but his eyes met hers unflinchingly. "It's what I called Griselda—what I still call her, sometimes, when I remember. Is anyone more off limits than the boss's wife?" His mouth twisted as he pocketed the note. "Satisfied, Dell?"

"Perfectly," she returned crisply, and stood up. "Let's look over the horses. I've reached a decision about some of them."

His eyes swept over her again appraisingly, and when he stood up, she was struck again by how tall he was. He towered over her, and she was tall, even in the low-heeled sandals she'd worn today. She thinned her lips, willing herself to discard her vague apprehensions about the man. "Follow me," she ordered, in her best control-freak voice, and walked out of the office.

"My pleasure," he murmured sardonically, giving her an insolent shrug when she turned to glare at his double-edged reply. "Hey, I'm just the hired hand, *jefa*. You lead, I follow." He laughed as her frown became more pronounced. "There's a lot to be said for following women bosses." Shaking his head at her, he waved down the hall corridor. "After you."

Clamping her lips together, Dell turned and walked toward the first stall, conscious of Jovi's eyes on her with each step she took. It was a relief to stop at the first half-open stall door. The big, sorrel mare inside nickered and came over to have her head scratched. Dell put a hand on the mare's broad cheek, reaching up to rub behind her ears with the other. The mare snuffled contentedly against Dell's chest, then reached her muzzle up and blew against her cheek. The idea of selling this gentle old friend brought sudden tears to her eyes, and she blinked them away grimly.

"This is Red Sugar Cash," she said. "She was my father's favorite."

He nodded. "Pete filled me in on names and a little history." He reached out to pat the mare's neck, his arm brushing warmly across her Dell's shoulder. "She's probably the best quarter horse on the place, too," he noted. "There's no reason to sell her—she's healthy, and still young enough to have another colt or two. Even if she isn't bred again, she's gentle enough for your teenagers to ride."

Dell turned to look up at him. "Well, well. I'm surprised at you, Jovi. Finding an excuse for me to keep a non-producer? I thought you'd give me that old saw about 'out with the old, in with the new' some men are so fond of."

He ignored her barb, moving instead toward the next stall with a business-like air. "You pay me to be heartless, Dell. In my line of work, it's absolutely necessary. Always has been." He paused, looking down at her, before adding, "If you expect to make any money at all with the horses. But, believe it or not, I'm a big backer of retirement in green pastures. I can't condone someone owning one of these animals for years and then shipping it off to the slaughterhouse when it doesn't bring in the bread." They stopped at the next door, and Jovi smiled ruefully, pointing into the shadows. The gray mare in the back of the stall looked at them with disinterest, then snorted at them with flattened ears and turned back to her hay.

"Now, Snow Mist here is another story," he said. "We don't like each other."

"So I see," Dell retorted, smiling a little at the mare's behavior and shaking her head. "Come here, Snow," she crooned, holding out a hand. The mare gave Jovi a baleful glare, but came over to Dell. Although she showed none of Sugar's affection, she let Dell pat the wide, white blaze that ran down her face. "She doesn't like men," Dell noted, a trace smugly.

"There's probably a name for that," Jovi muttered, and Dell gave him a false smile.

"There is—intelligence."

He laughed and reached gingerly into the stall to tug at the hay net.

"Snow's not quite nine years old," he pointed out, staying out of reach as the mare suddenly snapped at Dell, who swatted her muzzle gently and pushed her head away. "She has an excellent pedigree. She'd make a good broodmare—for someone raising quarter horses."

"She was in the foal crop born the spring Papi died," Dell said quietly. "He would have loved her and done wonders with her, but she's not really trained. I never had time. Pete and Danny try, but they were really just hired to clean and feed. Neither had experience training, just as grooms."

"She should go—and not because I don't like her," he insisted as Dell arched a brow at him. "She's probably the most valuable mare on the ranch that you could part with. Unless you've decided to keep the quarter horses and Appaloosas and get out of Arabians," he added. "Which, frankly, would make better sense in this part of the country."

Dell sighed, bit her lip for a moment, and then impulsively laid a hand on his arm. "Let me show you something about good sense," she said. She took him to the end of the corridor, temporarily ignoring the heads emerging from stall doors. At the end of the hall, she pushed open the door to the trophy room. Old trophies, most of them hers, were in cabinets and shelves, on tables and the floor. Ribbons, faded from the years, hung down the walls. She was surprised at how clean it all was, and he seemed to read her thoughts.

"I cleaned up a little," he told her. "I thought it was important to see what the horses had done before."

She led him over to the wall behind the still-cluttered desk at the far end and pointed. Two framed oil paintings took up a large section of the paneled wall. Both paintings were of stallions running across green pastures.

"The one on the left is champion Edwards Go Jet," she said, motioning at the bay quarter horse. "He was Dad's first stallion, and his get are still winning points in halter and Western pleasure and performance classes."

"I've heard of him," Jovi said evenly. "I believe the ledger shows he died, what, six years ago?"

"Yes. But look at him. Then look at Mojave." She swept her hand at the picture of the black Arabian flashing across a field, head up, eyes wild as he raced.

"Hmmm. Magnificent."

"Free. Spirited." She turned to him, her eyes intense. "Quarter horses keep their heads—they're supposed to. In Western pleasure, some of them almost drag their noses. They're so . . . so sensible. So useful." She shook her head. "I can't trade that"—she pointed at the Arab—"for that. I don't see how anyone could."

After a moment, her shoulders hunched in a small shrug, and she reached up to straighten a trophy of a rider taking a high fence.

He studied her thoughtfully. "We're not just talking about horses, are we?" he asked, and she shook her head.

"When I went to Columbia, it was all right. I really felt . . . okay. But I spent a summer at UT up in Austin—and would you believe my roommate moved out when she found out I was Mexican-American?"

He gaped a little, and she nodded. "I'm light-skinned and have money, so I get by. But I'll never forget that summer." Her voice hardened. "And I won't ever forget a dude ranch I visited. The woman who ran it had help from Mexico—illegal aliens." She turned away, looking at the pictures again, anger hardening her tone. "She used to joke at dinner about having 'out-of-state contractors.' But when she cursed them out, they had to just stand there with their heads down and put up with it. Because they had families back home, babies that needed food." She turned back to him grimly. "She never knew I spoke Spanish. She has no idea how much I found out about Beto and Lolo and the other illegals who worked there, and she wouldn't have cared anyway. It made a terrible impression on me, seeing them leading the horses—the quarter horses—over to all those laughing, uncaring people, and I wanted to shout at them to hold their heads up. But they couldn't, because she would have picked up a phone, called Immigration, and then found somebody else who was hungry." She drew a deep breath and ran a hand through her hair, tousling it. She glanced across at Jovi, tight-mouthed and still. A muscle twitched at the corner of his mouth, as if her pain and anger gripped him as well. "The saddest part is I realized the dude ranch owner wasn't a lot different from my grandfather. Or my mother. They were as arrogant and cold, and they humiliated just as many employees and associates. My father spent the last years of his life walking with his head down—but he loved my mother until the day he died."

Jovi couldn't think of anything to say, and he watched her silently as she turned away, almost shaking with agitation, to look blankly at one of the walls, decorated with the fading cascade of ribbons. "I could have grown up to be her," she said so softly he almost couldn't hear her. "To be them."

"But you didn't," he countered gently. "You grew up to be a woman who cares—apparently passionately—about people with problems." And then, trying to ease the mood, he grinned. "And about Arabians, obviously."

She smiled sheepishly and glanced again at the pictures before turning to face him. "Yeah. I want to keep the Arabians, Jovi. All of them. And the two Thoroughbreds. Red Sugar Cash. Those are non-negotiable. We'll do what we have to with the others."

He nodded. "In that case, let's finish our tour. But this time, you follow me!"

She laughed, but was a little disconcerted, as she walked out the door behind him, to find herself wishing his jeans fit just a little tighter.

CHAPTER SIX

The night was silent and sultry. Dell sat up in bed, listening for whatever sound had jolted her from her dream. She frowned, remembering abruptly what she had been dreaming, glad the room was empty and dark. Heat singed her cheeks as she blushed, remembering the passionate moments she had just shared with a brooding, annoying man named Jovani Treviño. *Inalcanzable?* Friends who'd given her the nickname so long ago had been dead wrong. In the dream, she'd been a wanton, lost in the power and passion.

She didn't believe the man's hands moving over her in her dream had awakened her, though. She thought she had heard a noise downstairs, but there was nothing now. She slid out of bed and padded quietly from her room. The girls' doors were open. After confronting Maribel about smoking, she had forbidden her to close her door, and the other three liked the hall light. They all were escaping their own dark fears, no doubt, and needed the reassurance in what must still be a strange place for them.

She opened the door to Becky's room and went inside, making a thorough search of the room. She paused to turn on the angel nightlight Rosa had given the toddler the day she came to the ranch. Had that been a year ago already? Becky had hardly been able to walk when she came, her little body weakened from malnutrition, her muscles undeveloped from being confined in a small crib for endless hours. Now she slept soundly, exhausted, no doubt, from her afternoon with Allison Gonzalez. After riding for hours, the girls had gone swimming with Karla, and the two had stayed for supper. Dell touched Becky's cheek as the child smiled in her sleep. She was dreaming with angels, Rosa would have said.

Dell's long nightgown slithered around her as she walked down the softly lighted hall, passing her upstairs study. Nothing seemed amiss. She hesitated on the top stair and considered going back for a robe, then decided she was being silly. After all, this was her house, and anyway, Rosa had undoubtedly double-locked the doors and windows as she did every night. The older woman was a worrier but a sound sleeper. Although the *Nueva Brisa* was relatively isolated from Laredo and the usual urban problems of burglary, vandalism, and, more recently, incursions from drug runners, Rosa insisted on all kinds of locks and bolts. Rosa's latest demand to buy a dog might mean problems with those overseeing the teens, but might be worth considering.

Feeling silly at her trepidation, Dell hoisted the hem of the floor-length gown enough that she wouldn't be likely to trip on it, and went quietly down the stairs. The spacious living room was dark and empty. Nothing moved in the shadows. She stuck her head into the den. Nothing seemed to be amiss, although she had the strange sensation of just having missed someone. She flipped on a light and glanced around. The windows were closed and nothing seemed out of place. Drawing in a deep breath, she headed back toward the living room. There was a sudden, muffled noise in the kitchen, as if someone had bumped something, and, unthinking, she sprinted through the dining room, hitting her own hip on a chair, and switched on the light by the dining room door.

On the other side of the room, a figure crouched beside the sink slowly straightened, holding a canister he must have knocked down.

"What the hell are you doing in my kitchen?" Dell spat, crossing the room toward him angrily, forgetful of her lacy, translucent nightgown.

"I'm sorry I woke you," he said, apparently unabashed at being caught in the house in the dead of night. He held up a flashlight. "I walk around a lot at night, watching things." He shrugged a little. "It was part of my job at Heaven's Thunder, being sure the place was secure. Dave and Griselda had received some threats." He looked around the kitchen. "Anyway, I thought I heard something, and I saw someone moving around with the lights off, so I came in. I guess it was my imagination—I didn't find anyone." He smiled. "Until you turned the light on. Then I found you."

"You did not find me," Dell muttered, wondering if she believed his glib story. Then again, why would he lie? What possible reason could he have for being inside except to have wanted to check on everything? Her brow furrowed as she considered his explanation, and she crossed her arms.

"What did you think you heard?" she demanded, not masking the suspicion in her voice. Something about this whole episode still didn't fit.

"I'm not sure. Just—it was more a sensation." He looked around the room again, then back at her. "Did Rosa tell you about the wrong numbers?" he asked after a minute, and was satisfied when she blinked in surprise.

"What?"

"I can see she didn't." He didn't want to cause Rosa problems, but she was his best way out of this current predicament. He formed his explanation carefully. "I'm sure she didn't want to concern you, but someone's been calling, breathing into the phone rather heavily, and then hanging up. It worried me when I answered, because of the girls." He shrugged. "You haven't said exactly why the girls are here. But anyone who reads the news these days would worry about all these stalkers and abusers who just won't give up their victims."

She shivered a little and looked grim. "Rosa should have told me. I'll check into it tomorrow." She let go of the last of her anger. "I'm sorry I sounded suspicious. Thank you for caring enough to check up on things."

He stepped toward her, closing the distance between them, leaning toward her as he answered, "My pleasure."

She blinked and stepped back, suddenly too aware of her wildly tousled hair, the sheer nightgown, and the memory of his body scalding hers in her unexpected, unwelcome dream.

"Jovi," she whispered, but he reached out a hand and cupped her cheek again. A simple gesture. That might have been innocent if it weren't so intimate. If his touch didn't burn. And it was too unreal, too much like a moment from her dream, for her to do more than gasp and step into his arms with a muffled moan.

For a moment, she just stood there, pressed against him, against his warmth, and then, hesitatingly, her arms moved up to clutch at his arms. He tilted her head up to him, and his lips closed over hers, gentle at first, then demanding. His tongue toyed with her teeth, her tongue; he buried a hand in her hair, supporting her head as he kissed her over and over, his other hand moving over her bare shoulders, sliding down her back, then urging her closer into the hard hotness of his body. It was her dream, replayed, but his fingers seared real flesh, caressed her insistently. She whispered his name again, desperately, and buried her face in the hollow of his shoulder, turning her head to press her lips against his throat in mute need.

And then, from a very far off place, she heard a snort of derisive laughter and jerked away from him, her face flaming as he slid one of the fallen straps back over her shoulder.

"Well, well. *Mira, no más!*" Maribel stood in the doorway, her face twisted into a sneer. "So this is what the judge thought would be appropriate for me? I saw this at home and everywhere else I've ever been!"

Dell struggled for composure, but it was Jovi's voice that asked matter-of-factly, "Did you need something, Maribel?"

The teenager shrugged, giving him a twisted smile. "Oh, no, I don't need anything, Jovi. I just came downstairs because I thought

I heard something." Her smirk was full of malevolence. "I guess it was just all the heavy breathing."

"Maribel—" Dell said, but the girl shook her head and held up a hand.

"You're older than I am. You can do it legally." She shrugged again. "No matter anyone could walk in for a drink or a snack." She waggled her hand again, turning away. "Have fun, guys. I would."

Dell sagged as Maribel walked out, clasping her burning cheeks in horror. "This is awful!"

"No." Jovi's voice behind her was soft. Comforting. Gently, he turned her toward him, pulling her hands from her cheeks. "It was beautiful, right up until a moment ago. And we'll all get over that." Very gently his lips brushed hers again, and then he stepped back. She could sense his reluctance, see it in his eyes. "Unfortunately, she's right. This isn't the place."

Dell's mouth opened to tell him there was no place, but his finger silenced her, holding back her intended denial.

"There will be a place," he said very softly, as if he had heard her unspoken words. "A time. Just not here. Just not tonight." He placed a whispered kiss on her forehead, then brushed her lips with his own. "We'll talk," he said. "Tomorrow." And then he turned and went out, leaving her alone in the strangely dark, empty kitchen.

CHAPTER SEVEN

Dell pulled her hair up on top of her head, pinned it securely, and studied her reflection in the mirror. Makeup covered most of the damage done by a sleepless night. She'd used one of her brighter lipsticks to call attention away from tired eyes, and the coral blouse under the oatmeal jacket was one of her favorites. She was wearing a business suit this morning; she had to escort Michelle to a court appearance. Personal friend or not, Judge Ovalle-Martinez always leaned toward family. Michelle didn't belong with her mother yet. So Michelle would stay here. Setting her mouth in determination, Dell turned and went down to breakfast.

The girls were all at the table. Not a morning person, she ate breakfast only because Rosa insisted it set a good example. But she did make sure the four girls were out of bed early in the morning, doing their chores and studying before they went out to ride or swim. Selina, Amy, and Michelle were huddled closely together on one side of the table, and Michelle's expression was one of apprehension. Maribel was sitting alone, and shot her a knowing glance.

"Good morning, Dell," Maribel said, her voice dripping with sarcasm. The other three looked somewhat embarrassed, and Dell could see at once that Maribel must have told them what had happened between her and Jovi.

"Good morning," she answered, forcing her own tone to be pleasant. "How are you feeling, Michelle?"

"Shitty." Michelle looked across at her, her face full of fear.

"Michelle—"

"Michelle, you never talk like me—" Selina sputtered, then glared at Dell. "And you never let me talk like that either! How come she gets to?"

Michelle ignored Amy and Selina as they pounced on her unusual choice of words. "They might send me home! Mom hates me—"

"Hate's too strong a word," Amy argued. "*Tu mamá—tiene que quererte*." She slapped her glass down on the table with a thud, repeating her words with insistence. "Moms love their kids. Period. *Punto*."

Dell pursed her mouth, biting back an unhelpful response to Amy's insistence. Michelle's mother didn't have to love her daughter. Dell knew better than that. But she'd never hurt any of the girls by disagreeing with Amy's evaluation.

"Don't you get it?" Michelle's voice wavered. "My dad left because of me—when he found Beto and me—" She stopped herself, looking devastated, and a tear ran down her cheek. Amy reached out to wipe it off her cheek, but Michelle swatted her hand away.

"Leave me alone!"

Dell came around the table and put a hand on Michelle's shoulder. "Your mom probably does love you," she said gently. "She just wasn't ready to deal with things—you having a boyfriend, her marriage collapsing—she didn't know how to cope. So she got a little crazy. But mothers don't just stop loving their kids."

"Hypocrite," Maribel muttered, and everyone in the room looked at her.

"Don't call Dell a hypocrite," Amy said angrily, surprising everyone.

"Why shouldn't I? We all know she is, don't we? Miss Saint Rosales, making out in the kitchen with the hired help—I don't see her mother around nowhere. *Saben quien*—you know who her mother is, right?"

None of the girls answered. Dell looked across at Maribel, dumbfounded. How could the teenager have found out about her mother? She raised a questioning brow.

"Who is my mother, Maribel?" she asked.

"That rich bitch. What's her name? Erika De Cordova."

The name didn't appear to impress the other teenagers, who just looked at Maribel with mixed confusion and anger.

"I'm thirty-something, Maribel. Would you expect me to still live with my mother?"

"She'd be around," the girl said heartlessly. "If she cared."

Dell took a deep breath. The judge and the court-appointed psychologist who had consulted with her before she had first taken in Selina had counseled against hiding anything truthful from the girls, saying they were all too well aware of the world and its sometimes ugly secrets.

"My mother and I don't see each other," she said levelly. "But that doesn't change anything I said to Michelle. I believe most mothers love their children—always. Maybe my mother loves me, and I've never given her the chance I should have."

"Or maybe she just hopes to get you out of this house and into someone else's," Maribel jeered to Michelle, sitting head down at the table.

"I don't think Michelle believes that," Dell said. "But most of the time, home is better than anywhere else." She sighed and went around the table, sitting down again. "I'm still a little puzzled as to how you knew who my mother is, Maribel. As far as I know, only two or three people on the ranch have that information—not that it much matters." The girl made no attempt to answer, just stabbed a fork into a piece of egg and swiped it across her plate, and Dell sipped her orange juice. "We'll have to discuss that later, though, because Michelle and I have to leave in a few minutes." She drank more juice, then put her glass down. "I think while we're all together, I should tell you about last night," she said. "I gather Maribel already mentioned it." The girl shrugged, but Dell looked squarely across at Selina, Michelle, and Amy. "You've heard me talk about bad choices before. I made one last night and I apologize. I should have been more responsible."

"*Responsible,*" Maribel snorted. "Shoulda just screwed in the broom closet?"

"No," Dell said coolly. "But if I were going to be . . . intimate with someone, it shouldn't have been there in the kitchen."

"I don't see what the big deal is," Selina shot back at Maribel. "It's her house, and it's not like any big deal. She kissed a guy. Even if she'd done it—everyone does it now, anyway."

"No," Dell protested. "Everyone doesn't."

"Now she's gonna tell you how you gotta wait 'til you get married," Maribel sneered, and Selina held up a finger with a gold band.

"I'm no *puta* like you—I *was* married," she said bitterly. "I just blew it, okay?"

"Sex doesn't just happen in marriages anymore, anyway," Dell cut in, "but I personally think there should be something more than hormones involved."

She turned to face Maribel calmly. "This conversation is over, but I still want to talk to you about some other things when I come back with Michelle." She smiled gently at Michelle, who had remained tense and quiet. "We're all counting on you coming back for a while, at least," she added, and Michelle forced a small smile and stood up.

She was wearing a dress she had picked out herself, and she looked very proper and very vulnerable all at once. Amy stood up and hugged her, and Selina pecked her on the cheek.

"Later, girlfriend," she said, and Michelle nodded, still without saying anything.

Dell stepped toward the door but paused momentarily as Rosa bustled in.

"Becky's still asleep," she announced, smiling. "That girl just hates to go to bed at night—and to get outta bed in the morning.

You both look perfect," she announced. She kissed Michelle, making the sign of the cross. "*Dios te bendiga*" she murmured in blessing. She turned to pick up Michelle's nearly full plate, then stopped suddenly, as if remembering abruptly to ask. "Did I hear noises last night? I thought I heard something, but then I fell asleep again just when I thought I'd better get up."

Ignoring Maribel's snort, Dell nodded. "Jovi, Maribel, and I were all in the kitchen. You must have heard one or the other of us."

"I guess," Rosa muttered. "Although it sounded more like it came from the study than the kitchen. Oh, well." She shrugged and started toward the kitchen. Hearing Rosa mention the study made Dell remember her own feeling of strangeness when she had walked into the room last night. Why hadn't she thought to ask Jovi if he'd also checked that room out? The thought of Jovi brought back another of her concerns.

She motioned the woman close and lowered her voice. "Rosa, have there been calls? Wrong numbers, or someone who doesn't answer?" she asked.

Rosa looked vague for a moment, then nodded. "Yeah, there have been. Jovi answered one when he brought the meat in the other day, and there was another that same night. I didn't think it was important. Then, yesterday, when it happened again, I was going to tell you, but I forgot." Rosa cast an accusing glance at Maribel. "Jovi suggested caller ID on all the phones. He thinks it might be some acquaintance of one of the girls. Trying to get in touch with someone without getting caught."

Maribel's expression didn't change as she glowered at Rosa. "I hope someone's trying to call me," she retorted. "I'd be gone before you could blink."

"You'd better remember the judge's orders," Dell reminded. "Your next stop is juvenile—out of town—until you're eighteen or until your parents prove they can manage you. The stay here should already be over, frankly." Dell paused, hoping her observation would sink in. "Here you have a private room, a pool, and your own music and clothes. If I were you, I'd make any new choices very carefully." She picked up her purse from the counter. "Come on, Michelle," she said, motioning for the girl to join her. "We'll see you all later," she added with a measure of conviction.

She waited while Michelle, unaccustomed to a skirt and dress shoes, settled into the front seat of the SUV. She fastened her own seat belt and maneuvered out of the garage, careful to maintain her composure. But as she turned onto the frontage road leading to IH 35 and Laredo, she couldn't stop thinking that only Rosa, Pete, and Jovani Treviño knew her mother. Pete had worked for her father virtually all his life. But he had no real time alone with the girls, and no reason to bring up Dell's mother. Rosa had worked for Erika Claudia De Cordova in Monterrey, but she'd quit when Dell was little and gone elsewhere, returning only after Dell's mother and father divorced. It was then, as a teenager, that Dell had found out how deeply Rosa hated her mother and how heartlessly Erika had treated Rosa and the other women who worked for her. *Criadas, servientes*—the names in Spanish were demeaning. Rosa called herself a housekeeper, and she said she never minded being called a maid, but she never wanted to be a servant again. Rosa would never have told Maribel—not her favorite of the girls, by any means—any personal information, let alone identified Dell as the daughter of a wealthy family.

True, Maribel knew her surroundings were comfortable—affluent, even. As a girl from the barrios, working the streets in spite of her age, she would have assumed Dell's family had money. But to identify her as De Cordova instead of Rosales . . . Dell's fingers tightened on the steering wheel.

That left Jovani. There was no way around it. Why had he told Maribel? How could the subject possibly have come up? Her brows furrowed into a frown. Just as disconcerting was the idea that he must have been alone with Maribel if he had confided that information to her. What was he doing alone with a troubled, belligerent woman-child who had been arrested for prostitution?

"Are things really going to be that bad?" Michelle asked suddenly, in a small voice, startling her. She shot a surprised glance at the girl.

"You look—I don't know. So worried," she explained, and Dell had to make a conscious effort to relax her clenched lips and smile reassuringly.

"Sorry, honey. I wasn't thinking about court, though. More about the little incident this morning. Is Maribel too much for you girls? Does she—I don't know—pick on you all? Do things she shouldn't?"

Michelle looked out the window for a minute, then shook her head and turned back toward her. "She mostly hangs alone. But she likes hurting people. She kept telling me they'd make me leave the ranch." Her hands knotted and unknotted in her lap. "I feel funny," she admitted. "What if she's right?" She paused again for a moment. "What if I have to go back?"

"Judge Ovalle-Martinez is a smart woman, Michelle. I've known her for years. It really won't be too bad. You'll see."

Michelle nodded without much conviction, and Dell forced herself to put everything aside but the girl's worries. She would get through this thing at court and then she and Jovi would talk. But she didn't think it would be the discussion he'd had in mind early this morning when he had said they would talk. Ruthlessly, she dismissed the image of his face, his eyes intent on her, his lips soft against her skin, from her mind. Something was very wrong with Jovani Treviño. She'd been stupid before. Been fooled. She'd been an unwitting enabler, briefly, for a man she loved. It wasn't a mistake she'd repeat. Ever.

Traffic picked up as they neared downtown Laredo, and she felt relieved to drop her efforts at cheer and just concentrate on the vehicles speeding around her.

CHAPTER EIGHT

It was almost six by the time Dell turned the SUV into the drive and slowed down as three white-tailed deer bounded across in front of the car. Seeing the graceful animals always gave her an unexpected dart of pleasure. They were so exquisitely formed, so much a part of this dry ranch country that still hadn't surrendered completely to Laredo's encroaching sprawl. Dell smiled in spite of her weariness. The slight bump as they crossed the cattle guard, put in years ago by her father and never paved over, made Michelle stir and sit up. She wiped a hand across her eyes and looked out. "We're home," she said, surprised.

She'd fallen asleep after the tiring day, and Dell wondered if she even knew she'd used the word "home." She thought back to the most awkward moment of the day, when the judge had spoken to Michelle's mother alone in her chambers. Apparently, the woman had accused Dell of trying to steal her daughter's affection, before being confronted by the judge, who reminded the woman sternly that she had thrown Michelle out because the girl had spent the night with her boyfriend—after doing nothing to prevent that situation in the first place. The woman had dissolved in tears and pleas for another chance. She explained she was taking parenting classes from her church, and she was trying to cope with her husband's abandonment after so many years. Michelle, she sobbed, was all she had, and she needed her back.

The judge had spoken separately to Michelle, who asked to stay with Dell. But, reluctantly, the judge insisted that, if Michelle's mother continued to take classes and try to overcome her own problems, the sixteen-year-old would have to return to her mother. Meanwhile, she asked Dell to allow weekly visits for

Michelle and her mother at the ranch. After the court appearance, Dell took Michelle out to eat and then to the mall, thinking it best that the girl have some time alone before she had to face Amy, Selina, and especially Maribel. Together, they walked the long corridors, not crowded on a weekday afternoon. Michelle refused to look for bargains at first, then shyly stepped closer to a window to browse the costume jewelry beckoning shoppers. Dell smiled when Michelle suddenly grabbed her wrist and urged her in to look at a T-shirt featuring the newest teen idol.

"You're sure you don't mind?" Michelle asked a second time as Dell paid for the shirt. She looked excited and a little abashed all at once. "Mom hated when I needed new clothes."

"I don't mind," Dell assured, letting the remark about the girl's mother slide.

"Thanks!" They headed back out, and Michelle glanced up at her. "I don't get it."

"Get what?" Dell paused to let a group of teens in saggy pants saunter past, and Michelle looked after them a minute, then remembered what she'd been saying.

"Why do you let us stay, Dell? Maribel says it's about money—"

Dell shook her head, stopping to peer through the window at a brightly colored sheath. "Not about money."

"Nah." Michelle looked at the dress Dell was looking at and wrinkled her nose. "Ugly. No, not the money, I can tell. But why?" She urged Dell away from the pricey store, heading toward the two-story merry-go-round nearby, with its benches and soda machines.

"Our own moms didn't want us," she pointed out after a moment. "And you're nobody—I mean, not to us. Yeah, we like you and stuff, but . . . " Another, pronounced shrug.

"You don't get it." Dell pursed her lips and ran a hand over her head. "Guess it's a little to do with what Maribel said," she answered finally.

"About?" Michelle colored. "All I could think about this morning was me," she admitted.

Dell grinned at her. "I think you're entitled to worry a little about yourself now and then." She walked over to the drink machine and peered in. "Thirsty?"

"Yeah. Water's good."

Dell retrieved two bottles and they sauntered on, Michelle quiet as she finished half the bottle in a gulp and wiped her mouth with the back of her hand.

"Your mom?" she said finally.

"Yeah." Dell thought for a moment. "Judge Ovalle-Martinez filled me in on some of your problems, Michelle. Your mother didn't pay enough attention to you, she said. She thought that was your main problem."

"Yeah," Michelle agreed. "No news there, though. Your mother—"

"My mother . . . dressed me up. Showed me off. And pretty much ignored me if there wasn't some special occasion. Some function, preferably with photographers in attendance. After she and my father divorced, I sort of pretended there was only my dad." Dell smiled at the memory of her father. "He loved me."

Michelle put out a hand, stopping her, and stared up at her. Suddenly she seemed to realize she was gripping Dell's wrist and dropped it.

"So you lied?" she asked, in a small, but determined voice. "About home being best? About mothers loving their kids."

"No," Dell said with conviction, and reached out to touch Michelle's cheek. "I meant it. I believe, mostly, home is best. Mothers love their little girls. Just not always, honey."

"Not always." Michelle nodded in agreement and pointed. "I think we parked out that way."

Together they started toward the exit, and Michelle moved close beside Dell as they neared the door. "So . . . what's up with Jovi?" she asked with a quick glance up at Dell.

Dell shook her head. "Oh, no. Just as you said—nobody's business."

"I didn't say that," Michelle pointed out with a quick smile. "Selly did."

Dell laughed. "So if you were only thinking about yourself, how can you quote Selina?"

Michelle giggled. "Selina's always got the good gossip—*los chismes*," she retorted. "She's how we know stuff."

"Aha! So I go to Selina next time I need a report on you girls?"

"That depends," Michelle said primly, clambering into the SUV. "Selina for good stuff, or girl stuff." She pulled the door shut and waited until Dell was in her seat. "But for the nasty stuff, stuff no one should know, ask Maribel." She flopped back against the seat, the conversation over.

Dell frowned as she turned the key. She didn't doubt Maribel would poison the waters whenever she could. And again, that nagging wonder—how had Maribel found out about her mother? And how had she known she could use it to hurt?

*

"Girls must be upstairs with the TVs on," Dell concluded when no one rushed out the door to meet them as they pulled into the garage. "I thought they'd be waiting at the door, as long as we've been gone." She smiled at Michelle and switched the ignition off. "They'll be happy to see you, though."

Michelle nodded and slid out. "Yeah."

Thinking about how hard it would be when Michelle returned home to her mother sent a shiver of apprehension through Dell. Could she even imagine losing Becky? The agency had been clear that there were no guarantees in Becky staying with her, and that they tried to return children to their homes if there were any way at all.

Surely in Becky's case that wouldn't be possible. Her mother had been in and out of jail, and, according to the case worker, hadn't even expressed a desire to know where or how Becky was last time the worker had spoken to her. Still, Dell was in a genuinely down mood by the time she got out. She waved Michelle to the rear of the vehicle with a half-smile as she stretched. She dug under the driver's seat for the low-heeled walking shoes she always kept there. Kicking off her heels with relief, she slid her feet into the loafers and walked back to peer in at the cluster of bags.

"I'll be in shortly," she told the girl. "Get everyone to help, will you? Tell them I just needed some air. And give Becky a kiss for me, okay?"

"Got it," Michelle called, already half way to the door with her bags. Dell left the car doors open so the girls could finish unloading and walked slowly down the drive toward the stable, letting the sun hammer away at her tense shoulders.

The stable door was open wide, and she could hear an excited commotion inside—hooves striking stall doors, Pete's shouts at the horses to quiet down and for Danny to hurry up. Feeding time—how long had it been since she'd carted food along that aisle? The three men must have it under better control than she and Pete and her father had before, though; she hadn't heard a single cuss word color the afternoon air. Grinning, she skirted the barn, then the riding arena, and took a path through the nearest pasture, relishing the feel of soft, spongy grass under her feet instead of the ungiving feel of asphalt or tile. This pasture was irrigated and had withstood the summer's heat well, but other pastures without a steady source of water were already burning and turning brown and dry. Off along the far fence line, three of the mares grazed peacefully, but she ignored them, walking instead in the general direction of the river pasture with its tangle of mesquite trees and tall reeds.

The river pasture was a long strip of sparse pasture hemmed in by the Rio Grande. Stock was seldom allowed to roam here, because no fence prevented animals from coming or going across the river to Mexico. When she had been a child, back when her mother and father had first started creating this south Texas showplace, the riverbank had been a virtual park. The native underbrush had been cleared, although the mesquites and stunted live oaks were left along the banks. Now vines, *carrizo* cane, and tangling grass were all over again, almost obscuring the picnic tables and grill that had been built near the bank. Nearby, a simple cabaña had provided shelter from the weather and housed party supplies; it was unpainted and relatively unchanged, although she couldn't remember the last time she'd actually looked for the key to the padlocked door and gone inside. The windows were boarded up; she had given Danny and Pete strict instructions to be sure no one could get inside the abandoned structure. She wouldn't have minded so much if the Mexican or Central American aliens swimming the river seeking work had used the cabaña for protection from a sudden storm or cold front, but the entire border was facing an onslaught from alien and drug smugglers.

She looked around carefully, but everything seemed much the same as it had when she was a teenager, riding down here almost daily to hide out from the world.

She had heard entirely too many tales of ranchers who had serious problems when their deserted riverbanks were used as staging areas by smugglers bringing marijuana and cocaine across the river. Although she suspected some of the property owners might not be as innocent as they claimed, she knew of one couple who had given up their ranch after being unable to keep traffickers away.

Relieved to find such calm, she walked down to the very edge of the river. Most of the bank here was steep, falling off with outcroppings of rock and dotted with cactus, but her father had leveled this one section out enough to allow easy entry into the waters. Her eyes stung with memories of her father, working in the sun to build this playground for her. Now the river's waters were so polluted that swimming was unsafe; factories here and upriver, as well as the *maquiladoras,* or factories, in Nuevo Laredo, had contaminated the Rio Grande and its banks with commercial toxins, while the area's burgeoning population had contributed to its pollution as well.

She drew a deep breath, then let it out slowly. Her father would have had trouble dealing with the loss of his river, she knew. On the heels of that thought, the fleeting image of her mother, uncaring that Samuel Rosales would have given his life for her or that he'd lived a life of loss and heartache without the woman he'd been married to briefly but had loved always. She squeezed her eyes shut, almost seeing her mother, lean and blonde, frowning and brushing imaginary grime from her arm. Her father, kneeling on the blanket there on the riverbank, holding out a strawberry. The smell of strawberry . . . she'd never forget that picture when strawberries teased her senses. And her mother pushing his hand away, pushing herself up, and slamming into the cabana. She'd been young then, but she could still see the pain in her father's eyes at yet another rejection.

She sighed and opened her eyes to gaze at the river again. At least he'd been saved the heartache of the river's demise, of the incomprehensible violence now confronting this one place that had given him peace.

Stepping back, she went back up into the shade of the trees, finding the conveniently bent tree trunk that had once been her throne, and boosted herself up. She felt material snag and belatedly realized she was still in her courtroom attire. Frowning, she extended a leg; the sheer nylon was shredded, and she'd probably just ruined her skirt. Oh, well. She shrugged the damage aside. It had been too long since she'd freed herself from walls and headaches and the daily business of problem solving. She stretched lazily, reclining more comfortably on the trunk, basking in the heated air washing over her body, soaking into her weary muscles. Small animals rustled and birds chirped; she closed her eyes, abandoning conscious thought completely.

She was blissfully near sleep when there was a sudden, heavy thrashing in the undergrowth, as if someone unfamiliar with the woods had stumbled through brush. Startled, she sat up, her heart beating heavily as she slid her feet to the ground, debating whether she should stand her ground or leave. Talk about hindsight. She hadn't even thought to bring the cell phone with her on this impromptu hike. She licked her lips to moisten them, then stood up cautiously, taking a step or two away from the trunk. The rustling continued, but not as loudly, and she paused, listening. Maybe her drowsiness had frightened her without cause, and the noise was simply a deer or a cow that had come across the river— some large animal, moving toward the water to drink. Hopefully it wasn't a *javelina*—that could be bad news. Her face screwed up at the prospect of facing a wild boar who didn't appreciate having his territory invaded.

Then the limbs of two closely placed trees parted, and Jovi stepped out into the relatively cleared space around her. She gasped—in relief or in surprise, she couldn't have said herself.

"You!" he said, obviously startled. And then his eyes swept over her, noting her hair, full of bits of leaves and twigs, which had come undone, as well as the shredded hose and snagged suit skirt. "Are you all right?"

"Of course," she replied coolly. "Why wouldn't I be?" The fact she had named a number of possible health hazards just seconds ago was none of his business. Somehow, letting Jovani Treviño know anything she thought or felt seemed inadvisable. But he just stood there, looking at her with a certain amount of derision in his dark eyes, although he answered her in a normal enough tone.

"Well . . . you're here." He stepped closer, then gestured toward her. "And you look . . . uh . . . "

"A mess?" she suggested helpfully, brushing at her hair and coming away with several pieces of debris.

"Maybe not a mess," he said. "But at least a little bedraggled."

She laughed, and a bird flew from its hiding place above them. "I haven't been called bedraggled in a while," she told him. Then she frowned, tilting her head up a little to see his face through the shadows that darkened it.

"Why wouldn't I be here, though? And how do you know about this place? I'm surprised, with as little time as you've been on the ranch."

He shrugged and walked over to where she stood. Her heart pounded more heavily than when she had considered being attacked by *javelinas*. His presence was unnerving, electrifying. She focused on ignoring his physical closeness and waited for him to answer.

"I've known about this since the afternoon you hired me," he said easily, leaning against the tree trunk beside her and looking down and out, toward the river, squinting a little. His sleeved arm brushed her bare one, and she tucked her elbow imperceptibly against her waist, resisting the urge to withdraw to a safer distance.

"That's surprising," she repeated, and felt his gaze return to her.

"I don't think so." He shifted, and his arm pressed into hers a little more closely. "I'd say it was only right that I toured the place. How can I run things if I don't know what I have? Pete gave me a complete ride around. I've already told them we need to hire a crew and clean out this brush." He looked around, and his voice took on a more solemn note. "Which brings us to why you shouldn't be here," he finished slowly. "At least not alone." He waved a bronze hand in front of her, sweeping it across her line of vision. "Do you know what drug smugglers, or even *coyotes*, might do to a woman they found down here by the river alone? Look at all the places someone could hide—anyone who wanted could use the cabin and the area here for—for whatever. You'd never know. Neither would Pete." He looked around again, and the heaviness in his voice was impossible to ignore. "I seriously doubt drug traffickers don't know about places like this anywhere along the river."

The fact he didn't mention Danny puzzled her, but she put that aside for a moment, turning to face him. "You sure became an expert on local matters in a hurry, Jovani. You're all but implying . . . " A frown slashed her face. "You had better not be implying drug trafficking goes on here! And as for why I'm here—it's my property, and I don't think women should stay inside and wring their little hands in the sanctity of their own house."

He sighed and wiped a hand over his face, then through his hair. When he looked down at her, his face was full of irritation.

"Look, Dell, I didn't imply anything. And, just for the information, I, like most normal, fairly well-educated men in this day and age, have no caveman perceptions of what women could or should do. But there's such a thing as stupidity"—he ruthlessly ignored her small stutter of protest—"and being down here alone with night approaching is stupid."

They were silent for a long moment. She didn't argue with what he'd said. Realistically, she supposed he was right, even if she had no intention of agreeing with him out loud.

"I used to come here alone a lot when I was a kid," she said eventually. "I suppose I forgot how much things have changed."

He sighed, looking around. "I bet you usually came on a horse, too," he said. "Something you could have gotten away on in a hurry if you needed to. Besides, when you were a kid, before you're parents divorced, I'm sure just being who you were was protection enough." His face was somber. "Now no one knows, Dell, and even if they knew, it's not enough. Now being Lionel De Cordoba's granddaughter might be an invitation to harm instead of protection from it."

She laughed shortly and moved away from him, then turned to face him. "No. I'm sure anyone who knows who I am knows my grandfather wouldn't pay a penny for me. My bridges with him are well-burned, Jovi." She shrugged. "I suppose I should head back. I don't want anyone at the house to worry, and I've been gone awhile." She took a couple of tentative steps, then remembered Maribel and turned back.

"Wait. There's something we should talk about first," she said. "Jovi, why—and where—were you alone with Maribel?"

"Maribel?" His surprise seemed genuine. "What are you talking about, Dell?"

"Maribel and I had an ugly scene this morning." She flushed. "About last night. What she saw."

"You had to have expected something of the sort," he said reasonably. "She's not the kind to just politely turn around and walk out of an embarrassing situation especially not one she thinks she can manipulate to her own advantage." He reached out and brushed at something on her shoulder without asking, his fingers warm through her blouse.

"That's not the point," she responded coolly, ignoring the small, burning spot where his fingers had just been. "I knew she'd have something to say. What bothers me is what she said." She took a step away from him, looking up at him. "Apparently, the two of you have been spending time together. Alone. And no matter how innocently, that's not smart, Jovi."

"Alone? With Maribel? How you can possibly believe . . ." He was furious, anger in his voice and in his eyes. He stepped toward her, and she could almost feel the rage coiling through him. She didn't back away, although she tried to visualize what the footing right behind her was like, in case she was forced to flee. Then she tilted her head imperceptibly, and confronted him with her own quiet anger.

"Maribel made it a point to tell Michelle my mother abandoned me," she told him matter-of-factly. "That *Erika De Cordova* abandoned me. You, Pete, and Rosa are the only three people on this ranch who know whose daughter I am, or that we don't have anything to do with each other."

His fierce scowl eased into an expression of puzzlement, and again he wiped a hand over his face, rubbing his chin thoughtfully. Then he sighed heavily and shook his head.

"Look, Dell, I can see why you'd assume, but I haven't said anything to Maribel. Why would I? And when would I? You can't honestly believe I'd be stupid enough to put myself in a compromising situation with her, can you? I'd like to think I'd made a better impression on you than that—that you were a better judge of people than that."

Unconsciously, Dell worried her lip as she went over what he'd said. How he'd said it. Finally, she nodded reluctantly. "Okay. Let's give you the benefit of the doubt—you weren't alone with Maribel." Her hand moved to her throat, and she tugged at the collar of her blouse, rearranging it absently. "Then how did she find out who I am?" She frowned. "It isn't that it really matters— there are people who know, and anyone could find out if they had some reason. I suppose Pete might even have told Danny, just shooting bull to pass the time. But they've worked together for years. Why *her*? And how?" She shook her head, agitated. "She's a sixteen-year-old with serious problems. She's not allowed online without supervision, and even if she were, the last thing she'd be interested in would be me."

Jovi shrugged. "Dell, I have no idea what the deal is." He tilted his head to glance up at the sky then at his watch. "Are you sure no one else could have told her?"

"I don't see who." She, too, checked the time. "I don't see why, either. I have to get back, though. I've been away from Becky too long already."

"I'll give you a lift—the pickup's just back up at the head of the path down here."

"I'd walk, but I guess for the sake of time . . . " She turned toward the path leading back and was startled when he laid a hand on her arm, stopping her.

"We didn't talk about this morning," he said huskily, his eyes dark and unreadable.

"There's nothing to say, is there?" She gently drew her arm from his grasp. "We made an error in judgment. One that neither one of us is likely to repeat." Her eyes met his challengingly. "I'm not likely to find you in the kitchen in the middle of the night again, am I?"

"No." His lips quirked, and the tiny *chispitas* danced in his eyes. "Unfortunately. But I can tell you where else to look, if you want."

CHAPTER NINE

Jovani gritted his teeth and dodged as Snow Mist made another pass at his arm. The mare was lightning fast with those teeth, and she wasn't being very ladylike about walking up the ramp into the trailer. The couple who had purchased her wanted to use her both for breeding purposes and as a riding horse. Right now, she wasn't giving any indication she'd fulfill either role willingly. He'd warned them about her temperament, but they insisted they were both experienced and could handle her. Still, he wasn't too sure they knew what they were letting themselves in for.

Snow put her front hooves experimentally on the wooden planking, then snorted and threw her head up, trying to bolt. Only the rope run through the front bars of the trailer kept her from escaping. And she'd already snapped one lead. Jovi smiled grimly. He'd hooked marlins down in the keys that hadn't fought like this girl. Loaded million-dollar stallions with killer reputations. Yet this one stubborn mare had him praying, cursing, begging, and sweating—to no avail.

At least Dell had walked over to the house with the couple, insisting they have a cup of coffee and some tacos after their early-morning arrival from Dallas. He had an idea she wouldn't hold up well to seeing the battle of wills that had been going on for more than an hour now. The mare's dapple-gray coat was lathered with sweat, and her breathing was becoming loud and labored. She snorted again wildly and drummed her hooves on the wood.

"Horse still won't go in?" Pete asked, reappearing from the barn with a wide canvas lead. He held it up for inspection. "Maybe we could winch her in," he suggested. A slight hint of a grin creased his leathered face. "Dell wouldn't much let us beat her in," he observed.

Jovi laughed. "No, that she wouldn't. I sure wouldn't want to be caught trying to do it, either." He took one end of the long lead, and Pete held on to the other. They looped it around the mare's hindquarters, ignoring the flurry of hooves aimed at them. Moving toward the front of the trailer, they pulled the lead taut against the mare's rear, but she dug her hooves in and didn't budge. Her large, gray body shook, and she flung her head as wildly as the taut rope attached to her halter would allow.

"Something's gotta give," Jovi muttered to Pete, then groaned as he heard the sounds of approaching voices. Dell was bringing Snow's new owners back down to the corral.

"I'd love any ideas you might have," he whispered to Pete, who was clinging tenaciously to his lead, and just shook his head.

"Oh, dear," the woman said, coming over to them. "I thought sure she'd have given up by now."

"Perseverance is a trait," Jovi pointed out, although he wasn't sure he meant it at all.

"Stubbornness, though, is a fault." The man was frowning a little at the mare. "Honey, are you sure about—"

"Well, of course I am." The woman nodded vigorously. "This is just the most beautiful mare we've ever had. Can't beat her bloodlines." She brushed past Jovi to pat the mare's lathered neck, ignoring the threat of injury. "She's upset, that's all. We'll work with her. She'll be fine." She stepped back again.

Jovi kept most of his attention focused on the mare, but when the mare snorted pitifully again and tried unsuccessfully to throw herself backward, he saw tears glisten in Dell's eyes before she bent and brushed at some invisible substance on her jeans. When she straightened, her face was grim. If the couple didn't back out, Jovi guessed, Dell would. He nodded across at Pete.

"Let's put her in," he said quietly, as if they were in charge. The older man nodded, and together, muscles straining, they pulled on the ends of the lead. Snow Mist snorted one final protest, then clattered up the ramp into the trailer.

Fighting the urge to shout, "Yes," and do a childish fist pump, Jovi helped Pete raise the ramp and lock the mare in, while the new owners retied the head rope to take out some of the slack. Then he stepped aside, brushing his hands together, pretending to be completely unruffled by the frustrating battle of wills he had barely won.

Minutes later, the couple drove off, with a weary Snow munching hay from a net inside the trailer. Pete returned to his duties, and Dell stood silently by, watching the car and trailer disappear. The sadness on her face hurt. Without thinking, he draped an arm across her shoulders and hugged her gently.

"She'll be fine," he said gently. "They really wanted her."

Dell sighed. He was right, and she understood that. But the sadness lingered. Piece by piece, her past was disappearing. The De Cordova past had gone long ago; now she was losing the part of her life that had mattered most. The horses had been freedom, triumph—her mother had watched her win her earliest ribbons. When her mother's interest faded, then vanished, the wind in her face dried the tears when loneliness taunted her. On a horse, she had outrun everything. For just a moment, she sagged against Jovi's arm, still wrapped protectively around her. The strength and warmth isolated her momentarily from the sense of loss.

So she let him hold her. But only for a moment. Then she straightened within the warm grasp and stepped away. "She will be fine," she said, reassuring herself as she agreed with him. "I wouldn't be surprised to see some of her babies in the show ring." She managed a slight smile that almost wasn't grim. "So . . . Mist is gone now. And most of the others you thought we should sell, too. What now?"

Jovi regarded her thoughtfully even as he wiped the back of his hand across his sweaty forehead. "Well, the next logical step would be . . . ” He paused, wondering how she would react to what he’d decided to say. “Going to South Padre Island.”

Her reaction didn’t disappoint. Shock widened her eyes, and her mouth opened. Then a frown drew her brows together before she regained her usual pleasant but unreadable expression. When she spoke, her voice was tinged with puzzlement, but not with alarm. Or angry denial.

“Excuse me?”

He shrugged, then fished his handkerchief from a pocket and wiped his face. “You need to get away,” he said sincerely. “I always find the beach soothing. You’d enjoy being there. We could fish . . . or swim.” His lips twitched slightly as he visualized her in a bikini, wading into the warm gulf waters. Or just lying on the warm, white sand. Of course, she’d undoubtedly turn him down flat. Still, the idea was tantalizing.

To his absolute amazement, a slow smile spread across her face, turning her lips up at the corners. The dark brown eyes danced with sudden excitement. “South Padre,” she repeated softly. “How long has it been since I’ve even considered . . .” Just for a second, the smile faded. “But I don’t know . . . ”

The unspoken worries came and went, and he was surprised how easily he could read them—Becky, the ranch, and the girls. Guilty because he had ulterior motives for luring her away from the ranch, he ticked off reassurances.

“The girls and Becky will be fine. Pete and Danny have taken care of the horses for years. We could drive down just for the day—”

“We?” She frowned at him. “You’re including yourself?”

Her tone was teasing, though, and he lifted a shoulder. “Well, why wouldn’t I? It was my idea.”

Dell pursed her lips and brought a hand up to cup her chin as she studied him. The idea of walking barefoot in the sand was appealing, and she hadn’t been to the popular beach in years. She loved swimming in the warm gulf waters, and getting away from the sadness of parting with Mist and the others would be good for her. But putting on a bathing suit and lying on the heated summer sand next to Jovi Treviño . . . The thought of him in swimwear made her mouth dry, and the fingers she still held pressed to her face shivered against her skin.

South Padre, she thought again. He was watching, sure now she would accept his invitation. He must somehow have known the idea would be too enticing to discard. But had he invited her out of concern for her bruised feelings over Snow's ordeal, or simply because he thought she'd be vulnerable and willing to fall into bed with him after an enjoyable day away from the ranch?

She arched a brow at him. "I don't know about the day part. Couldn't we get a room and stay overnight?" she asked mildly, and almost laughed at his astonishment.

"Well, of course, if there are rooms." Jovi couldn't quite quit staring at her. He hadn't expected her to agree to going. And here she was, asking to spend the night with him? Heat swept through his body, and his heart pounded. *Caray*. His idea to get her away from the ranch was working better than he could have hoped.

Dell smiled. "Good," she said, almost purring. "I'll go tell the girls to get ready."

"The girls?" he asked blankly.

"Of course, the girls," she replied easily. "They've probably never been. I think it was wonderful of you to suggest it. I'm sure they'll all appreciate it." Stifling laughter at his stricken demeanor, she turned and headed back toward the house.

"Damn," he said, with feeling, and kicked the graveled drive in disgust.

CHAPTER TEN

Damn delays, anyway. Jovi glanced at Dell, twisted in the passenger seat to point out a glimpse of bay water and long-legged herons to the chattering girls. He'd expected to woo her from the ranch yesterday, not be chauffeuring a noisy horde of kids on a pleasure trip. Dell's laugh at something one of the girls said gave him a twinge of guilt. The girls obviously needed a jaunt like this as much as Dell.

Still, a weekend alone with Dell, even if it was just a fantasy weekend—giving that up was hard. In spite of her sudden animation as they neared South Padre, she had seemed distant and lost in thought for most of the trip. Again he wondered if anyone or anything could ever really touch the woman inside those carefully constructed walls. If only he'd been able to spirit her away. Alone. He shifted in his seat as he thought of how deliberately he'd planned to seduce her . . . or try. Whether or not he would have succeeded was anyone's guess now. She turned, sensing his discomfort but mistaking it for weariness.

"Would you like me to drive?"

No. I'd like to make love to you on some deserted beach. I'd like to hear you scream with the need and the heat and the pleasure of it. He shot a sideways glance at her, glad she couldn't know what he was thinking. "No. I'm fine." He even managed a smile. "Just restless, I guess. But we're almost there."

The girls overheard him and squealed with delight. He was glad in a way that Maribel had won her fight with Dell and stayed behind. Although it meant Rosa had stayed, too, he imagined the girl would have been her usual sullen self. The other three deserved a break, and so did Dell. Becky certainly didn't need Maribel, either, although, in all fairness, the girl was usually careful of her language around the toddler.

Thinking of Maribel creased Jovi's face into tight, grim lines. The girl was bad news. He didn't think Dell understood the extent of the girl's problems, even now. He had surprised her in the barn office trying to make a phone call when she should have been mucking out stalls. He didn't know if she'd had time to get through to whomever she was calling. And he didn't tell Dell, because he wasn't sure what good it would do after the fact. And it would make her wonder all over again about whether or not they'd been alone before—would she believe he'd caught her lurking around in the barn alone?

It worried him. It worried him even more that she'd offered herself to him if he didn't say anything and let her make another call. Even the fact Danny had come into the office to ask something hadn't deterred Maribel at all. How did a girl that young become that hardened, that desperate? The girl needed more help than anyone at the ranch was able to provide. He was sure of that.

And of course . . . His frown deepened. Leaving Maribel meant one more person on the ranch. Actually, it meant three more, since Dell had invited Karla and little Allison to stay. One more chance for something to go wrong tonight when Hampton made his quick, secretive visit to see what information could be gleaned from the ranch books. Jovi had made copies of them, and they were in a folder in the office. Brock Hampton was good, and it was unlikely anyone on the ranch would know he'd come and gone. Still, the fewer people around, the better.

Guilt twisted through him. He glanced again at Dell, who had turned around to smile at Becky. She didn't have a clue he wasn't who he said he was. To Dell, he was the ranch foreman, but he'd taken that job only to help old friends at DEA. His objective was to incriminate her if she was involved in the drug trade. That was harder for him to accept by the day. But the evidence against her was strong, if circumstantial. He didn't even realize he'd shaken his head until Selina leaned over the seat.

"No, what?" she asked.

He forced himself to laugh. "Nothing. I was just thinking of how hot the sand is this time of year."

Selina nodded. "I bet it is. But I made all the girls bring their sandals. And we have gallons of sunscreen, too."

"Good job," he assured her, and the teenager settled back in the seat, beaming at his praise.

Dell grinned across at him, blissfully unaware of his unsettled, uneasy frame of mind. "I love it," she chided. "Big, macho men, so afraid of the little things. Like blistered feet." She shook her head at him. "You're nothing but a big baby, Jovi Treviño."

He managed a smile. "That's me," he agreed affably. "A big baby when it comes to hot sand." *Or heartbreak*, he thought, and then cursed himself silently. He was her employee, not her lover. She was attractive, yes, but the world was full of attractive women. She had no hold on him. Where had the idea of broken hearts come from? He turned the volume up on the radio and made a show of singing along with the song as if he were really wrapped up in the music, taking himself out of any further conversation.

Dell's teasing smile faded, and she turned to look out the window again, making him wonder just how badly he sang. But the pretense served its purpose—no one was paying any attention to him, and his dark thoughts were safely stashed away. At least for the moment. When the towering bridge that would take them to Padre Island suddenly rose in the distance, and the girls gasped in excited surprise, he was as relieved as they were.

*

The sand *was* excruciatingly hot. Dell winced when she stepped out of her flowered flip-flops and scooped Becky up off the towel again, holding her close as she dashed for the damp, cool sand at water's edge.

Becky smelled like a baby coconut thanks to all the lotions smeared on her little body. She also glowed bright pink, thanks to some new lotion all the girls loved. What would they think of next? Dell smiled as she set the toddler back in the gentle lap of the waves and turned to glance at their belongings, stashed under two of the bright orange shades they'd rented from a beach-side concession.

Jovi was leaning nonchalantly against an ice chest, mirrored sunglasses glinting in the sun. She'd felt strange when they'd first arrived, discarding the beach robe that covered her swimsuit. Jovi hadn't commented, but she'd seen the open admiration in his gaze. The heat had burned almost as intensely as the sand under her bare feet. But it had been years since she'd indulged herself like this, and she had pushed away her uneasiness. He, too, had stripped down to his form fitting trunks and headed straight for the water, although he apparently had tired of swimming in the rocking surf faster than she and the girls. At least she felt comfortable now, immersed in water up to her waist, holding Becky as she pounded the water with her tiny feet and hands.

Nearby, Selina bobbed over the top of an incoming swell, followed by Amy and Michelle. The girls had been hesitant at first, unsure of the swimming skills they had acquired back at the ranch. That had been hours ago, though. Now she wasn't sure she'd be able to drag them out if she needed to. They were as relaxed and as happy as she had ever seen them, and although she knew Jovi hadn't meant to include them in this trip, she was glad he'd suggested it. She'd have to tell him.

"Let me take Becky," Amy offered, coming over and holding out her hands to the little girl, who laughed and changed arms willingly enough.

"She'll be fine," Michelle assured, seeing Dell's slight hesitation. The water's only up to Amy's waist, and she's the shorty." She ignored the tongue Amy stuck out in her direction. "Besides, we'll all help. You should have fun." She nudged Dell with her elbow. "Swim, or go keep poor Jovi company."

Dell flicked another glance toward the beach. There were briefly clad female bodies all over the sand; she doubted Jovi was suffering. Many of the beauties were unattached, although there were some couples dotting the beach. Children ran everywhere, dodging the prostrate bodies of sun worshippers as they chased the seagulls or each other. Smiling, she decided to let the girls watch Becky for a few minutes. The tide was going out gently, protected by the jetty that extended out into the bay, and swimmers were everywhere. A quick glance showed that most of the nearby swimmers were families, grownups paying careful attention to their kids and the surroundings. The girls would be safe, and she could use something to drink.

She sloshed out of the water, realizing when she hit the sand that her legs were starting to ache from the vigorous exercise. The first two trips into the water with Becky had been a piece of cake, she realized. Third time in was the challenge.

She bent to pick up her flip-flops, able to bear the sand against her wet feet long enough to pad over to the sunshade. She ignored the dubious, mumbled compliment of a beer-bellied man sitting alone burning in the sand, and was glad she couldn't read Jovi's expression as she made it to her towel and sank down beside him. So much for being comfortable, she thought wryly as he smiled lazily at her and repositioned himself, his oiled muscles rippling and tautening.

"Had enough?" he asked, and she shrugged. He took off his glasses then, focusing on her, and the tiny flames dancing in his eyes seared her. Determinedly she fought back a blush, aware the scanty top of her bikini wasn't designed for shrugs—not with any modesty, anyway.

"No. You're the one up here all alone," she retorted. Then she remembered she'd come up to thank him. Out of the water, the heat was blistering. She touched her dry tongue to salty lips, and he watched her with unwavering interest.

"Would you give me a water?" she asked, and he smiled and turned to open the ice chest and rummage in it. He pulled out two dripping bottles and handed one to her, watching as she pressed the bottle to her face.

"Hot," he said, and she opened the eyes pressed tightly shut against the sun, wondering exactly what he meant. He had turned his attention back to the water, though, so she let the comment hang in the air between them, as sultry and provocative as the day itself.

"So if you're not exhausted, what brought you here?" he asked after opening his bottle and draining most of the contents in a long swallow.

She took a more moderate sip, letting the cool liquid re-moisturize her mouth, then caught herself just before another shrug. "The girls thought you looked lonely."

He cast a glance around the beach, his gaze lingering pointedly on a couple of unaware sunbathers, and then grinned devilishly when her lips thinned. "That was kind of the girls," he told her. "But I'm actually doing okay."

She didn't reply at once, trying to position herself comfortably while still keeping the girls with their bright pink skin where she could spot them easily. She couldn't find the right angle and wiggled futilely against the bundles of towels and clothing behind her to no avail.

"Let me help," Jovi said, and scooted off the ice chest to sit beside her on another towel. Fixing himself comfortably against the ice chest, he reached out a warm, bronzed arm and propped her against his shoulder.

She would have protested, but the fit was perfect. And there was really nothing overtly sexual about his move, just a comfortable heat that seeped slowly into her neck, shoulders, and back. Sighing a little, she relaxed against him, still gazing out toward where the girls were sitting at the water's edge, laughing when the idle waves washed up over their legs.

"Perfect," she said, and turned her head up to cast him a quick glance. "Don't get a swelled head, though, Mr. Treviño. You're a perfect recliner, and the day is perfect. I'm not talking about perfection of any other kind."

"Shucks." He smiled down at her and moved a hand to rearrange a wisp of hair that blew across her eyes, blurring her vision. "I thought you meant my body was perfect. You know? That Greek god kind of stuff? Movie star stuff?"

Off hand, Dell couldn't think of a body, from the heavens or Hollywood, quite as attractive as the hard, sculpted one insinuated against hers. But there was no way she could admit that and still keep any distance between them, she knew. Emotional distance. The physical distance had completely disappeared, and the initial innocence of their skin touching was quickly turning into burning awareness. She knew she should simply stand up and walk back to the girls. She didn't want to, though. She wanted to sit here, with the scorching sea breezes whipping their bodies, and the gulls crying overhead as they circled, and feel Jovi's body pressing more closely against hers.

As if he knew her unspoken thoughts, Jovi's arm tightened around her, and his lips brushed her windblown hair in a kiss. Startled, she looked up at him again. This time he bent down, and his mustache pricked her skin as he feathered a kiss against her cheeks. Then, unexpectedly, he eased her away and pushed the ice chest behind her to support her.

She said nothing, just stared at him in surprise.

"This is a really good time for me to go take care of the girls," he muttered, and waved a hand toward a couple necking nearby on the sand, oblivious to the world. "I'm assuming that was not on your list of things to do at South Padre," he added, and she blushed. It hadn't been, but she wasn't entirely sure she should have left it off. *Inalcanzable*, she reminded herself. She couldn't lose herself in Jovi's sensual embrace with the four girls just yards away, turning occasional glances their way.

She bit back a sigh and stood up, too. She even managed a slight smile.

"No. Definitely not on the list," she agreed. He turned to go, and she touched his arm. He turned back, something both startled and hopeful in his expression. "Jovi?"

"Yes?"

"Thanks for suggesting this. I don't think the girls will ever forget today." She smiled, but from a distance again, and turned toward the water. "Come on. We'll go try to pull the girls out before they become permanently wrinkled."

She didn't look back at him again. For a long moment, he just stood there watching her beat him down to the water's edge. He should have said something, pushed a little harder to get closer to her. Instead he followed after her, not sure he would forget, either.

*

Getting the girls out wasn't just difficult—it seemed impossible. Dell argued for a futile minute or two before giving in to the clamor to stay in, wrinkles and all. When Becky giggled and kicked up a waterspout, Dell laughed and splashed water back at all the girls. The splashing quickly became a battle, and the girls had the upper hand in number and effort.

"Let me help," Jovi said behind her, and pushed Amy under an oncoming swell. She surfaced sputtering and laughing, and Selina and Michelle grabbed Dell, determined to dunk her. Becky giggled as Jovi snatched her out of Dell's arms and waded into deeper water, a little removed from the battle.

"Smart girl," Jovi said approvingly, as Becky clapped when Dell disappeared under the water. Becky turned her attention from Dell and the girls to a careful inspection of his ear, then crowed in excitement when she spotted a tour boat sliding off in the distance.

"Boat," he explained, and then, with a smile, "and dolphins—look! By the boat."

He stopped, feeling a little silly, but Becky was looking where he pointed almost as if she understood him.

"Dolphins," the older girls chorused, swarming around him.

"Porpoises, actually, but—"

"I never saw—"

"They seem so tame—"

The touch of a warm hand on his shoulder called his attention away from the boat, the dolphins—even the other girls.

Dell's eyes sparkled. "Thank you."

"For?"

"Realizing three-year-olds are people, too," she explained. "Talking to Becky. She isn't talking much yet, but she needs to hear the words."

He shrugged it off and ran a hand over Becky's water-flattened hair. "It's nothing."

The girls were entranced, staring after the boat and its escorts. Dell eased Becky back into her arms and thought of Maribel, alone at the ranch with Rosa. How could anyone not be touched by the beauty of the blue water, the dolphins surfacing unexpectedly and then disappearing, and the contentment so apparent on everyone's faces? She shook her head and noticed Jovi watching her instead of the water.

"Problems?" he asked perceptively, and she shook her head again.

"No," she assured him, "not really. I wish Maribel had come. Something like this might have helped her."

"Maybe," he said, without conviction.

"Dell, Jovi, look—over there—" Michelle pointed at the jetty. "Look at all those people over there watching the boats. Can we go?"

Grasping at the girls' sudden willingness to climb out of the water, Dell nodded in agreement. "Sure. We'll walk over. I think our stuff will be safe."

"I could stay," Selina offered, glancing in the direction of the lifeguard's tower. The bronzed, bleached kid in the chair shot her a brief smile before refocusing on the swimmers, and Dell managed not to laugh.

"Nope, not necessary," she insisted. "Let's stick together."

Selina's mouth twitched, but she shrugged and obediently struck off across the sand, leaving the others trudging behind.

"She seems level-headed," Jovi commented as the girls fanned out and left them to walk together.

"She'll be eighteen in a few months." Dell shifted Becky and glanced up at Jovi. "Patricia—

"Patricia?"

"The judge, but I went to school with her."

"Oh."

"Anyway, Selina will be free to go when she's eighteen. She's at the ranch sort of like she might be at a halfway house." She smiled. "I think she'll be okay, in the end."

"Yeah." He glanced out over the water, squinting a little at the freighter outlined against the horizon. "Might grow up to be a good mother, if the way she shepherds those other girls means anything."

Dell didn't answer, her attention caught by Amy's precarious footing on the rocky edge of the jetty. She hadn't thought to warn them how slippery—

Even as the thought occurred, a wave broke over the rocks. Amy shrieked in horror as the water hit her. She floundered, trying to regain her balance, but her shoes slipped and she fell into the surf, flailing and grabbing at the rocks.

Instinctively, Dell sprinted toward the scene, but Jovi spurted past. "Careful with Becky," he admonished, and clambered down the rocks into the water, grabbing Amy and hoisting her out.

Another wave slammed into the jetty, and onlookers drew back, still murmuring and apprehensive. Selina and Michelle grabbed Amy and pulled her back toward Dell as Jovi scrambled back up over the rocks.

"Are you all right?" Dell demanded, hugging the girl as well as she could with a baby in her arms.

Amy nodded, but shivered. "Just scared," she said shakily. Then she managed a small smile. "No waves at your pool."

Dell closed her eyes momentarily with relief that the girl seemed unharmed and could even manage a joke. *Dios protégé tontas.* God protects fools. The saying fit—she should never have let the girls get so far ahead. Becky fussed as Dell bent to examine a scratch on Amy's arm.

"*No es nada,*" Amy assured her. "Nothing—it doesn't even hurt."

Dell frowned. "We'll put stuff on it from the first aid kit anyway." She motioned the girls in the direction of their umbrellas. "Let's go, girls."

"Let me take Becky for a while. She must be heavy by now." Jovi grinned teasingly at her when she hesitated. "Come on, Dell. Fork over the kid. I've proved I'm harmless, haven't I?"

Dell surrendered the toddler, and they started back up the beach toward the hotel. Trudging through the sand required some effort, Dell acknowledged, glad Jovi had offered to help her with Becky.

"You're good with little ones," she noted, catching up with them. "Have you had a lot of practice?"

"Pure instinct," he boasted with a wink, but the sight of him carrying the little girl so tenderly brought a lump to her throat. She slowed and turned back to the girls, determined to maintain her composure even in the face of exhaustion and unwelcome emotion. She wouldn't think about how sweetly Becky nestled against Jovi, pulling his hair when he didn't answer a question quickly enough, then surrendering to sleep and letting her little head fall to his shoulder.

Dell had splurged on a suite at the King's Palm; she knew the beachfront hotel was pricey, but the girls deserved something truly special. The King's Palm featured rooms just yards away from the beach, a truly appealing feature to girls who were getting their first look at the ocean.

The rooms were elegant, and the girls were delighted with the spaciousness and vivid décor of the suite. After spending so much time in the salty gulf water, they were all exhausted, and took turns trying to stay awake long enough to shower and change for dinner.

Dell had claimed one of the three bedrooms for Becky and herself, and she showered and dressed while the toddler napped on the huge bed. Aimlessly, she wandered out to the balcony and leaned on the railing, watching the beach, still full of sunbathers and swimmers enjoying the late summer light. The breeze blew in off the water, warm and strong, wrapping the gauzy turquoise material of her dress around her and pulling at her upswept hair.

She closed her eyes in contentment. She loved the ranch, and wouldn't change it for even a beachfront home. But she hadn't allowed herself a change of scenery for much too long. And she couldn't have chosen better company.

The door opened, and Jovi stepped out to join her. He'd changed from his trunks and cotton T-shirt to a crisp cotton dress shirt with slacks, and his hair gleamed darkly, still wet from the shower, apparently. Aftershave swirled around on the evening breeze, mingling with her own perfume.

"We have a problem," he announced, and then held up a quick, reassuring hand when she jerked upright. "Not a major one, though. Minor. Very minor."

She arched a brow at him. "Minor? You ruined my solitude and my utter lack of interest in moving for something minor?"

"Sorry." He was completely unrepentant, though, and just smiled at her complaint. "The girls have decided they're too hungry to wait for food, and too tired to go out."

"Which means?" Dell prodded.

"They want pizza. It could be here in half an hour, and they wouldn't have to get up except to answer the door." He shrugged. "Selina said so," he added. "And we know who's really in charge, right? I told them you—we—wanted to take them out to a really nice restaurant. They weren't particularly interested."

"But they could have pizza at home," she protested.

"They're teenagers. Well, except Becky, who might not wake up to eat anyway. They can't have too much pizza."

Dell thought it over and nodded slowly. She really didn't want pizza, and hadn't dressed so carefully to sit on the sofa in the living area and stain her clothing with grease and tomato sauce. Still, if the girls were set on staying in the room, she supposed it wasn't fair to force them out to an unfamiliar restaurant with food they might not enjoy.

"Let's go call," she said, determined not to let her disappointment show. They went back in and found the three lying on the carpet, shoeless, and laughing uproariously at cartoons they must have seen a million times before.

Selina looked up when they came into the room and then clambered to her feet, her face glowing.

"We're having a blast," she announced promptly, and then gaped a little at Dell.

"You look beautiful," she gasped, and the other two girls turned around to gape, too. "Even Jovi looks super nice," Selina added.

"Thanks," Dell said, replying for them both, and Jovi smiled at the girls and sent them a quick wink.

"Our pizza party clothes," he explained with a grin.

Selina smiled back, but then suddenly frowned.

"Gee, you probably didn't want to stay here and eat," she realized, flushing a little. "I'm sorry. We can go out—"

"Don't be silly," Dell said quickly. "Pizza's fine. We want you to enjoy yourselves, after all."

"Can't eat pizza like that," Amy declared, pushing herself up to her knees and surveying them. "You know what I think, Selina?"

Selina turned to look curiously at Amy. "What?" she demanded.

"We eat pizza, but they go out and eat. Somewhere really *elegante* and *romantico*. With candles and stuff, just like in the movies." She grinned at them. "Just don't stay out too late and get in trouble."

"Cool, Amy," Selina beamed with pleasure. "Awesome. Y'all get a break. We get pizza. We can babysit—no danger, right?" She looked around the regal accommodations again, still in obvious awe at her surroundings.

Dell frowned. The idea of going out to dinner with Jovi was tempting. But she could hardly leave these troubled girls and a toddler alone in this unfamiliar place.

Selina was waiting for her answer, her face full of hope and excitement. Amy and Michelle were waiting, too, hanging on her words. Besides her, Jovi shifted his weight and laid a hand on her arm.

"Hey, we're not babies here," Amy pointed out, and Michelle nodded.

"Aren't you and Rosa always telling us to grow up—to learn to make our own choices and figure out stuff by ourselves? What's wrong with us choosing tonight?"

"What about it, Dell?" he asked, his voice husky. "A dinner date for us, and pizza for the girls? Then I could hand feed you squid."

The girls laughed at the face Dell made, but sobered when she sighed and shook her head. "I don't think so."

Selina seemed the most upset by her refusal. "Dell, we really wouldn't do anything wrong," she insisted. "I used to babysit."

"It isn't that," Dell protested quickly, recognizing Selina considered her answer a sign of distrust. "Look, I know that the three of you could be trusted. And you'd take good care of Becky. But I don't like leaving you alone in a strange place—"

"There really isn't much danger," Jovi said thoughtfully. "We could stay until the pizza came and then eat in the hotel restaurant. We'll leave my door locked from the inside, and lock the connecting door. They could lock this door, and we'd be come right back after dinner." He didn't say it, but she could almost hear him thinking it. *We could show we trust them.* She turned to confront him but found herself unable to argue with his unspoken logic.

"All right," she conceded, and was a little surprised when Selina hugged her with uncharacteristic affection.

"This is so cool," the girl chortled. "Bring on the pizza! Have fun." She released Dell and headed toward the door, pulling it open with a flourish.

Dell laughed, but walked over and shut the door. "Not so fast, young lady," she protested. "After the pizza comes, okay?"

"Sure." Selina hugged her again then bounced over to fall on the sofa. "But I'm calling for food right away. Some of us are in a hurry to feed our faces." Amy and Michelle crowded around her, telling her what to order, and, smiling, Dell slipped into her room to check on Becky. The toddler was still sleeping soundly, her little hands closed into fists as she slumbered.

Dell bent down and brushed a kiss on her cheek, then turned to find Jovi in the doorway, watching her with a bemused expression. She thought she saw tenderness in his eyes and in the half smile touching his lips. But she saw something else, too, the trace of an emotion she couldn't identify. Suspicion? Melancholy?

Silently deriding herself for being overly imaginative, she smiled. "This girl's a doll," she told him easily. "Big eater, sound sleeper—no problems." He stepped aside to let her back into the living room, where the girls had gone back to their cartoons. Although she didn't quite touch him as she brushed by, heat flooded through her, and she sent him a startled look, wondering if he felt the tiny electrical charge as well. He looked at her with hot brown eyes.

Where's my distance now? she thought, but she didn't really want anything between them. Jovi Treviño had invited her here, intent on seduction. An affair with the man was out of the question. But she could certainly make dinner memorable for him—and for herself. An old college acquaintance claimed there wasn't ever any harm in flirting, but she'd never acted on the impulse. Had never felt the impulse so strongly . . . never. The night seemed perfect for testing that theory now. Grinning, she went back to sit with the girls until the pizza came.

*

The waiter placed a salad in front of her, and Dell nodded at him as Jovi checked his cell phone, then turned his attention back to her. "Sorry—"

She waved away his apology. "I know your mother hasn't been well."

"Thought the girls wouldn't let us leave," he ventured after a bite of lettuce. "Between wanting you to wear more makeup and you wanting a sentry—"

"Not a sentry," she protested. "I slipped a few bucks to a hotel babysitter to check on the girls a time or two, that's all."

"With such marvelous excuses to stick her head in," Jovi agreed somberly. "She wanted to invite the girls to the sunrise buffet? She couldn't remember if she'd left her name and number in case she was needed another day?"

"So I'm cautious," she retorted, smiling. "Selina wasn't crazy about me sending her, either, but we did have one close call—

Amy falling into the gulf like that." She picked up her wine glass, wrinkling her nose.

"Bad bouquet?" he asked, and the waiter materialized from somewhere behind them.

"The wine is bad?"

Dell bit back her laugher and shook her head. "The wine is fine," she assured him.

"Fine," Jovi confirmed when the waiter shot him a questioning glance.

"So what *is* wrong with the wine?" he asked, when someone else summoned the waiter to a nearby table.

"Nothing. I just haven't drunk wine in—in ages. The smell—the *bouquet*—caught me off guard."

"You're pretty lowbrow for a high-class chick," Jovi teased, and she scowled.

"I'm a rancher, remember? Nothing high class about that, right?" She poured more dressing on her lettuce, ignoring his amused glance at her drenched salad. "I don't muck stalls in my gowns, for godssake!"

"Hmmph. You don't muck stalls at all from what I've seen." He pushed his plate away and watched her blot salad dressing off her lips. She straightened a little in her chair, and he hoped his taunt hadn't irritated her. He knew he should probe, prod, find out who and what Dell Rosales was. He didn't want to, though—didn't want to hurt her, to lie to her, to think about anything but the moment. And the need.

"Shoveling manure wasn't ever my favorite chore," she admitted, then grinned. "Except when I could do it right in front of my mother's guests."

The waiter came back with their orders, giving Dell a steak and placing Jovi's seafood platter in front of him. The smell of the grilled peppers and onions on Dell's plate swirled around them mingling with the smell of shrimp and garlic. Hunger flared.

Then Dell shifted her legs, her foot bumping his momentarily, and he saw an entirely different kind of hunger in her dark eyes.

Or imagined it. He couldn't tell, only watched as she cut her meat into careful bites.

"You're not eating," she noted as his food sat untouched. She raised her brows. "Couldn't have been the mere mention of manure," she teased. "I mean, you must be in it up to your ankles most days."

In his pocket, his cell phone vibrated. Hampton? *How about up to my neck?* He forced himself to spear a shrimp, realizing his decision to leave DEA had been right. Agreeing to help them on the De Cordova-Rosales mess had been every kind of stupid, though, because it meant lying to Dell. More and more, he had trouble excusing himself for that.

Across the table, Dell suddenly looked troubled and embarrassed. "Sorry, did I offend you?" Subtle color stained her cheeks. "I . . . " She bit her bottom lip. "Don't date much."

"No, you didn't offend me." He managed a smile and another bite of food. "But the day I'm ankle-deep in manure, I'm firing everyone on the ranch, girls included."

Hating the part of himself that was still more agent than man, he waved his fork at Dell. "So—what's the deal with them, anyway, that you get unpaid child labor to help clean the stalls?"

"Unpaid child—oh. You're kidding." Dell finally took a gulp of the wine she'd picked up and put down several times, chasing it with the glass of water right next to it. "Not funny!"

"Sorry." He winked at her. "I don't joke much."

"It shows!" She tore her dinner roll in half, but set it aside and leaned toward him. "The girls—remember I mentioned my friend, Patricia?"

"The judge, yes?"

"Yes. She and I went through Catholic school together from Kinder on."

"So . . . she knows your family?"

"Patricia worked her way up to the bench," Dell explained. "Her parents weren't particularly important, but my mother didn't object to her as much as to some of the other kids' parents." She paused to finish her vegetables. "Once my mother picked me up for a photo shoot for a Monterrey magazine. Came right over to Patricia's house and took me away from her birthday party."

Dell's face clouded, but she shook aside old memories. "Anyhow, Patricia thought a lot of the girls she saw in court needed something besides being sent home to their folks."

"Juvenile—"

She snorted. "Juvenile—there's constant overcrowding, half the kids there are hard-core—Jovi, some of the kids there are rapists and murderers. You have to know."

He nodded. Most juvenile systems couldn't handle the caseload, the social changes that turned innocence into cynicism and evil. Drugs were involved more often than not, whether through the absence of parents or the corruption of the kids themselves. That, he reminded himself grimly, was the crux of the matter. Why he could force himself to sit across from someone he could care about and lie. *Damn drugs.*

"Well, to make a long story short, Patricia thought the girls could gain from getting away from their peers for a while. And their parents."

"So you offered to keep them?" He managed to keep the questions light. "Still, I bet you jumped through hoops to get approved."

"Not so much. The system is overburdened, and Patricia— Judge Ovalle-Martinez—had discretion over how to handle the girls. She just doesn't think sending them home made sense."

He finished his food while she talked.

"I guess knowing a judge could come in handy," he said thoughtfully when she finished.

"How so?" she asked, drawing back a little.

He made light of the thought that had crossed his mind. "Oh, you know, speeding tickets, parking citations . . ."

Across the table, though, Dell stiffened and frowned, obviously not finding the flip reply amusing.

Jerk, he scolded himself. Obviously not the right tone.

"Would you like dessert?" Their waiter was back, his expression hopeful.

Dell cast him a small smile. "No, thank you."

"We have a wonderful flan—"

"No," Jovi repeated, more firmly, standing. "Dance with me?" he invited, holding out a hand.

Dell glanced at her watch. "The girls—"

"Have your creative babysitter watching their door like a hawk," he reminded. "Didn't she say she woke Selina up last time she checked?"

Dell hesitated, then nodded slowly and stood. "Okay," she agreed. "But only a few minutes."

"A few minutes," he agreed, taking her hand and leading her toward the floor.

Dancers on the floor were gyrating to a throbbing salsa, moving legs and bottoms seductively to the pulsing rhythm. Dell nudged Jovi in the side with her elbow as they headed toward the corner of the floor, nodding at one uninhibited couple doing their version of dirty dancing. While the woman followed the music, the man squatted and danced around her, planting frequent kisses on her rear and pelvis. Some of the onlookers clapped and encouraged with catcalls, while others looked away.

"I'm guessing we're not going there," Jovi murmured, ducking his head to speak into her ear as they stood aside, watching the frenzied activity.

The whisper of breath against her cheek singed her skin. She wondered why anyone would waste time in a mockery of passion when the real thing could be so subtle and unexpected. The thought drifted away as the music ended, though, and the small orchestra in the corner of the room struck up an old Spanish ballad.

Jovi moved onto the floor, and Dell settled into his arms as if it weren't their first dance. Eyes closed, her lips touched with contentment, she suddenly wasn't untouchable. Unattainable? The nickname seemed laughable right now. As their bodies slowed and moved with the music, everything faded but the moment. The feeling. The need. The distance fled, and when she leaned more closely against him, his arms tightened slowly.

*

Dell sat up in bed, unable to sleep. Careful not to disturb Becky, curled up beside her and prevented from a fall by a barricade of pillows, she slipped out of bed, her ivory nightgown slithering around her. Quietly, she eased out of the room and across the living area, her steps muffled on the deep carpet. She went to the kitchen and poured a glass of water but pushed it away after an experimental sip. Sighing, she retreated back through the silent room and paused only briefly before stepping out on the balcony.

No one was likely to see her at this hour, and the black wrought iron provided a privacy screen of sorts. Going back inside for her robe held absolutely no appeal, she decided. She still peered around carefully, but the balconies adjoining other rooms were all empty. The balmy air washed over her, and she smiled and sank into one of the loungers, stretching out and closing her eyes, listening to the sea sounds down below. Faint laughter drifted up, too, and she sat up again, frowning. Even at this hour, there were obviously revelers coming and going from the beach to the hotel. Lounging around in her nightgown wasn't a good idea.

Regretfully, she stood back up, stretching, and went back in. The restlessness that had driven her out of bed still bubbled through her. She didn't want to sleep, didn't want to stand here alone in a darkened room. She wanted . . . The realization made her heart pound, and her ears seemed to echo the drumming roar. She wanted Jovi. She didn't want to be *la inalcanzable*, unreachable and untouchable. And alone. Aching with need.

True to his word, Jovi hadn't insisted on spending the night dancing. After another *cumbia*, he'd folded her into his arms again for one last dance. A slow dance, not the frantic beat of the *cumbia*. Sensual music. They'd melted into each other, felt desire pulse between them like the music itself. Then they'd walked together to the connecting door separating his room from the open area of the suite. He brushed her lips fleetingly.

"If I asked . . . " he whispered, and she held a finger to his lips, silencing him and shaking her head.

"No. We can't," she said, firmly and with only slight regret.

He smiled. "I thought I'd ask, though," he returned as he pushed the door open.

"No harm done," she'd whispered lightly, and they had each gone their separate ways. But the harm had been done, with that last dance. What had her buddy Karla said so long ago about nothing mattering when you wanted someone?

With sudden conviction, Dell slipped back into her room and plucked up her robe. On silent feet she went to each door and peered in. All the girls slept soundly, Becky still surrounded by her pillow fence. She closed each of the doors quietly then went down the short hall to Jovi's room. She knocked, but no one answered. She tested the door knob; the door was locked from his side. Not wanting to knock harder and risk waking the girls, she went back and searched the table for the key cards. They each had duplicates—a convenience, she'd thought, for fetching and leaving things. Teenage girls, she knew, never had what they needed or wanted at any given minute. In the empty corridor, she swiped the card and watched the light go green. Tried not to wonder what she'd do if the chain were on. For just a moment, as her hand found the knob and turned it, she wondered what spell she was under, what craziness possessed her. Then she shook the uncertainty aside and gave in to the raging need.

The chain wasn't on, and she pushed the door open just enough to slip through and turned to close it quietly. With shaking fingers she slipped the lock into place and then turned back and took a few decided steps toward the bed. Halfway there, she froze, staring blankly. The bed was empty, its bedspread unwrinkled and unused. There was no light on in the bathroom, no sounds of use. Still, she walked across, feeling stupid and out of place, and tapped on the door, opening it when no one answered. Jovi was not there, not in the room at all.

Realization of a totally different kind slammed her as hard as desire had minutes earlier. Where was he? Bars must be closed—had he just found someone else's bed to share? Unable, he thought, to take her to bed, he had simply sneaked out like a college kid to find someone more agreeable. *Her fiancé Jeremy all over*. Had she learned nothing from trusting too easily?

Shaking with embarrassment and anger, she walked over to check the locks on the outside door. Then she let herself out through the connecting door, her fists clenching and unclenching in the silky softness of her nightgown. What on earth had she been thinking? Jovi was no one, nothing to her—just the man she'd hired to help her take care of her horses. An arrogant devil who'd blithely believed he could seduce her while she was away from her own protective environment—and who'd almost succeeded, she admitted, more furious with herself than with him.

Grimly, she walked to the girls' bedroom, looking in. All three of the girls slumbered peacefully, uncovered even in the air-conditioned coolness. Selina, alone on one of the beds, was almost falling off one side, but her awkward position obviously didn't bother her sleep. Dell tiptoed out, closing the door again, then went into her own room. She tossed aside the sheer lace robe and replaced it with thick terry that covered her completely. She repositioned Becky in the middle of the bed, soothing her when she stirred and waiting to be sure that the little girl didn't wake. Then she slid on her slippers and went back out to the darkened living room and sat down on the sofa. To wait.

*

Jovi glanced at his watch and frowned. The luminous dial showed the hour clearly, and he hadn't expected to be up until four waiting for Hampton to call him. He'd lurked in the shadowy bar for most of the night, downing a glass of scotch and trying to avoid conversation from other patrons while he waited for his call. Bored and impatient, he'd finally gone out and walked along the beach, and it was there Hampton had finally gotten in touch.

As if the hour weren't bad enough, the news was even worse. Nothing had been accomplished. Hampton used the key to get into the stable with no problem. But while he was going through papers Jovi had left in the desk drawer, easily accessible, the alarm in the house had gone off. Hampton couldn't explain what had happened, but the alarms brought Pete and Danny running into the barn to grab lights and head up to the house. He'd hardly had time to snatch the folder and conceal himself before they arrived. Minutes later, a sheriff's patrol car, obviously in the vicinity, had pulled up in front of the house. Hampton had decided to get away before anything else went haywire. No one knew he had been there, but none of the questions had been answered.

And that was frustrating, damn it. Jovi massaged his neck, glanced a final time at the bar, closed now that he actually wanted a drink, and walked over to the elevator. No point in staying out any longer and having someone miss him. The elevator doors opened, then closed quietly behind him. He pushed the button for his floor and leaned back against the wall. How could he have gone to dinner so thoughtlessly with that woman? Even with his eyes squeezed shut, he could see her face laughing at him across the table. She was beautiful and enticing, and he didn't want to wonder who she really was or what was behind her easy charm or quick, throaty laugh when he amused her.

She hadn't laughed when he'd suggested they spend the night together, though. He wasn't sure if that was bad news or good, and it didn't ease the frustration he felt. He could still feel the touch of her finger silencing him halfway through his proposition, and he couldn't remember anger or condemnation in those dark, quiet eyes. He felt his body stir just thinking how close they might have come to making love. Maybe, with time . . . He sighed. There might not be time. He knew that, even if she didn't. And maybe she wasn't nearly as drawn to him as he thought . . . as he was to her.

He thought about Becky. She obviously had been very involved with someone. There was undeniable proof of that. But there was no marriage, no mention of the absence of the child's father. Maybe she wasn't the kind of woman who wanted commitment. Given her family situation, maybe she didn't even find the idea of family particularly appealing, though she clearly did adore the child.

Frustrated and annoyed with himself, he pulled out the key he'd pocketed earlier and tried to open his door, startled when he found the chain on from the inside. Apprehension niggled. They'd agreed to lock the door, but—if the chain was on, did that mean—? He walked the short distance to the main door and unlocked it. He slipped in, sliding the deadbolt home as silently as possible.

"Well, hello, Jovi," Dell said, behind him, venomously, and he started, but managed to choke back a heartfelt, "Oh, shit," before it slipped out.

"Hi," he said, turning to face her. "You're an early bird."

For long moments, she didn't answer, just pinned him with an unwavering stare.

"I didn't know you planned on going out," she said eventually, and he shrugged and came across the room, bending over to flip on a lamp on one of the end tables.

"I didn't know I needed permission," he countered. "I'm a big boy." He paused, looking for something sufficiently annoying to ruffle her and make her stop staring at him so intently. "Besides" He shrugged. "I didn't know I was on duty."

The taunt worked; he saw faint color come and go in her cheeks, and anger tightened her lips.

"On duty?" she echoed in disbelief, standing, even more agitated. "No, you certainly aren't on duty—but I didn't expect you to be gone."

"Where do you think I went?"

He settled himself on the sofa where she'd been sitting, ignoring her frown, and propped his shoulders comfortably against the corner of the high armrest.

She made a sound close to a snort and paced over to the door then came back toward the sofa.

"In my experience," she retorted grimly, "men who are gone all night don't spend it alone. Engaged men, married men—most men wind up in someone's bed. And with the girls here—"

"The girls are asleep," he pointed out gently. He was silent, and outside, the surf rumbled strongly. "Could it be that you're upset because you think I went from . . . wanting you to finding someone else so easily?" He stretched and rubbed a hand over his face.

She glared at him, wanting to lie but unable to. "It certainly wasn't very flattering," she gritted. "But that's not the point. Even if the girls are asleep—"

He stood then, putting a finger to her lips just as she had done earlier and stopping her sputter of indignation.

"Dell, you're insulting us both," he said quietly. "How could you think I'd actually walk out that door and go find someone just to shack up with? Wanting you is on a whole different level than just wanting—someone."

"But . . . " She wasn't convinced. "It's after four. I've been up . . . for a long time." She didn't look away. Didn't ask him where he'd been. And he didn't know when she'd first missed him.

Damn her. Couldn't she just drop it? Again, guilt twisted in his belly. Yeah, he'd wanted her. And no, he'd never have picked up someone on the beach or at the bar for casual sex. Not when he was here with her. But he also couldn't give her the reassurances she wanted. He couldn't even give her the truth. He sighed and went back to the couch, sitting and letting his head flop back against the cushions. He stared for a moment at the ceiling before answering her unspoken questions. "I went out . . . I couldn't sleep . . . thinking about you." He turned his head without lifting it, looking back at her. "You really can't blame me for being . . . restless."

"Out where?" she asked, unmoved by his blame placing.

"I went to the bar—had a drink. A couple, actually. But that didn't really help." He smiled at her. "That last dance, damn it. If it hadn't been for that last dance, a drink or two might have worked."

Dell blushed, uncomfortable with the memory both of that last dance and her own reaction to it. Unwilling to dwell on their shared time, she waved vaguely at him. "Okay. You had drinks." She glanced at the clock on the wall across from them.

I walked. Up and down the beach."

Without me? Dell thought, but subdued the indignant whisper and rubbed her temples, considering his explanation. She wouldn't have left the girls. He seemed sincere enough. He wasn't drunk, so he must not have been in the bar the whole time. And he had wanted her. She wouldn't pretend not to know that. Unbidden, she thought of the expression she'd seen briefly when he saw her with Becky earlier. Almost as if he had reason not to trust her. She bit her lower lip in momentary agitation then decided to drop the issue.

She believed him. He hadn't slept with somebody else. *He wasn't Jeremy.* The thought was much more comforting than she would have liked.

"Well, I'm glad we got that cleared up." She yawned, finally ready to sleep. "Guess we call it a night—Becky's up with the sun."

Jovi stood again, also smothering a yawn, and nodded. He headed toward the hall, then looked back at her.

"I just have one little question about all this."

"A question?" Dell repeated, disconcerted. "What could you have a question about?"

He stepped close to her, and she could see the glint in his eyes, even in the lamp's low light.

"Yeah, a question," he repeated, his voice a husky whisper near her ear. "How did you know I was gone, Dell?" He reached out and caressed her cheek with a feather light touch. She pushed his hand away.

"You won't ever know," she retorted, and walked to her own door. With a hand on the doorknob, she turned and smiled at him. "But you'll always wish you did."

*

Early the next morning, Dell drove back, assuring herself she wasn't doing it to annoy Jovi or put him in his place. She liked driving, and besides that, she didn't relish three or four hours of time spent staring idly out a window at mostly barren scenery. Jovi joked with the girls and commented on the trip with them, and he turned frequently to check Becky, who grumbled at being constrained in the carrier, but he rarely spoke to Dell, and only when she directed a remark to him.

"Are you two guys mad at each other?" Amy asked curiously as they pulled into a gas station on the eastern edge of Laredo.

"Should we be?" Dell asked lightly, not answering the question directly.

"Beats me," Amy said, clambering out and stretching. "But you sure don't seem as friendly as you did in South Padre." Shrugging at Dell, she climbed out and followed the others, already on their way to the ladies' room.

"So how do I answer that?" Dell wondered out loud, asking herself, really. Jovi was pumping gas, and he looked across at her.

"The truth usually works," he suggested.

"The truth?"

He replaced the gas hose and closed the cap before leaning against the roof of the SUV and regarding her cynically.

"Tell her I'm the hired help, and the excursion is over," he said. "How hard would that be to understand?"

"You're ruining what was a really wonderful time—for all of us," Dell gritted. "Don't feel sorry for yourself, Jovani Treviño."

He had the grace to look abashed, if only momentarily. The girls came out of the gas station just then carrying Becky and a bag of drinks and chips, and they all scrambled back into their respective seats.

"Here's your change, Dell," Selina said, handing over a handful of coins and dollar bills.

Jovi wiped his hands on his jeans and gave a final, dark glare before going around to climb into the passenger seat, and Dell buckled herself in with annoyance. Just who did Jovani Treviño think he was, anyway, she asked herself. She pulled out into the heavy traffic on Zapata Highway with care, but she couldn't wait to get back to the ranch.

CHAPTER ELEVEN

Dust puffed up around the horses' hooves as they cantered through a shallow draw, shoes clicking metallically when they hit loose bits of rock. Dell rode behind the four teenagers, partly to keep an eye on them and partly because she was carefully holding Becky in front of her in the saddle. Sugar was a calm, easygoing sort, but Dell wasn't about to risk the toddler's safety if the mare shied at a rattlesnake or stumbled unexpectedly.

Jovi rode ahead, controlling the pace as he reined the big, brightly spotted Appaloosa to a trot and said something to Selina. The other girls gathered around him in a cluster as he pointed off toward the tree line that ran along one edge of the pasture. The girls were shading their eyes and looking, too, and when Dell squinted, she could make out the well-concealed outlines of several white-tailed deer.

The deer weren't uncommon on the ranch, of course, but seeing them during daylight was unusual. She looked at Jovi consideringly. For someone who denied having much experience on local ranches, he sure did have good eyesight. She bit her lower lip and resisted the urge to sigh. Their relationship had definitely chilled since that fateful trip to South Padre. Annoyance twisted her mouth. Relationship? He was her foreman, for heaven's sake. Hardly a relationship to worry about there.

She shifted in the saddle and cursed silently at herself. Since when had position mattered? If she wanted to avoid a relationship with Jovi, it wasn't because he wasn't good enough. It would just be awkward, with the girls. And if they were involved, she couldn't very well boss him around, treat him the way her mother had treated her father. No. Jovi could be a man she admired. A man whose honest opinion and knowledge about horses mattered. Nothing more.

Except, of course, she admitted honestly, that he'd been one missed opportunity away from being her lover. She shivered a little at the thought, in spite of the blazing summer heat. All the girls wore wide-brimmed hats and sunscreen, and Becky glowed with the remnants of the sun lotion. But she supposed they probably should head back to the house, if only for the horses' sake. Funny, she chided herself wryly, how quickly a stray erotic thought could ruin a perfectly lovely day.

She eased back on the reins, and Sugar slowed, then stopped. Ahead of her, she caught Jovi's eye and saw him circle the girls back around toward her. Maribel moved her horse alongside Jovi, leaning too close to him to say something. Apparently what she had said had irritated him, because even at a distance, Dell noted the frustrated shake of his head, and he kneed his horse into a quicker pace to get away from her. Dell's lips tightened. What kind of fool was she, not to send the belligerent—and apparently brazen—girl back to authorities who might be better able to help her? Or at least control her.

Maribel lagged behind as the others caught up to Dell.

"We're not going back, are we?" Michelle protested, wiping a hand across her forehead, sweaty in spite of the hat's shade.

"I think we should." Dell patted Sugar's neck. "The horses don't have much of a voice in this, and it's hot out here."

"But, Dell—"

"Dell's right," Jovi said firmly, and the girls exchanged disappointed glances but didn't argue with him. "There's always another time—if we don't overdo it today." He headed his Appaloosa back toward the drive that led to the home pasture. "Anyway," he went on, as all the girls except Maribel trotted along close to him, "we need to be back before seven."

"Do we?" Dell resettled Becky. "What happens at seven?" She

kept her tone light and smiled pleasantly across at him, but the smile didn't reach her eyes. He was pushing her away, and had been since they'd returned from the beach.

He forced a smile of his own and shrugged. "Business," he said. "Mine, not yours," he added, as if teasing, and the girls giggled. But Dell caught the slight challenge and arched an eyebrow at him.

"Maybe we should define terms," she muttered, reining Sugar in between Amy's pinto and Jovi's horse, turning toward him so she could speak privately to Jovi. "On my ranch, on my time—my business."

"Maybe we *should* define terms," he concurred, but the concession was an undisguised taunt. "I answer to you about horses, and I put in enough hours to oversee the stable's affairs. Anything else—my business, not yours."

"So what are they whispering about?" Maribel demanded, edging closer. Selina, Amy, and Michelle drew their horses closer together, slowing them and forming a barrier that kept Maribel out of earshot, much to the girl's disgust.

"We wouldn't know," Selina said loftily. "They're having a private conversation, and we have manners."

Maribel snorted profanely, but the other girls, unperturbed, just laughed and refused to yield any ground.

Dell fumed silently over Jovi's refusal to talk, but she said nothing, and her expression remained unchanged as the horses' hooves churned up small explosions of dry soil. The girls rode with confidence, pointing out skittering lizards or clumps of browning wildflowers to each other, happy with the day's outing. She wouldn't upset the girls or herself over some stupid argument with the *help*, she told herself bitingly, even as she admitted Jovi never had been just *help*. He was annoying and arrogant and not easily enough managed, and she wasn't sure exactly what he was or wasn't. But he wasn't just an employee. And that was a shame, she thought grimly, because if he were just the ranch foreman, she could fire him in a minute. Damn Jovi Treviño, anyway, she thought, not for the first time.

As if feeling her scathing condemnation, he turned back and cast her a long, appraising glance. For a second his face softened, as if he were going to relent and treat her with the old mix of friendliness and innuendo, but when he did finally smile, it was at the sight of Becky, fast asleep in Dell's arms. With a slight shake of his head, he turned and went on ahead to open the gate leading up to the barn.

*

The girls had argued over coming back, but once the horses were cooled and stabled, they seemed to agree two hours in the afternoon heat was more than enough and headed almost immediately for the house to change into swimsuits.

Dell refused Jovi's offer to take Becky up to the house, although by the time she laid the toddler in her crib, her arms ached from the strain of carrying her the whole distance. The girls urged her to join them at the pool, but Dell regretfully decided on a shower and change, knowing she had work stacked up on her desk in the study. A glance out her window showed her Rosa was sitting on a lounger, a glass of tea in her hand, watching the girls, so they were safe enough. With no real excuse to waste more of the afternoon, Dell headed for the study.

The room had always been her favorite, and she was surprised at how little time she'd spent there recently. The girls needed attention badly, but Dell realized when she glanced at her bank statement that finding a source of income wouldn't be a bad idea.

She wasn't desperate, she acknowledged, noting with mild surprise how much she'd spent on the girls. The state sent minimal reimbursement for the girls' lodging, but she had decided on the summer classes herself and had gladly provided more than necessities. She didn't begrudge any of the money, and the energy bills always soared during the summer anyway. This year, with the higher fuel prices, the electricity bill was almost frightening. Still, she'd received four thousand for Snow Mist. Jovi had driven a good bargain, given the mare's temperament, and he'd deposited the money in the ranch account for her. There was interest income on her inheritance, too. She frowned at the thought of her father's legacy. It was so much more than she had supposed he would have. Until she knew more about it, she hesitated to use it. She drummed her fingers absently on the polished wood. There had been stories circulating—rumors Lionel De Cordova had become involved in the lucrative drug trade. She didn't believe it. The man had millions of dollars. What need for more could he possibly have?

The younger De Cordovas were another story. The lure of fast money had certainly enticed many, and she was sure many of her unknown cousins and assorted distant relatives were as greedy as her mother and grandfather. But she knew nothing of the De Cordovas. She didn't want to know. Turning the past over again in her mind always led to the same heartache, and she wished wondering about her father's money weren't so painful.

Blood money, she decided, again, pure and simple. Money paid to Samuel Rosales so that he wouldn't go to the Texas courts to make community-property claims against any of the De Cordova money. Hush money, to be sure he didn't go around reminding the world that, at least briefly, Erika De Cordova had been his. Maybe Lionel had provided Samuel with the money as damage control, too, hoping Dell would be well enough satisfied with her inheritance, paltry as it was compared to the bulk of the De Cordova money, that she wouldn't seek more.

Her lips twisted, and she stood up, agitated. She would work tables or clean toilets before she'd take a penny of Erika or Lionel De Cordova's money, and surely they knew it. But if she didn't want to touch her father's inheritance right now, she thought, dragging herself away from the hurt, she'd better consider going back to work.

She reached over to straighten the framed photo of her father. The horses wouldn't pay for themselves for some time, she knew. Given the economy and her lack of concentration on the ranch, the horse operation was between pitiful and non-existent. The sale of some of the stock would go toward ranch bills and the purchase, hopefully, of another good mare or two. And a stallion. In a year or two, maybe the books on the horses would improve.

Her commitment to the girls would actually end when school started, except, of course, that Becky's placement was indefinite. Not indefinite, she told herself, permanent. Even as she thought it, she breathed a prayer for success with her adoption bid. And, even though the teenagers would be finishing up their programs soon, Judge Ovalle-Martinez had left open the option of keeping them for a longer time, or accepting new teens who might need a temporary home.

She still had contacts in the trade industry, she reminded herself, walking over to the window. A tiny hummingbird darted by, an iridescent blur that hovered over the bright flowers outside. She watched it absently, ticking off previous successes. She'd helped set up offices in Monterrey and Mexico City. Her services had been in demand. Of course, the world she had known was now in free fall, with the economic chaos and the horrific violence as drug cartels ran over anyone in their way as they plied their trade. The environment was toxic, and she had the girls to consider. Traveling as much as she had was out, clearly. Still, Mexico's biggest cities beckoned investors, and many of the people she'd worked with were undoubtedly still running businesses. In all likelihood, much of her job could be done electronically. If it could—problem solved. The horses she loved, the girls—and good use of her negotiating skills. With sudden excitement, she went back to her desk and started jotting down notes.

She was engrossed in her planning when the phone shrilled. Absently, she reached for it, glancing at the caller ID information almost as an afterthought. Her hand froze when she recognized her grandfather's Monterrey number. How many years had it been since someone from that number had called here? It was almost as though her reminiscing had conjured up all the old monsters from her past.

"Hello?" she said briskly into the receiver, her voice curt and cold.

There was a pause on the other end, and she supposed that whichever of the De Cordovas had deigned to call had assigned the menial task of dialing to a subordinate. After the silence, her mother's voice, seeming surprisingly edgy, although Dell wasn't sure she even remembered right anymore, addressed her.

"¡*Hola, amor*!" Erika paused, apparently already at a loss for words. "How are you, darling?"

"Why are you calling, Mother?" Dell asked baldly, ignoring her mother's small sound of protest. "You haven't for years."

"Mi'ja—" The endearment came through the line falsely. "I'm your mother. You really didn't meet me half way after your father's death. I—I've wanted to call. But I just haven't."

Dell drew a deep breath, pressing her eyes tightly shut. "But you did now, Mother. Why?"

The silence on the other end lengthened, and then Erika sighed noisily. "Just to say hi, I suppose." Something about the conversation was all wrong, apart from the obvious fact her mother hadn't called in all those years. After a moment, Dell decided it was almost as if she were being given instructions on what to say.

"We should consider getting together, Dell," Erika went on. "We're family, and we really shouldn't have let things come to this."

"Mother, you're at home with your father. You're surrounded by De Cordovas. You don't need me. In fact, you haven't needed me ever." Dell's tone was calm and unemotional, but her fingers tightened around the receiver with growing anger. Why this woman had called was beyond understanding.

"Dell, I'm not getting any younger," her mother argued. "You're my only child. We shouldn't be strangers. We should talk." When Dell didn't answer, her mother sighed again. "Your grandfather would love to see you again, too. He was wondering just the other day about the horses, and how things were going . . . "

Dell shook her head in bewilderment. Lionel De Cordova had asked about the horses? Nothing made any sense to her at all.

"Why would he do that?" she asked into the phone, not bothering to hide either her confusion or the anger she felt at this unexpected contact from her past. "Last I heard, I was a Rosales, *not* a De Cordova! And, as I remember, all he ever said about the horses was that my father wouldn't know quality if he saw it."

Erika was silent again, and Dell suspected she wanted out of this conversation, too. The faint sound of someone else speaking in the background confirmed her suspicions that Erika was being coached, although for the life of her, she couldn't imagine why.

"Mother, what's going on?" she asked again, curtly. "Did someone—my grandfather—have you call? If so, why?"

"I already told you why." Erika's voice turned sulky, and Dell remembered that tone all too well. Samuel must have heard it most of the married days of his life, and when Dell had been old enough to defend him against her mother's unreasonable demands, she, too, had been forced to listen. "You're my daughter, Dell. You can't escape that, no matter what. I made some mistakes, and now I'm trying to fix them. To make things right again."

Dell massaged her forehead with her free hand, wanting to slam the phone down and cut off her mother's petulant complaints. "Look, Mother, why don't we just leave things alone?" she suggested as civilly as she could. "We really have nothing to say to each other. Maybe some day . . . " Her voice trailed off. She couldn't honestly see a time when she would feel differently.

Erika apparently decided to give up the battle as gracefully as she could. "*Bueno, mi'ja*," she sighed. "We'll talk again, then. Later." There was a lengthy pause, almost as if her mother were debating whether to lie baldly enough to claim maternal love. Then she just said "ciao" and hung up. Still somewhat stunned, Dell held the receiver to her ear for several long seconds—long enough to hear a faint but definite click somewhere off in the distance. Someone had been listening to the conversation. Rosa didn't know how, and wouldn't have, anyway. Besides, she was outside with the girls. Only one other name came to mind.

Frowning, she got up. And went to look for Jovani Treviño.

*

Pete was alone in the office when she stalked in, and his weathered old face showed his surprise when she asked for Jovi with unusual agitation.

"He went over to his house for a little while," Pete explained, waving a hand in the general direction of the foreman's comfortable house, set a short distance away from the barn. "I could call him." He reached for the phone with a gnarled hand.

"No, don't bother." Dell laid a hand on his arm and managed a composed smile. "It's really not urgent. I'll just walk over. I'd meant to check with him and see if those repairs he needed on the kitchen sink were ever finished, anyway."

"Well, all right, if you're sure." Pete still looked a little concerned. "If something's the matter—*si hay algo*—"

"No. Everything's fine," Dell insisted. She wondered what this man, who had been so loyal to her father for so long, would think of Erika's call. He'd be furious, undoubtedly, and worried about her to boot. Pete was as loyal as anyone could be. He wouldn't be particularly happy if he'd caught Jovi listening in on a private conversation, either, she knew. Frowning, she turned toward the door, then turned back, remembering the shovel in the barn corridor she had tripped over.

"Pete, who was cleaning the stalls?" she asked.

"Danny," he answered.

"Well, he didn't finish, and someone could get hurt with him leaving the equipment just lying around."

Pete's expression turned to disgust. "I'll speak to him," he promised, and went out of the office, mumbling under his breath.

Troubled, Dell followed him out of the small room, but turned toward Jovi's house. She was a little surprised the tools had been left there so carelessly. Danny seemed responsible enough, and Pete had never mentioned anything to the contrary. The groom hadn't worked for them nearly as long as Pete had, but he wasn't new, either. Well, she'd have to take that issue up with Jovani Treviño, as well as a number of other concerns, she thought grimly. After all, he was in charge, as he seemed quick to point out when it served him, so Danny's mistakes were his responsibility.

She stepped up onto the small, neatly kept porch and rapped sharply on the door. There was no answer, and so, after a moment, she pushed the door open and went in. She hadn't been in the foreman's house in years, but little had changed. Apparently Jovi considered his mother's house in Laredo his real home, because the furnishings here were still the original ones, without personal pictures or adornments to make the house Jovi's. In spite of its spartan appearance, however, it was immaculate; Dell was a little surprised to see all the flat surfaces were spotless. Gritty caliche dust sifted in the windows in virtually any of the buildings in the area, and ridding a place of the white powder could be a never-ending job. Without fully realizing she was doing it, she ran a finger over the top of a small bookcase and held it up for inspection. It was clean.

"So do I pass muster?" Jovi asked sardonically. Blushing, Dell spun around, only to find her breath catch and her mouth go dry.

Oh, yes. He passed muster and then some. She stared at him, leaning against the doorframe, dressed only in tight, short denim cut-offs. His chest glistened, and there were tiny beads of water in his hair.

"I didn't know we were doing dorm inspections, or I'd have come dressed," he added, crossing nonchalantly toward her.

"I knocked," Dell told him, regrouping. "You didn't answer, but Pete said you were here." She shrugged. "I was trying to find you."

"Here I am," he offered, with an expansive sweep of arms that rippled those sculpted chest muscles.

"I noticed. Jovi—"

"Have a seat," he offered, interrupting her to indicate one of the neatly kept chairs. "What can I get you to drink? Chilled wine? Followed by a pitcher of water?" Sparks of laughter danced in his eyes, and for a moment he was the old Jovi.

"I think I'll pass on that," said Dell, relieved he wasn't being antagonistic for the moment. "I think I'll sit down, though." His state of undress made her knees weak; she didn't need to add alcohol to the equation. His lips twitched, but he made no comment, just settled himself easily in the chair across from her, turning it so he could straddle it. He propped his chin on the back of the chair and stared at her.

"So. What can I do for you?"

Dell hesitated for a moment, trying to focus her attention on the things she had come here to discuss. She made herself quit staring at his torso and shoulders and concentrated on his face. That didn't really help, since his sensuous lips were touched with amusement, and humor glittered in the depths of his eyes. Unwilling to anger him right away when he was so utterly appealing in his current mood, she decided to begin with the easiest issue first.

"I just came from the barn," she said, and realized he already knew that. Scolding herself for an unusual lack of mental composure, she shrugged. "You knew that. But did you know some of the stalls weren't cleaned, and the tools were just lying in the corridor?" She stopped, realizing the complaint seemed a little petty. Pete had already seen to it, undoubtedly, and she doubted it was a recurring problem with Danny, or she would have heard.

He straightened a little, calling attention to himself all over again. "Well, no, I didn't," he said slowly. "If I had known, I would have picked up the equipment. And addressed the problem." He paused. "I'm guessing the problem was with Danny, not Pete?"

"Yes. Pete was really upset."

"You can't blame the poor guy." Jovi's sympathy was immediate and sincere. "He's not young, he loves the horses, and he's too loyal to complain. He probably should have asked for Danny's hide years ago."

Dell arched an eyebrow. "That's a pretty strong condemnation. Pete's never mentioned any problems."

"No." Jovi shrugged. "Like I said, he wouldn't have. To him, that's a lack of loyalty. But that's an easy problem to fix. Consider it done."

Dell nodded. "Okay. One down."

"Is there a list?" Jovi's tone was light, but she sensed his surprise. She shook her head, and he stood up, pushing the chair back under the table.

"Not exactly a list. But I thought I'd tell you that my mother called. Out of the clear blue."

Jovi frowned a little, and his expression turned grim. "I'm sorry to hear that. I gather it wasn't a pleasant experience."

"No." Dell had meant to tell him about the click and the suspicions she'd had about him having already known. And yet he didn't react nervously, as if he were worried she might have known someone had listened in on the conversation. And his concern for her feelings seemed real.

"The funny thing," she went on, "is that I have absolutely no clue why she called. It didn't make sense."

"Didn't you ask?"

"Yes, of course." She looked down at her hands and absently began to twist her ring around her finger. "She said she wanted to patch things up. Because I'm an only child." Dell looked up then, her eyes hard. "She was lying."

Jovi didn't say anything at first, just stood abruptly and walked over to the door, then turned and came back, massaging his neck. He didn't sit down again, but stopped near her, and his nearness and tallness and maleness were overwhelming. Dell pulled in a slow breath and twined her fingers together to keep from jumping to her own feet.

"What other reason could there be, though?" he asked levelly, and she shook her head, still not looking up at him.

"I can't think of any," she admitted.

There was another long silence, and again he paced around the small room. She watched him this time, bemused. His air of concentration was disconcerting. If he had listened in on the call, he was an excellent actor. But she was sure now he hadn't. He seemed too intent on figuring out what sinister motives had driven Erika De La Cordova to reenter her daughter's life.

This time, when he got back to her chair, he shook his head. "Strange, I'll give you that," he offered, then held out a hand. "Come into the kitchen with me. I need something to drink."

He drew her to her feet with a gentle tug and led her into the kitchen. He smelled of soap and freshly applied deodorant and aftershave, and she wondered for a moment if he was going out. Then she remembered he'd said he had a business appointment at seven, but had refused to discuss it with her.

She bit her lip, fighting back an immediate surge of annoyance. Maybe sugar would catch more flies than vinegar, she thought.

"I've got tea, cold water, or orange juice," he offered, pulling open the refrigerator. Like the house, its insides were sparsely filled, but spotless.

"I'll take a glass of tea," Dell said, hoping that stalling over a drink would give her an opening to probe into Jovi's unexplained business. She sat down at the table and watched as he carefully poured two glasses of tea over ice.

"Sweetener on the table," he said, placing one of the glasses in front of her and then pulling out the chair beside hers and sitting down. She wished he'd chosen the chair across the table. His bare arm brushed hers, and she resisted the urge to turn and flatten herself against him. So much for unreachable, she thought darkly. She was well within reach. The trick would be to keep him from knowing just how close she wanted to be. Still stalling, she sipped her tea, wrinkling her nose without meaning to.

"Too strong?" he asked good-naturedly, and she managed a slight smile.

"No, it's all right." But she put the glass back down and reached for the sweetener.

"Never water it down," he said huskily, and she knew he didn't mean the tea. She stirred the sugar substitute into her drink with great concentration, hoping the infinitely small circles she made would hide the slight quiver in her fingers.

"So . . . " Jovi apparently had decided she wasn't going to acknowledge his innuendo and went back to their earlier conversation. "If you don't think she called to see how you were, what do you suppose it could have been?" He took a huge swallow of his own unsweetened tea. "I know you said you couldn't think of any reason, but there has to be something."

Dell shrugged and shook her head, not turning to look at Jovi. "No. I got the impression someone told her to call. But the only person who bosses Erika De Cordova around is her father. And there's no reason in the world why Lionel should have wanted her to call. No reason," she repeated emphatically, finally turning enough in her chair to meet Jovi's eyes again, her boot toe idly tapping the floor.

He was quiet and tense, and she wondered what on earth he was thinking. His dark eyes devoured her, but she didn't think his tautness had anything to do with desire. At least not at the moment. His scrutiny made her uncomfortable, though, and she pushed her chair back abruptly and stood, momentarily forgetting the business appointment she'd meant to question him about.

"I guess I should get back to the house," she said, brushing a few stray hairs away from her forehead.

"Without finishing your tea?" he chided, his mood lightening. He reached out, catching her wrist. "Don't go. The second half of the glass packs the punch."

She grinned. "That sounds like a threat, not an invitation," she pointed out, relieved he wasn't staring at her so intently, and that his fingers fell away from her burning skin almost at once.

"A promise," he said loftily, and then stood up too, stretching his arms. Then he smiled at her. "You're breaking my heart," he announced, winking at her. "I thought you snuck over here for a little afternoon delight."

"Hardly," she scoffed. "You had your chance at that, and you blew it." Too late, she realized what she was saying. She clamped her lips together, but his eyes gleamed.

"So that's what South Padre was all about," he said. She neither confirmed nor denied his suspicion, just raised her chin and returned his dark gaze with her own.

"Dell—"

She held up a slender hand. "Let's not go there, Jovi," she said evenly. "Whatever South Padre was or wasn't, it's over."

He took a step closer. "Why? Neither one of us has been happy with what's happened since, have we?"

"What does that matter?" Dell retorted with frustration. "Jovi, no matter how . . . attractive I might find you, we can't change the obvious. We're not in a position to be involved."

"No?" The throaty taunt made her shiver and press her eyes shut for a fleeting moment.

"Jovi, I don't mean to be condescending. It isn't about snobbery or prejudice. But you're the man I hired to take care of my horses. An employee. We can't . . . carry on an affair in front of four troubled teenagers who were all taken out of unhealthy situations with partners of one sort or another."

He regarded her steadily. "You're sure it's not the De Cordova, Dell? Telling you not to make the mistake your mother did and set your sights too low?"

She supposed she couldn't blame him for asking. But the question stung anyway. "How can you think that?" she demanded. She laid a hand on his arm. "Do you think I see my own father as less of a person than my mother? It isn't about you being a ranch foreman, Jovi. It's about you being—being an employee—"

"Ah," he said, nodding sagely, and the mischievous glint was back. "Harassment. You're worried about making me feel obligated to sleep with you." His lips twitched then eased into a grin. "I'll sign a waiver," he offered cheerfully, and Dell shook her head at him.

"Very funny," she retorted. "Jovi, there's just something—not right—about being involved with someone who works for you." She sighed. "Besides . . . the girls . . . "

"The girls were with you in South Padre," he said quietly, the laughter gone again. He took a step closer and reached out to draw her against him. His warm skin burned the length of her body as he held her close, and she trembled against him.

"Dell, don't use the girls as an excuse. We can work it out with them—if that's what you want."

She said nothing, leaning her forehead against the warm wall of his chest. She wanted him. But she didn't want to. Reluctantly, she lifted her head.

"South Padre is over. It would have been a mistake, anyway. Wrong. I'm glad you'd gone out."

"Liar," he said gently.

She shrugged. "My story," she said, and took a half step back.

"And you're sticking to it?"

"I don't have a choice," she gritted, and he shook his head.

"Yes, you do." He bridged the distance between them, brushing his lips across hers teasingly. "There are always choices."

"Not good ones," she argued. His hands cupped her face gently, and his lips teased hers again.

"Yes," he insisted, the word warm against her mouth.

She meant to step away from him. Instead she found herself moving forward, her own hands sliding lightly over his bare, muscled arms. She sighed and gave in to temptation, pressing her lips into the rock hardness of his chest. He let out a long breath, and she felt him shudder.

Maybe we can, Dell thought, her eyes closed tightly as she lost herself in the feel of his hardness and warmth. He crushed her close, and she pressed more kisses up his chest to his throat, shaking against him as he returned her kisses with growing urgency.

"Damn," Jovi said suddenly, in her ear, and eased her away, holding her while her legs steadied and their breathing slowed.

"Hold on," he called, and Dell realized that the faint drumming she had heard moments ago had been someone at the door. She glanced at the clock. 7:05.

Jovi's rueful grin confirmed her suspicion as he indicated his bare chest and shorts. "This is no way to conduct business, is it?" He touched her forehead with a caressing finger and sighed.

"Dell, do me a favor, will you?" He straightened her hair and turned her toward the door. "Will you let him in and ask him to wait just a minute?" He winked at her. "You can even offer him some tea if you want."

"Who is this—this man I'm supposed to entertain?" she demanded, following him out of the kitchen.

He turned on the bottom stair. "Name's Rick Ortega," he replied, continuing up the stairs. "And he's DEA." He stopped at the top and peered down at her. "Just so you'll be expecting it if he flashes ID at you." And he disappeared into his room, leaving her gaping after him.

CHAPTER TWELVE

Rick Ortega was as tall as Jovi, but strikingly thin. Dell couldn't help but wonder how the man would fare if someone attacked him. He seemed almost frail, physically. His eyes were shrewd, though, and he responded to her questions with polite, noncommittal answers while they waited for Jovi to join them.

Jovi changed quickly, coming back downstairs in casual slacks and a knit shirt and taking control of the situation immediately.

"I'm sorry I lost track of the time, Mr. Ortega," he apologized as he shook the agent's hand. "I'd been doing some yard work. Would you like something to drink? I have tea." He carefully didn't look across at Dell, and she had to bite back her own grin. She doubted this man had come to be party to their inside jokes.

The urge to smile quickly changed to a genuine frown when she remembered that she didn't know why Ortega was here, and that Jovi had intended to exclude her.

Almost as if he'd read her mind, Jovi waved a hand in her direction. "You'll have to excuse Ms. Rosales for not knowing about your visit," he ventured. "I hadn't told her."

Ortega looked at her thoughtfully from behind his wire-rimmed glasses, but made no comment.

"After I spoke to you, I thought I probably could answer any questions and that we'd only call her in if you wanted to." Jovi turned to Dell, then, directing his explanation at her, unperturbed by her sudden unsmiling demeanor. "We had a report of suspicious activity along the riverbank near the property line. Not by the cabaña, but near the corner of the pasture where your property joins the Simmons' place."

Ortega nodded. "You understand, Ms. Rosales, that we're not sure illegal activity occurred. But there have been instances of ranches along the river being used by smugglers."

"Yes, I'm aware of the problem," Dell agreed. "But Mr. Ortega, a couple of things about this visit concern me. One of them is why Mr. Treviño chose not to tell me—but I'll discuss that with him later. What I don't understand is how anyone could have been on the property. I'm not an absentee owner, as some of the ranchers who have problems are. I try to keep up with what's going on around the place, and I know Mr. Treviño and Pete, my other stable hand, have done a lot of clearing and inspecting of the river property recently."

"We're not sure what we're dealing with, Ms. Rosales," Ortega said easily. "I called Mr. Treviño primarily because I thought the person who was most involved with land management would be the one to meet with. A Border Patrol flyover reported a small group of people who crossed from the Mexican side to the U. S. side in a boat. They landed in the corner of your property. They could have been alien smugglers, drug smugglers—we don't know. Border Patrol ran their Marine unit up and down the river for a couple days and didn't see anything themselves. But Mr. Treviño was quite concerned when I spoke to him. He said that you ride along the river bank frequently."

Dell cast an annoyed glance at Jovi, but his expression was unreadable. "I wouldn't really say frequently," she muttered. "And it is my property, Mr. Ortega."

"Yes, of course." The agent shifted his lanky form uncomfortably. "Mr. Treviño asked me to come by to discuss possible measures to assure the riverbanks would be safe. Unfortunately, I don't see that much can be done."

"I think Mr. Treviño's overreacting, frankly," Dell said. "Jovi, if there really were a problem, I don't understand your rationale for not telling me." She turned her attention back to Ortega. "So these reports, these sightings," she pressed. "Besides the most recent one you mentioned. Have they been frequent?"

"No." Ortega shoved a hand through his sandy hair. "We only know of the one instance, Ms. Rosales. And we only had that information because of a pilot's report on the situation." He shrugged. "We just thought if we brought it to your attention—or to Mr. Treviño's attention, anyway—further problems could be prevented."

"Is there anything that can be done? Because of course I'd cooperate—"

"No, Ms. Rosales." The agent shook his head, then stood slowly. "The thing is, the river bank's so long. There's no way to patrol it all, all the time." He sighed. "Not short of vigilante patrols, anyway, and those are a crime waiting to happen in and of themselves." He shook hands with her and then with Jovi, and they walked him to the door.

He paused on the porch, turning back to her with affable concern. "The only thing is, Ms. Rosales, if you ride by the river, please be careful. And call us if there's any problem."

She agreed and then stood by Jovi while they watched the car disappear back down the drive toward the highway. When Ortega was gone, she turned to confront Jovi, but he held up a hand.

"Don't. Yes, knowing you have this need for control, I should have told you. However, I saw it as my responsibility, and as an isolated incidence. I agree with what you told the man, Dell. We're around too much for anyone to set up housekeeping there along the river, at least on our land. If the pilot had his location right, then it was probably just a one-time encroachment. *Coyotes*, probably, landing someone who escaped off into the brush. We'll keep working on clearing the riverbank and fence lines."

"Jovi, it's not a matter of control. It's my property and my name. If there's ever another 'business' meeting with some law official, I'd like to know. And be included," she said crisply.

"Suits me." He watched as she reached a hand up to massage the tense muscles at the base of her neck.

"Let me," he offered, stepping close and cupping her chin with one hand while he kneaded her neck with another. "I suppose that inviting you in for more tea would be pointless?"

She sighed, opening her eyes again and reluctantly stepping away from his soothing fingers. "Pointless," she agreed. "The girls are probably wondering where I am." She turned to go, wishing fervently that their afternoon together had ended differently. Much differently.

"Jovi—don't hide things from me again," she warned as she reached for the knob. "Deception and dishonesty—I don't deal with them."

He shrugged off her admonishment. "Deception and dishonesty weren't involved here, Dell. I was just earning my salary. My job is running the ranch." He glanced at the clock on the wall and sighed. "As much as I hate to admit it, I think you're right."

"Right? About what?" Dell asked, pulling the door open.

"Right about waiting to have any more of that tea. I need to go help Pete with feeding and be sure Danny's pulling his weight." He glanced around. "As late as it is, I'm sort of surprised not to see Rosa or one of the girls here looking for you." He bent to touch her lips with his own, and the gesture was at once sexy and full of tender concern.

"Take care, Dell. We'll talk again later." Without giving her a chance to respond he clattered off the porch and headed across the drive to the barn.

*

The next morning, Dell's fingers flew over the computer keys, and she hummed under her breath as she typed. Getting back to work had been easier than she had anticipated—almost as easy as letting the idea take root and acting on it. In spite of downturns in tourism to Mexico, there was still so much traffic between Laredo and points south that several of the largest brokerage firms in Laredo were chronically short-handed. It was difficult convincing some of the freight-forwarding firms that she wasn't applying for a regular job with them, but that she wanted to help develop contacts and work with various Mexican businesses right from the privacy and comfort of her own home.

The incident with Jovi still bugged her when she took time to think about it. She had been on her own for years and certainly didn't need his misguided paternal protection. She had also wondered, after the fact, why the agent had come at all. Didn't the Drug Enforcement Agency officers cloak themselves and their missions in secrecy? Why would one have come forward to admit the ranch was being watched? Even given that Jovi had worked for the agency, she didn't think he could have any connections here in Laredo that warranted receiving special information from his ex-colleagues. He hadn't been stationed in Laredo, anyway, but in Florida. The DEA probably hadn't wanted to speak to him, but to her. She was the property owner, after all. A slight frown twisted her lips when she thought of how easily Jovi manipulated situations.

Still, she had little time to dwell on her reservations. When she contacted several local firms she had worked with in the past, the demands on her time were immediate. One of the firms, *Garza y Landin*, was in the midst of an ambitious expansion from Nuevo Laredo into Monterrey. The owners were from Mexico City and had put the manager of the Laredo office in charge of finalizing details for office space, staff, and the actual physical movement of several pieces of equipment.

Dell hadn't really wanted to accept overseeing that sort of an operation. As she told the harried Laredo manager, she had lost any real awareness of the Monterrey labor and real estate market.

But he insisted he could use her just to handle the Laredo end and make general recommendations, and she knew a reliable employment agency in Monterrey, which seemed to ease the manager's mind almost immediately.

Given the value of computers and the Internet, with newer satellite technology thrown in, she wound up being helpful to the manager without having to drive down to Monterrey, which she had been willing, if not eager, to do. When she finally hung up from a lengthy call to the employment agency, where she had renewed some old acquaintances as her call was channeled, she couldn't help smiling in satisfaction. The sense of accomplishment and the anticipation of new challenges were invigorating. Going back to work seemed financially prudent, if not really a matter of urgency, but the pleasure in accomplishing what she set out to do so easily was rewarding in itself.

"You look happy," Rosa remarked as she came into the study carrying a glass of freshly made lemonade.

"I got a lot done without much time or effort," Dell admitted. "It feels good to actually work again."

Rosa sniffed. "I'd call the girls work," she pointed out. "When it wasn't one thing it was another, when you started helping that judge friend of yours. And then the horses—"

"It seems all I've done recently is watch the girls and attend functions with this person or agency or that. Not that I'm complaining," she added quickly, aware Rosa still didn't really approve of having the girls at the ranch. Rosa might enjoy the girls' company, but she wouldn't admit it.

Rosa made another faint sound of disavowal and patted Dell's arm. "Well, as long as you enjoy yourself. People should do what they like best. Which is why"—she made a face—"I'm going to go tackle the laundry."

"Get the girls to help you," Dell suggested. "They need to learn."

"No, no. I don't mind it too much. I just put it in the machine, anyway. The only part of it I don't like is sorting it. Selina would help—she always does. Amy and Michelle do a lot. Maribel's face would curdle cow's milk, so forget that." Rosa shook her head. "No way in the world I ask *la princesa* Becky to sort. Nothing would ever match again!"

Dell laughed. Becky did enjoy separating and taking apart more than she liked to put things up. "Well, all right. But don't spare the girls if you need help. Three of the four don't mind, and the other needs it the most."

Rosa went out, and Dell sat for a minute, trying to decide what to do next. Finally she decided she'd walk down to the barn and see how the horses were. She had no intention at all of seeing how Jovani Treviño was doing, she told herself. Nevertheless, she found herself checking her makeup and hair in the hall mirror on the way out.

*

The barn was quiet and shadowed when she went in. Some of the horses had been let out to roam the pastures, while others dozed, waiting for feeding time. She stopped, as she always did, to pet *Carbón's* graying head.

"Old lug," she crooned, and went into his stall. "You should be out to pasture, not hogging the best box in the barn."

He snorted disdainfully, and she laughed and scratched his ear, knowing in spite of his rugged nature, she'd never have the heart to turn him out. She wondered if she should saddle him up and see what he'd do. Becky loved to ride when Allison Gonzalez came over, or when Dell had time to swing up on a horse and carry her around, but *Carbón* had once been gentle and safe. Maybe Becky could ride him on her own in the near future. If the old guy didn't mind. Dell had heard often enough that horses were actually a better choice for children than ponies. Ponies could be as obstinate as mules, and more devious. Still, it wasn't nearly as long a fall from a pony, she acknowledged, grinning. She'd certainly had her share of falls from both distances, but coming off *Carbón* hadn't hurt quite as much, if she remembered correctly.

Still smiling, she opened the door, half turning to give the pony a final pat and push him gently back, since he wanted to follow her out, and she walked right into Jovi.

He was leading one of the Arabians, a fidgety bay mare who reared and tried to pull away, but he somehow managed to hold the temperamental horse with one hand while steadying Dell with his arm.

"I'd say hi, but I'm busy." He grinned, and before Dell could manage a reply, he bent and pressed an unexpected kiss on her upturned lips. Then he freed her, switching the lead and catching the halter up close to control the dancing mare.

"Think quarter horses," he admonished, and went on down the hall, cursing at the mare in gentle tones as he tried to quiet her.

Bemused, Dell wandered into the office and sat down at the desk Jovi had cleared off. She picked up an issue of *Western Horseman* and leafed through it without real interest. She didn't like Western horses. She liked Eastern horses—hunters, jumpers, the hot bloods.

The irony of it made her smile. Men who asked her out without success had insinuated that her blood must be glacial. Cold as they come, one rebuffed pretender had sniffed. But she had no use for the gentle warm bloods or the big, plodding cold bloods when it came to horses. They had to be hot and fast. Her breath caught momentarily in her throat as she visualized Jovi in his trunks at South Padre. Or in his shorts in the foreman's house. Hot . . . and fast. Her taste seemed to run that way where men were concerned, too.

He walked into the room just then, and she blushed. Dark

eyebrows shot up. "Did I interrupt a private fantasy? I hope?" He walked over and perched on the edge of his desk, towering over her.

"Not exactly." *Memories aren't fantasies, so I'm not lying.* "I was just thinking something funny. About the horses." To prove her point, she picked up the glossy magazine and waved it in front of his nose. "These horses."

"Ah." The glint in his eyes told her he didn't buy it, but he moved from the desk and sat down in his own chair, and she felt more comfortable. Looking across at him was a little less unnerving than being forced to look up at him.

She put the magazine back down and fidgeted with it, trying to find a way to tell him to stop kissing her. She didn't want to be kissed. She glanced at the door. What she really wanted was to get up, walk to the door, and latch it. But she couldn't do that.

"I didn't mean to bump into you," she began finally. He grinned at her, boyish and unrepentant.

"You just didn't see my six-foot frame coming down the hall with a horse," he offered, nodding. "Of course."

Dell expelled a slow breath. "You really irritate me sometimes," she muttered. "I'm serious." She frowned at him. "You shouldn't have kissed me, either."

He shrugged, and something of the humor seemed to fade, although she wasn't sure why. "No," he agreed. "I probably shouldn't have. But I couldn't help myself."

At a loss for a rebuttal, or for anything intelligent to say at all, Dell stood slowly and walked over to the office window, looking out at the empty riding arena. "You have to help yourself," she said finally. She didn't add, *because I can't,* but she thought it. "If only you didn't work for me," she added impulsively, turning to face him.

The mischievous gleam was gone completely, and humor had turned into grimness. She remembered when he had called himself *un enojon,* someone easily angered, and was a little more inclined to accept that now than she had been then.

"But I do work for you," he said, slowly and heavily. "And my job matters. I've always considered myself a professional. Matter of pride, I guess. So I'll try to keep my mind on business, Dell. For both our sakes."

He sighed and reached for a neatly typed letter lying on one corner of his desk and stood to hand it to her.

"Look this over," he suggested. "A ranch just up I-35 is going out of business. They're liquidating their stock—and they have Arabs."

She made a show of looking at the letter offering him the chance to come view the horses before they were consigned to a local auction house. She had already known about the horses, but they didn't interest her. Jovi Treviño interested her. And infuriated her. And fascinated her. She handed the letter back.

"What do you think?"

"Most of the stock is only fair. But the broodmares are used to this south Texas heat. And two of them look really good on paper. I think it's worth checking out."

She nodded. "Go, then. Let me know when you get back, or call if you think you need to."

He shifted a little, studying her thoughtfully. "Can you afford new stock?"

She looked startled at the question. "We've sold most of what I had, Jovi. Why wouldn't I be able to?"

"It was just a question." He shoved a hand through his hair and glanced at the clock on the wall. "I think I'll try to go up today. Might as well beat any competition. Do you want to go with me?"

She shook her head. "I don't think so. I've been locked up in the study all day. Becky needs some quality time. I think I'll take her and the others into town to eat." She smiled faintly. "It's a kid thing, but they're in heaven if we go somewhere with fast food. "I'll take Rosa, too, if she'll go. Mostly she won't."

He sat back down at the desk, reaching for the phone. "Have fun," he said absently, already punching numbers in. She nodded and left, wishing he'd put her—them—before the horses.

CHAPTER THIRTEEN

Two days, later, though, Dell couldn't fault Jovi for his attention to his job. He'd picked up the only two horses they'd agreed were worthwhile and talked the farm owner into throwing in a trailer he no longer needed. Dell smiled at the girls' excitement as Jovi pulled to a gentle stop by the barn, the horse trailer rocking a little as its occupants shifted and moved inside, unseen. Michelle and Amy were giggling and hopping around, and even Maribel had come down to watch as the two new mares were unloaded.

"Horses," Becky crowed, as Jovi lowered the ramp, and Dell kissed her cheek.

"Yes, Becky, new horses."

"Are they tame? Can we pet them?" Amy demanded, clearly the most excited of the girls.

"Jovi said they're very gentle. But we need to let them get settled in. They've never been moved before," Dell warned gently. "Let's let Jovi and Pete bring them out."

Actually, she would have loved to go up the ramp and help unload her new purchases personally, but someone had to supervise the teenagers and keep Becky at a safe distance. She smiled again as she heard Pete complaining to Jovi about Arabians. He just couldn't help himself, she knew; to him, quarter horses were a south Texas tradition that should be honored above all others.

The first mare down was gray, her coat fading in patches with age. She pricked her ears and looked around with interest but without alarm. Thinking of the nervy, overly excitable bay mare in the barn, Dell was relieved this old girl seemed perfectly docile. Jovi was stroking her neck, and when she showed no signs of nervousness, he led her over to the girls.

"Meet Desert Snow. It never snows in Laredo, but I get stuck with all these gray horses named Snow," he said, then grinned wryly at Dell. "*She* loves men."

"She has beautiful lines," Dell approved, reaching out to stroke her forehead gently. "Of course, I'm not sure about her intelligence . . ." Becky squealed in delight and stuck out a chubby hand. The mare lifted her nose and sniffed the toddler's cheek, ruffling wisps of her hair, and Becky laughed happily and patted the mare. Amy and Michelle came up quietly, the way they had been taught, extending their hands and talking to the horse. Although they were careful with their movements and voices, their faces glowed with excitement; it was almost as if the horse had been bought just for them.

Maribel leaned back against the fence and sniffed in disdain, her mouth a dark red frown as she watched.

Pete unloaded the second, a taller, younger mare, but she danced skittishly and seemed more upset than her stable mate, so he took her into the barn right away, and Jovi excused himself and led the gray mare in, too.

"They're nice," Michelle said.

"Nice?" Amy sounded outraged. "They're beautiful! *Bien bonitas!* They're incredible. They're—" She stopped suddenly.

"What's wrong?" Dell asked, seeing the stricken expression on Amy's face.

"Nothing!" Amy colored a little. "It's just . . . I suddenly realized. What I want to do."

"Oh?"

Amy nodded, her young face full of sudden conviction. "A vet. I want to be a veterinarian." She stopped for a minute, unsure again. "I think."

Dell smiled. "You've got time to be sure. But you'd be very good at it."

Maribel snorted. "Good at it! Like she's smart enough—hey, Amy—you dropped out, no? You gonna pass medical school and stuff? Even vets have to go to school, I bet." She chortled. "I can just see you, stickin' your skinny arm up some horse's ass—"

Amy ignored her and Dell frowned at Maribel.

"There aren't any dropouts here, Maribel," she reminded the girl. "And Amy will do well. I'm counting on it."

Maribel shrugged insolently. "Whatever," she muttered and stalked back toward the house.

Dell put Becky down, careful not to let the toddler pull her hand free and rush toward the barn.

"Well, girls, don't be afraid to go help the guys," she urged. "I know mucking stalls isn't anyone's favorite job, but the effort's always appreciated."

Michelle and Amy exchanged amused glances.

"That sounded like a suggestion," Michelle groaned, and Amy nodded.

"I thought so, too," she agreed. "Or an order. Do we get to ride if we help?"

"Sure. But in the arena, and don't choose those two new girls. Give them a day or two," Dell warned, and they nodded happily and ran toward the barn.

Becky tugged, wanting to follow, and Dell reluctantly picked her up again. "Not this afternoon, sweetheart," she said reluctantly. "We need to go get some work done at the house."

Becky's face puckered, and she squirmed, pointing at the barn. Then she reached up and pulled Dell's face close, kissing her on the check.

"'Kay," she gurgled. "Me work."

Dell laughed and hugged the little girl, wondering yet again how anyone could give up a child. Holding Becky close, Dell headed back to the house.

*

Light from the moon flooded the yard. Dell stood outside by the pool, staring up at the golden sphere, transfixed. She could understand where the ideas about moon madness came from. Walking out into the hot summer air and seeing a full moon could literally freeze her in place with amazement. And contentment, she thought, stretching. She shook her head slightly. Some of her acquaintances claimed to be unimpressed with the moon, the summer heat, even the scent of the honeysuckle and gardenias, which were almost overpowering at the moment.

She didn't believe them. How could anyone not relish this sense of perfection? Shrugging, she slipped off her beach robe and padded over to the edge of the pool. She rarely swam, and since she had started picking up odd jobs with the forwarding companies, she hadn't been in the water at all. The problem was that when she made time to dive in, she couldn't drag herself out again. So she avoided the pool and saved the hours of time she'd lose if she gave in.

She didn't dive in, just walked over to the shallow end and stepped in, testing the water experimentally. Not surprisingly, the pool was as warm as the night, and it rose around her, liquid and soothing. Sighing contentedly, she flipped over on her back and floated, moving her fingers occasionally just to steady her position on the unmoving surface. Any idea of exerting herself was gone. Floating mindlessly and timelessly under the clear, south Texas sky was just too appealing.

Far off, a coyote howled, and she thought once, briefly, of Jovi, but pushed him determinedly from her mind. After floating lazily for a blissful eternity, she reluctantly put her feet down, standing up and looking across the length of the pool. She had come here to swim, she reminded herself sternly. She could use the exercise, and maybe a little physical activity would make it easier to sleep when she went back in. If she went back in. She really couldn't imagine leaving the pool. A good breaststroke would burn off a lot of calories and wear her out in a hurry. She sighed. Then she took a deep breath and dove instead, gliding effortlessly across the pool under water.

A long time ago, her father had teased her about being half dolphin, she remembered suddenly, because she had preferred those short, rolling surface dives to the rigor of the "real" swimming her mother practiced to maintain her own figure. Frowning at the memory, she dove again and again, almost with anger, until she was gasping for breath. She came up for air in the middle of the pool and stood motionless until the beauty of the night slowly reclaimed her consciousness and attention. When her eyes kept looking up to check the moon's position again instead of squeezing shut against the pain of some new memory, she hoisted herself to the tiled edge of the pool to take a breather, idly circling her feet in the warm water.

"Sneaking a swim's going to be awfully hard now," a husky masculine voice drawled behind her, and she started so violently that she slipped off the edge and back into the pool.

"Sorry." Jovi reached out a lean, muscled arm. "Shall I help you out?"

Dell felt her chest tighten, cutting off her ability to breathe normally. At South Padre, Jovi's trunks had been passably decorous. The trunks he wore now seemed sprayed on with a half-empty can of spray paint. The low, low cut showed too much torso. And too much hair. Not to mention way too much of everything else. She made herself refocus her gaze on the extended hand, and when she thought she could meet his eyes without blushing, she looked up at him.

"What are you doing here? It must be . . . " Her voice trailed off. The question was lame, and she herself had already decided that on nights like this, time was of no importance at all.

He smiled cheerfully. "It must be two in the morning. Early, not late. And, as I already explained, I'm sneaking into the pool. At least I was trying to."

He shrugged his massive shoulders and crossed his arms when she still didn't take his hand. "What can I say? You caught me."

"Do you do this often?" She asked, and watched as he had to make his own effort to refocus on her face.

"No, not often," he said, seriously. "Actually, this would be the first time. That I've ever seen you in a bikini like that."

She grimaced. "Funny. I meant, do you sneak into the pool very often?"

"Oh, that. Yes." He sat down on the edge of the pool and slid his legs into the water. "Almost every night, as a matter of fact." He struck a bodybuilder's pose, fists clenched and arms tautened to show off his muscled torso. "I have to maintain this perfection somehow." Then he laughed. "God, I sound arrogant, don't I? But I love to swim, and I didn't think you'd mind."

"Of course not. But every night?" She couldn't mask her surprise. "I've never seen you."

"How often are *you* here?"

"Never," she admitted. "But now and then I do look out my window. Maybe not at two." She cocked her head to see him from a better angle. "You don't sleep nights, or what?"

"I sleep. When I have to." He waved an expansive hand at the lush greenery and sparkling water around them. "But why squander time sleeping when you could enjoy scenery like this? And a night just made to perfection."

She smiled. "Spoken with the soul of a poet."

"All men in love are poets," he announced grandly, then laughed at himself again. "Not that I'm in love, but that's a good line. I'll have to write it down before I forget it." He kicked, spraying her with crystal rain. "So . . . do you want me to leave?"

Dell turned away for a moment, considering. Whether or not she wanted him to leave, it obviously would be far safer if he did. Or she did. He worked hard with the horses, even given that some of his chores confined him to the air-conditioned office. But she'd often gone down to the barn to see him cleaning stalls with Pete and Danny, or moving equipment around outside. He wasn't a shirker, and it seemed unfair to keep him from enjoying what was apparently a ritual for him after a hard day. And the water was divine, so soothing and tantalizing, that she didn't want to leave, either.

She ruthlessly silenced the tiny voice whispering to her that the man posed at pool's edge, waiting for her answer, was both divine and tantalizing himself. Soothing, no. The man definitely was more upsetting than soothing. She managed a sedate shrug.

"Suit yourself," she said loftily. "But stay out of my way."

"Yes, ma'am," he agreed laconically, and slid into the water. She turned and dove away, swimming toward the deep end of the pool. He waited until she had almost reached the other end, then thrust himself away from the wall and raced across the pool, arms and feet churning the surface as if he were chasing an Olympic record. When she surfaced, he was already there, arms hooked nonchalantly over the pool's tiled lip.

"Hi," he said, and laughed when she just frowned and turned away. This time she used a lazy sidestroke, and he swam alongside, not talking, just smiling across at her. She was a little surprised the water didn't bubble and boil, since the heat in the pool had climbed steadily, and he was swimming so close to her their legs brushed occasionally.

If she rolled, changing sides, she thought idly, she would roll right into his arms. The temptation to do so was strong, but she also knew it was stupid. She had the girls and Becky to think about, and in spite of his occasional, reluctant flirting, he seemed to be unwilling to initiate a physical relation himself, now, even if she didn't know why. Provoking him would be inexcusable.

He reached the edge of the pool and reached out a hand lazily, pushing himself upright and watching her as she did the same. She, too, leaned against the wall, feeling the heat of his body across the few inches of space between them, wishing he would give some indication of feeling it, of feeling her. Of wanting her.

She couldn't imagine how he could stand there, so silent and motionless, when she felt shaky and breathless. Unable to deal with the treacherous fire igniting deep inside, she braced her arms on the pool and swung out.

Her abrupt departure apparently startled him; he glanced at her, then swung out after her, following her to the lounger where her towel was.

"You're not leaving, are you?"

She reached for the towel and blotted the water from her face. "Yes. It's late."

He didn't dispute the time, but cast a thoughtful glance at the sky above them, then looked at her.

"I didn't mean to chase you away," he apologized.

She tried an indignant snort, but it came out soft and unconvincing. "Don't give yourself too much credit. I've been out here for a long time, and I'm ready to go. That's all."

"You weren't thinking about leaving when I first got here," he pointed out matter-of-factly. "You don't allow yourself enough little luxuries like this." He cast a glance at the loungers. "Stay," he insisted. "We'll talk."

Dell sighed and ran her fingers through her wet hair. Then she shrugged. "Okay. I'll dry out for a few minutes. After that, I'm calling it a night."

He nodded. "Me, too," he agreed, and sank into the lounger closest to him, stretching out with apparent indifference and waving at the other. "Make yourself comfortable."

She shook her head at him but sat down carefully on the flowered cushions, too aware of him to lie down. To cover her uneasiness, she began toweling her hair dry, rubbing the dark strands of her hair in the fluffy towel over and over again.

Behind her, she heard Jovi breathe out a deep, heavy breath. "Quit torturing your poor hair," he ordered. She heard the faint noise of the cushions on the lounger behind her as he stood and came over to drop to his knees behind her. His hands, strong and warm, pulled the towel from her unprotesting fingers and tossed it on the ground beside the lounger.

"Quit torturing me," he whispered, and she jerked upright as she felt the prickle of his mustache on her bare back, followed by the soft warmth of his lips trailing a line of fire up toward her neck. He didn't hold her, though, kept his hands planted on the lounger, although she could feel them on either side of her hips. She could get up and walk away, and she knew he wouldn't stop her.

Instead, she drew in a deep, shuddering breath, then twisted her head around just as his lips brushed the side of her neck. Slowly, slowly his hand came up, brushing up her arm to catch and hold her chin. Gently, he touched his lips to hers.

She whispered his name and twisted, kissing him back, sliding her fingers over his shoulders and holding him close. With a muffled groan, he pressed her back against the cushions, reaching out to lift her legs, then stroking them with teasing fingers as she stretched out. His kisses grew deeper, more demanding, and his body pressed into hers, bare flesh heated and electric. She kneaded his shoulders, gasped his name.

The lounger tipped under them, and he muttered a curse and rolled Dell into his arms, easing her down on the smooth, hard tile. She barely felt the ungiving texture under her arms and hips—she was too aware he had drawn away from her. She tugged gently, and he obligingly leaned over her again, touching her mouth with his, then bending closer to kiss her throat, taste the salt with the tip of his tongue.

Then his head moved lower still, and he felt her body tauten with surprise and go still as he pressed his lips to the soft swell of her breasts, kissing each one softly, then nudging the brightly flowered fabric of her bra until it gave way. She gasped, arching toward him, her fingers knotting in his hair as he teased each hardened peak in turn, crying his name, pressing up into him, seeking contact with his hard, masculine body along her entire feminine length.

Shaking with need, Jovi tugged and teased her nipples, a hand sliding gently down her flat stomach, caressing, sliding beneath the band of her bikini. He heard her cries, soft and pleading, as his fingers found her. He dragged his mouth back up toward her mouth, intent on silencing her, and from a faint, far-off distance, he heard the tiny click.

Not the click of a gun, he thought foggily, his body still hard, still trembling as he fought to control his need for completion. It had been the small click of some kind of camera. He hadn't seen a flash, but he wasn't sure there hadn't been. And the moonlight and yard lights would have made it easy to shoot pictures with any good, low-light camera even without a flash.

He shifted and moved away, propping himself to screen her from whomever had been watching from somewhere in the plants behind them. He heard a slight rustle and glanced over his shoulder to see the shrubs that surrounded the side gate move even though there was no wind. The opportunity was lost; he knew he would find no one now. But he knew that someone had been there.

"Jovi," Dell murmured, her eyes refocusing, and her lips swollen and parted. "What?"

Reluctantly he leaned over, touching his lips to hers again, then pushing himself to his feet.

"Someone was here, on the patio," he said, not wanting to frighten or embarrass her, but unable to lie. "Somebody was watching us. I heard a camera click."

He saw the shock in her face, followed quickly by disbelief, then anger. Turning away, she refastened the bikini top and started to stand up. He held out his hand, and she didn't take it, so he caught her wrist, pulling her up gently.

"No," she said with a decided shake of her head, looking around the serene patio. "There's no one here. There couldn't have been." She looked genuinely puzzled, but only slightly concerned. "How could there have been? Why would there have been?" She shook her head again, more slowly and more hesitantly in spite of her denial. "You're imagining things, Jovi."

He didn't point out he'd been a cop. She knew from his resume, and given his real reason for being here, he didn't want her to dwell on his past. But even though he had decided he didn't want to spend his life in law enforcement, he'd been good. He still had the skills and the instinct. Someone had been watching. Anger flared through him, but he kept it carefully hidden. It had been inexcusable for him to forget why he was here, and he had endangered both his investigation and Dell by giving in to temptation.

Breathing deeply, he turned again, squinting into the shadows along the tall, wooden fence that enclosed them. The carefully tended plants were still again. Sighing, he shoved a hand through his hair. He wasn't sure who would watch, or why anyone would want pictures. Maribel? He dismissed her as soon as he thought of her. She might stumble on them and stay to gather ammunition to hurl at Dell, but he couldn't imagine either that she'd walk in on them a second time or that she'd be armed with a camera in the middle of the night. No one else on the ranch had reason or access. His frown deepened. So why was someone shooting pictures, and was Dell the target—or was he?

Reluctantly, he turned back to Dell, aware of her disbelief, of her withdrawal. Again. He fought the urge to sigh loudly and heavily. Their relationship tottered precariously on a high wire, and each time they took a step forward, the wire threatened to snap, sending them hurtling to destruction. He'd never wanted a woman as much as he wanted Dell. He knew she was physically attracted to him. How strong the attraction might be, he didn't know. She was so damn distant sometimes, so remote. But the worst thing he could do was take her to bed. She'd regret it in the end because of the girls. And because he'd lied to her from the get go.

And he'd regret it too, if it were just a matter of a few hours or nights, if it were just sex. Because he wanted so much more from her. He straightened imperceptibly, tensing, as that thought slammed home. He wanted more. He didn't know whether it was the emptiness and lack of connection in his own life, or the untouchable distance she projected that made him want to reach out and draw her close. Whatever it was, though, had worked its way deep inside, and he doubted he'd ever look at her and not want her.

She was still watching him, her expression somber and a little hurt. Her breathing had returned to normal, and she had draped herself in a towel.

"There was someone here," he told her again, knowing she still didn't quite believe him. He forced a thin smile. "You can't think I just wanted to stop. I invent headaches, for that, not cameras."

He could see her try to fight back a faint smile. "Somehow I don't believe that," she retorted, then shook her head. Her hair, just beginning to dry, slapped wetly against her towel-covered shoulders. "You have to admit it doesn't make sense, though. Why would anyone bother? Why would they care?"

The shrug was one of disavowal this time. "Who knows? Perversion? Unrequited love? But it happened."

Dell snorted. "If it's unrequited love, don't look at me, buster. There isn't anyone *that* interested, trust me."

He slanted an eyebrow. "And what? Am I beating women off with a wet towel or something?"

Dell thought of Karla Gonzalez and frowned. If the man didn't have women fighting over him somewhere, she'd be surprised. But she bit back the thought and tried to focus on his worries instead.

Her face tightened as she thought of something. "You don't suppose Maribel—"

"No." He shook his head and ran his hand over his face again with irritation before swatting at his bare arm. "I thought of her," he admitted. "But she couldn't just happen onto us twice. She'd have to be a pro to luck onto us twice, and she's not." He shrugged, and then swatted at his shoulder. "Damn mosquitoes."

Dell cast a speculative glance at the house. All the windows upstairs were dark, except she could make out the faintest glow of light coming from what she knew was Becky's room. The angel nightlight—she'd turned it on herself. Thinking of Becky made her realize she'd been within seconds of making love to Jovi in the middle of the patio, with bright lights shining all around them. And without protection of any sort. She flushed, appalled at the thought, and her lips thinned as she silently cursed her stupidity.

"Regrets already?" Jovi's voice was low and gentle, the mocking tone he'd used minutes ago gone. "Nothing happened."

"I wouldn't say nothing," she returned shortly, not able to meet his gaze. She glared at him. "Did you come here expecting— ready—to make love?"

He looked at her blankly for a moment, then shook his head. "Don't carry condoms in my trunks," he admitted, his tone light but his expression abashed.

She snorted. "Couldn't fit even a foil package in those," she muttered, glaring at the too-tight trunks. She shouldn't be thinking about what could or couldn't fit *there*. She should be upstairs in her room. Asleep.

She looked again toward the second-story windows. "Hopefully no one was awake."

He glanced at the house, too. "I'm sure no one was," he said soothingly. "We'd probably better get to bed." She looked back at him. "Our own beds," he amended quickly.

She didn't seem particularly appeased, and the steadiness of her regard was discomfiting. But after long, silent seconds she merely nodded. "Good night," she said, and walked toward the house, leaving him standing alone by the pool. When he was sure she was gone, he allowed himself a long, loud sigh. Then he cursed for good measure, and headed back to the dark, lonely foreman's house.

*

Dell leaned her chair back and stared listlessly at the wall. She had come to the study to busy her mind and her fingers, because rehashing what happened—or almost happened—on the patio with Jovani was driving her stark raving mad, and she'd been doing it for two days straight. She didn't like feeling vulnerable or threatened. Her lips twitched. She also didn't like feeling unwanted or discarded, she admitted. Jovi's apparent ability to forget how close they had come to making love was irritating, in spite of her grim determination to regain control of her senses. And her body.

She shifted in the chair, aware the incessant ache of wanting him was back, throbbing through her, painful in its intensity. She thought of her other fleeting relationships. Even her fiancé had not made her tremble with need from the inside out. No, Jeremy's appeal, overwhelming at the onset, had faded into a morass of lies, broken promises, and disregard for any future they might have together. She'd do well to remember he'd merely used her—and she let him. Pretended not to see the drug use. Believed he'd give it up for her if she waited. Excused the deception, because he'd soothed her doubts with loving words and the promise of forever. Forever had been just a few short months, and he'd taken his life in her apartment, shattering her belief in herself and in love.

Sighing, she looked down at the paper, covered with neat notes. She had promised Judge Ovalle-Martinez to allow Michelle's mother to visit the ranch. The judge had arranged for a mediator to drive the woman out the first time. The teenager was unhappy and nervous about the visit, but Selina and Amy rallied around her, assuring her time would pass quickly. The visit specifically required private time for the two, and although Michelle looked apprehensive, Dell offered them the study or the patio for their time together. After the two had had a chance to talk, Michelle's mother stayed to dinner. She was timid and unsure of herself and kept casting furtive glances around what had become her daughter's temporary home. While they ate, she told them about the classes she was taking, and her face glowed with her newfound success and independence. Dell could see the woman was seriously trying to make amends to her only child, and she suspected it was only a matter of time before the court decided to send Michelle home.

Logically, Dell knew it was for the best. She believed children should be with their mothers, or fathers, even if they were young adults. Most parents loved their own, even when they lacked the tools to convey that feeling. She closed her eyes, breathing a troubled little prayer as her thoughts turned from Michelle to Becky. Did Becky's mother ever miss her? Did she want her home again? Would it matter to her that Becky was learning colors and could count to five in English and in Spanish? Losing Becky now would be more than she could bear, no matter how deeply she believed families should be kept together.

Dell drummed her fingers on the desktop. She could do any number of things. Her contacts were widening. A number in Houston now graced the top of her "to do" list. A woman had called earlier, asking her if she could provide advice on which locations in Monterrey would provide suitable housing for employees who were being moved there to staff a branch office. Asking about security arrangements. Dell agreed to work on recommendations, but for the first time since she decided to start offering her services again, she resented the intrusion on her time and thoughts.

She knew herself well enough to know why, too. She was still upset and frustrated over the whole situation with Jovi. For two days, they'd tiptoed around each other and their frustrations, losing themselves in their separate tasks. She'd bumped into Jovi on several occasions, taking the girls out on rides or walking through the barn to visit the horses, and he'd been civil and distant.

A sharp pain lanced through her head, and she stopped drumming to massage her temples. His behavior was exactly what it should be, she thought with a trace of bitterness. Deferential. Accommodating. She didn't understand his withdrawal. She had always been distant. *La inalcanzable.* He'd been warm and provocative. Well within reach. He wasn't role playing or engaging in payback. He'd physically distanced himself, and for reasons she didn't want to analyze, it angered her. And hurt her.

Frowning, she got up and walked over to the window. The drapes were open in spite of the strong slant of the sun. The heat outside would be oppressive—it always was. She glanced at the clock. In spite of the brightness and the scorching temperatures, it was already almost seven. The horses would have been fed, the stalls cleaned. Danny and Pete would be in their rooms for the night. The girls were watching television, oblivious to the world. Becky was asleep, and Rosa sat in her corner in the living room, embroidering with her slow, careful fingers. Day was done, and everyone was at home.

She thought of Jovi, dressed in his skimpy shorts, coming down the stairs at the foreman's house. Completely at home. She looked around the elegant, empty study, suddenly unwilling to live with the loneliness any longer. She wasn't a teenager, and she could make responsible choices. She could be discreet. What she couldn't be anymore was alone. Unloved.

She checked her watch, verifying the time. Giving herself a few extra seconds to change her mind. Then she slipped silently out of the study and out through the front door. She could call Rosa later if she needed to, and present some reason for her abrupt absence. But she wouldn't waste precious time now, trying to explain the emotion or the desire that drove her.

By the time she reached Jovi's door, her chest was slamming painfully in her chest, and she was breathless. She made herself breathe deeply once or twice and brushed at her damp forehead with the back of her hand. She knew it wasn't exertion that had caused her pulse to accelerate and her legs to buckle momentarily; it was the enormity of her decision. She raised her hand to knock, knowing her decision to spend most of the night with Jovi was irreversible. Karla's friendly jab had been right after all—nothing mattered except the need to make love to Jovani Treviño. With one final, deep drag of air into her constricted lungs, she rapped the door sharply.

The porch light was on, but the front room was dark. She supposed Jovi was either in the kitchen, eating, or upstairs. Couldn't be watching TV in the living room—there was no telltale glow or flicker of changing scenes. She listened, trying to hear him make his way to the door, but could hear nothing. Her heart slowed and each beat was a separate, painful blow against her chest.

Then the door swung open silently, and he looked at her with undisguised surprise. But, she noticed, without real invitation. He didn't seem pleased to see her, really, just surprised.

"Hi," he said finally, and moved out of the door. "Come on in." He closed the door after her and then walked over to pick up some scattered magazines from one of the chairs. "What's wrong?"

She shook her head, noticing with some disappointment that he wasn't in shorts. Actually, he was in jeans, a clean shirt, and polished boots, as if he were on his way out. The burning sensation low, low in her stomach that had been desire was slowly cooling, hardening. Into a premonition of disaster. Still, she had walked into this. She wouldn't go without letting him know why she had come. Not this time.

Biting her lip a little, she gave her head another brief shake. "Nothing's wrong," she replied, her tone cool and level. She looked him over again. "But am I keeping you from doing something? You look like you're ready to leave."

He didn't deny it, just returned her appraisal. Then he motioned toward the chair he had just cleared. "Well, I have some time to kill, so make yourself at home," he invited. Courtesy. She hadn't wanted or expected that from him. Not tonight. Still, she wasn't sure how to tell him what she did want, so she walked over to the chair and sat down obediently.

"Well, if nothing's the matter, let me get us something to drink," he suggested. He tilted his head. "Tea?"

She thought for a moment, trying to think of a subtle way to announce her intentions. "I don't suppose you'd have any wine," she said, after a moment, slowly, feeling the slightest trace of warmth push up her throat into her cheeks.

He obviously read between the lines, because, just for a minute, both his eyebrows shot up, and his eyes widened. His mouth, full and sensual under the mustache, twitched. But just as quickly, he managed a slight, regretful smile.

"No wine. That's fancy lady stuff." He gave her a wink. "I could get us a couple of cold brews."

Dell's nose wrinkled in distaste. She didn't even like the smell of the stuff. He laughed at her.

"My bar stock obviously isn't up to snuff," he admitted. "But you're in Texas, honey. Texans drink beer."

"Not this one," she said primly, and then smiled back at him, taking the arrogance out of her retort. "How strong is the tea this time?"

He shrugged expansively. "A babe could drink it," he assured her with another quick wink.

She sat uncomfortably in the chair, listening as he clanked ice into a glass. He was back in no time, carrying a beer and an impossibly tall glass of tea. Freshly cut lemon and artificial sweetener graced the small round tray he handed her, and she put it down on the table beside her before he could notice the slight tremor in her hands. She'd always credited herself with being thoroughly modern, honest, and efficient. But her insides were shaking at the thought of asking Jovi to take her to bed. How did women proposition men, anyway? She was abruptly convinced that this equality of roles, sexually speaking, was for the birds. She would much rather he do something, say something. She couldn't. But he just perched himself on the couch, opened the beer bottle, and chugged most of it down in one swallow.

Then he set the bottle on the coffee table, propped up his feet, and gave her an affable grin. "Good. I'd wipe my mustache with my sleeve, but I'm being polite."

She nodded. "I noticed." There really wasn't anything else she could think of to say. Why was he so far across the room? And why did he watch her so intently from the unfathomable depths of those dark eyes?

She'd seen movies where a woman simply stripped off her clothes to announce she wanted someone. She lifted her hand to brush absently at her hair. His eyes followed the slight movement, but his expression never changed. Somehow, fighting her way out of the buttoned cotton blouse and tight jeans didn't strike her as seductive, but embarrassing, if the moment wasn't just right.

Although he said nothing, she had the impression he was in a hurry; she saw him sneak a quick peek at his watch. Was he going out with someone? Did he have plans to spend the night in some other woman's bed? She wouldn't let him do that.

She stood up abruptly, without speaking, and he started. She walked over to the couch, sitting at the end farthest away from him. He put his feet down and turned obligingly, but again she sensed his surprise. And his discomfort.

"Jovi," she said, "you know . . . why I went to your room, when we were in South Padre." It was a statement, not a question, but he nodded slowly anyway.

"Yes."

He knew where this was going, too, why she was here, but he wished he didn't. Not tonight. Because when he turned her away tonight, he knew she wouldn't be back. He considered not turning her away. He didn't work for DEA, not really. His convictions were strong: drugs were destroying the country. He'd seen things in Florida he hadn't seen in the military, in countries at war and suffering through genocide against one or another group. Drugs were killing his countries—killing Mexico, destroying the States. He believed that absolutely. He also didn't believe that he, or any one person, could do a damn thing about it. Hampton and Ortega wanted him to look at some new surveillance photos. There had been another small boat landing in the same, isolated corner of the ranch. Dell hadn't even been on the premises at the time; she'd been in Laredo. But they clearly wanted him away from here— away from her—before they shared the specifics.

He could tell them to go to hell. He could stay here with Dell tonight, spend the night making love to her, breaching the distance she kept between herself and the world. Reaching her, touching her. Hearing her cry out his name. His jaw tightened, and he forced the muscles to relax. He couldn't, and he couldn't tell her why.

She had left him an opening, had tried to draw him into what she was about to say, but when he said nothing, she fidgeted on the couch, twisting her graduation ring around on her too-thin fingers. The paleness of her hands had never really held his attention the way it did now. But he didn't want to look at her lips . . . or the softness of her breasts under the crisp cotton shirt . . .

When he continued to sit silently, waiting, she looked up at him again, and groped for words. "I'm not sure why or how, but things have changed since then," she said. "We're not . . . as comfortable as we were."

"No." Jovi didn't deny it, didn't rationalize it. She bit her lip, but her eyes didn't waver.

"I want what we had again." The words were almost a whisper. The honesty in her eyes was painful. He reached out a hand, curving it around her cheek, stroking her lips with a gentle thumb, sealing her words away, unspoken.

"We can't have that," he said quietly. "We've reached that decision . . . I don't know how often. And it's the right one."

Her chin lifted defiantly. "Why?" she demanded, her voice soft but insistent. "Because you're on your way out and it's not convenient? Because I said no the first time?"

"No." His tone was curt, and he stood up, putting distance between them, not wanting to face the accusation and hurt in her eyes. He paced around the room once before turning and walking back over to her and catching her gently by the shoulders, then shaking her lightly.

"Because, believe it or not, someone was watching us. Someone was taking pictures when we were in the patio. Someone wants to know if we're screwing around!" He used the vulgarity cuttingly, deliberately, wanting her to back off, but she didn't.

"Even if that were true—and I don't believe it—what's the worst that can happen? We're adults, we're free—" She froze suddenly, and her eyes narrowed. "I'm free. As far as I know, you are?" This time she was asking, and he scowled at her and gave her another, less gentle shake.

"Yes, damn it, Dell, I'm 'free!' There's no wife hidden away somewhere. Get this straight—if I ever marry, there'll be one woman in my life! I'm not my father's son, Dell—running off or hooking up with any woman that walks by."

He released her shoulders and spun away, frustrated and angry. "This isn't about whether or not we're free, or even whether or not we want each other. Don't you understand no one could want to watch us together except for really twisted reasons?"

"Of course I realize that. I'm not stupid, Jovi. I just refuse to believe you heard what you thought." She took a step toward him, gesturing emphatically. "And I won't believe it without proof, or a reasonable motive and a reasonable suspect!"

"The motive? I'm sure you could come up with one or two, if you sat down and looked at things logically," he returned coolly. "And suspects? Only one makes sense. Your grandfather."

Dell gaped at him.

"Maybe Lionel is a little more involved in your life than you want to believe," he suggested grimly. "Quite frankly, from what I've heard of him, he sounds like the type who'd spy on his own family for his own sick reasons." He didn't add that Hampton and Ortega had questioned whether or not the two were really estranged. Hampton had intercepts of a few calls from Monterrey to the ranch. They were to a cell number, not the main phone, nor Dell's cell. But Dell paid the account along with all the other bills.

She considered what he said, then shrugged. "I'm not my mother," she said, her voice thin. "No one would drive me away from . . . " She stopped. *From a man I love,* she'd almost said. "From a relationship," she finished slowly. "Certainly not the man who destroyed my father's life. Not Lionel De Cordova."

She sounded very sure of herself. Jovi thought of his own mother, clinging tenaciously to the man she had loved. His mom had given up so much for such brief happiness. Could he and Dell have more than that? He swallowed hard, thinking of having her and then losing her. Worse, of having her and betraying her.

"You might be burning bridges that will cost you later," he warned. "Years have a way of changing how we see things, especially when family's involved."

She shrugged. "Family? My family's dead, Jovi. I mean that. Family isn't about blood and genes. It's about love and caring. The

De Cordovas aren't family. There's only been one person in my life who ever loved me, and he's dead. "

"Still." He couldn't let go of it. Partly because of the past, and partly because it was the only excuse he could think of to explain why he didn't sweep her up in his arms and carry her to the bedroom. Or just pull her down to the floor. Faint color was seeping into her cheeks, and he knew she was beginning to suffer. He hadn't been turned down very often, but he remembered all too well how humiliating rejection could be.

"Let's leave it alone," he suggested. "For a few days. Then if it seems safe . . ."

She took a deep breath, then nodded. The movement was robotic, a slight mechanical motion. "Maybe," she said. "Or maybe not."

Jovi rubbed the back of his neck. "You're not going to fire me, are you?" he asked.

Dell looked at him. "Why?"

He grinned. "My second career choice was as a stand-up comedian. Glad I went into horses. I was trying to be funny."

"Funny . . . Oh." She managed a faint smile. "You're job is safe, yes. Somehow I don't think I'd care to defend myself against sexual harassment charges." The faint smile slipped. "After tonight, I probably wouldn't have much of a defense." She walked back over to the table, picked up her tea, and downed most of it in a single gulp.

"Not nearly strong enough." The distance was back, he noted with relief. He had been sorely tempted to try to comfort her, to hug her, and touching her wouldn't have been smart. Not when he was already late for his meeting with Ortega and Hampton.

"I'll do better next time," he offered glibly as she crossed the room toward the door.

"Next time won't help tonight, though, will it? Tonight I think I'll drive into town and get falling-down drunk."

He stiffened slightly, but she noticed anyway and arched an eyebrow at him. "Am I shocking you again?"

"No, uh . . . " He floundered, apparently trying to avoid coming across as judgmental and chauvinistic. But obviously at a loss for words.

"Relax," she said after a minute. "I didn't mean it. Good night, Jovi." She didn't look back as she walked out the door and stepped carefully off the low porch. He sighed heavily and cast another glance at the wall clock as he, too, headed out the door.

CHAPTER FOURTEEN

Embarrassment seldom kills, Dell thought wryly. She looked out the window, watching Jovi try to saddle her thoroughbred mare, Josie. The mare was almost seventeen hands, tall and beautifully proportioned. She'd never raced, although she'd been a fairly successful jumper when Samuel Rosales brought her home to Dell. But the mare didn't like working these days, and she kept turning around and nipping at Jovi's rear. When he'd jump out of her reach, the mare would shy, prolonging the process and making Dell laugh in spite of herself.

So he said no, she told herself for the hundredth time as she started out to offer a hand. *If I told someone no, I wouldn't expect him to be all bent out of shape.* Of course, she had offended more than one overly ardent, would-be suitor with her refusals. So she supposed she could forgive herself for being hurt. But Jovi had been unchanged this morning, unthreatening and casual. Comfortable again, almost. Why he had turned down her invitation was a puzzle, but it was one Dell wasn't quite ready to dwell on. He'd suggested waiting a few days; rationally, the idea was sound. Maybe she'd be able to exorcise the demons of desire curling through her body and making her ache with need.

Jovi turned at her approach, his face beaded with sweat and his mouth tight with irritation. She grinned, unable to help herself, and he muttered a curse under his breath and thrust the reins out at her.

"I saddled a Derby winner last year, and this—this—" Words failed him, and he just glowered at her.

"Josie, you're being bad," Dell crooned, easing around Jovi and laying a gentle hand on the mare's glossy neck. She patted the broad cheekbone, and Josie turned to nuzzle her leg, without nipping. Continuing to talk to the mare, she ventured a glance back at Jovi. "If you'll put the saddle on, I'll cover your . . . backside."

He growled something unintelligible but lifted the saddle again slowly, settling it over the mare's withers. Dell smiled as Jovi carefully drew the girth under the chestnut stomach and buckled it.

"She doesn't kick," she assured him. "You're way too timid about those hooves. Biting is her only vice."

"You shouldn't let her get away with it," he groused.

"I don't sweat the small stuff," Dell retorted cheerfully.

"Small stuff? My leg and my butt are black and blue and you—you're grinning!" He sounded so plaintive that Dell couldn't bite back a low laugh.

"Men are such babies," she said, shaking her head at him. She nudged him out of the way with an elbow, caught the stirrup, and swung into the saddle easily, then looked around.

"You're not coming?" She asked the question lightly. She didn't want him to think she was still after his body.

He considered her question, then shrugged. "I could, I guess. My research can wait."

"Research?"

"Tell you in a minute. Let me get a horse." He cast a glance up at the sun, frowning. "Although I don't understand this penchant for afternoon excursions in hundred-degree heat."

"When else can you ride, here in Webb County? Even December's hot."

"True," he conceded. "Wait for me, okay?' She nodded and trotted Josie around the ring while she waited for him. He returned quickly, leading the one remaining Appaloosa and carrying an extra hat.

"Here," he said. "You'll burn to a crisp if you're not careful."

"Afraid I'll wrinkle?" she teased, and he frowned at her and swung up onto his horse.

"Wrinkles don't worry me," he muttered. "Skin cancer does."

"You're in a somber mood today," Dell noted. "Thanks."

"Where are we going to ride?" he asked as she headed Josie down the drive to the pasture gate.

She hesitated, not sure she wanted to tell him. She planned on riding across the pasture, over to the fence that intersected with the Simmons' place. And seeing if anything looked amiss. Even though that Ortega man had said he didn't think the property had a real problem with unwelcome visitors, looking couldn't hurt. But Jovi didn't like her to visit the cabaña, so she didn't know how he'd feel about her current plans.

"You have no sense of adventure," she protested, stalling as she urged Josie back into her ground-eating trot.

"I proved that last night, though, didn't I?" Jovi asked, riding alongside her. She turned, startled. His eyes met hers, and his lips twitched.

"Regrets?" she challenged, and he shrugged and reached out to touch her arm.

"Of course I regret it. You know I want you, Dell. But we're doing what we have to."

She was silent, unsure what to say. His fingers, light on her arm, burned through the cotton of her long-sleeved blouse.

"Maybe," she said, finally, shifting her arm to hold the reins more comfortably. His hand fell away, and she turned her attention back to their path, but she could feel him watching her. Wanting her. He wasn't lying about that. She knew he still wanted her. "Jovi . . . if it's wrong now, it's going to be wrong in a day. Or a week." She faced him again, her gaze level. "You need to know that."

He sighed, loudly enough that she heard it over the horses' hooves striking rock, deeply enough that she watched his chest heave under his patterned Western shirt.

"We'll see."

"Yes." She tightened her knees, and Josie sprinted ahead of the

Appaloosa, startling Jovi. The rush of hot wind in her face was exhilarating. Dell leaned lower, letting the horse run, heading in the general direction of the fence line. Jovi's horse didn't have a chance to keep up, and she reluctantly reined Josie into an easy lope, circling around to let him catch up.

"Not funny," Jovi gritted as he slowed the winded gelding to a walk. "You shouldn't race off like that."

"Why?" Dell demanded. "Josie's not even hot."

"You should have let me ride her, so I'd have had a chance."

"Ride her?" Dell asked in disbelief. "You couldn't even saddle her!"

Jovi frowned and tugged at the brim of his hat. "Control freak," he muttered, without real ire. "What now, Ms. Rosales?"

She looked across the field and back at Jovi. Now was as good a time as any. "Uh . . . we keep riding toward the fence." She waved a hand in the general direction of the river. "Then we follow it and make sure everything's . . . okay."

He raised an eyebrow questioningly. "And if it's not? Have you ever asked yourself on one of these daring excursions just what you'd do if you ran into some kind of trouble?"

"I'm guessing I'm safer with you than without you, wouldn't you say?" She smiled sweetly at him. "So wouldn't you rather I invited you on one of my daring excursions?"

He gave up. "Sure. I'm delighted you want me to ride with you in two-hundred-degree heat, unarmed, in danger from alien smugglers and drug smugglers and rabid coyotes—"

The appaloosa shied suddenly, violently. He managed to stay in the saddle, although he slid precariously in the worn stock saddle and clutched at the horn to keep from coming unseated.

"—and frightened horses," Dell offered, adding to his list of dangers. She looked around carefully, but didn't see what had caused the usually placid animal to shy. "Rattlesnakes, too, maybe, although I don't see one."

He shook his head. "Tell me again why I left Florida," he groused, heading his horse on toward the fence line. "Stay with me, Dell. Don't you dare go charging off again. You could get me killed like that."

She grinned cheekily at him. "The idea has merits—especially after last night." Ignoring his startled expression, she clicked to Josie and trotted on past him. She wouldn't race off and leave him, but she wouldn't ride next to him feeling his heat burn along the length of her body, either.

*

A few minutes later, they entered the scraggly tree line with relief. The trees were a mixture of stunted live oak and mesquite, hardly towering shade producers, but they were well established and offered some respite from the heat. Birds rustled and complained in the branches above, and little lizards darted here and there, scattering from the danger of the horses' hooves. Dell smiled at the tiny, flustered inhabitants, but sat up and paid more attention to Josie's demeanor; thoroughbreds were known as hot bloods for a reason, and Josie was skittish.

"The ride must have mellowed her," Dell told Jovi, when a snake, sliding across the path in front of them, failed to raise even a snort of alarm. "She should have gone bonkers by now."

They followed the ill-defined path along the fence, dodging branches and guiding the horses carefully over the rough terrain. The ground began to slope down toward the river, and Dell looked around with careful attention. According to what Ortega had said, this rough trail would bring them to the corner of their property, where some kind of unusual activity had recently occurred.

As they rode, Dell squinted and peered into the brush, looking for telltale signs of campfires or food containers or any other evidence of human encroachment, but she saw nothing. She sensed rather than saw Jovi's heightened awareness as he rode behind her, and remembered how easily he'd spotted the deer on the ride with the girls. Must be the military or law enforcement training, she realized, annoyed she'd never thought about it before. No wonder the man was so observant.

As the land leveled out onto a trail that ran parallel to the river and toward the cabaña, the horses broke into an easy trot, and Dell relaxed in spite of herself. There certainly didn't seem anything amiss. If anyone had crossed her property illegally, they were gone with none of the signs that would have pointed to frequent or lengthy use of the area.

"Well, I won't say that pilot was wrong, but I sure don't see anything that shouldn't be here," she told Jovi, and he shrugged and looked around again.

"Not now, anyway. Whatever it was must have been isolated." He still seemed tense, though, more wary than she was. "And it can't hurt that we're here. If there's a regular presence of any sort, I'm sure visiting more should help keep away trespassers."

"Are you saying I should come here more often?" she asked sweetly, and he glowered at her.

"You know better than that." He reached out, catching Josie's reins and stopping her. "Dell, you can kid about it, but this is really not a place you should come at all."

She frowned at the grim warning and shook her arm to free her reins. "That's ridiculous, don't you think? Being careful is one thing, but this is my ranch, and why should I stay away?" She shook her head decidedly. "I'll ride anywhere I want to, Jovani Treviño. No one is going to stop me."

Jovi sighed, and gazed out at the placid river, wide, green, and scarcely moving in the afternoon heat, then turned back to her. "Foolish, foolish pride," he muttered, and kneed his horse forward. "At least, that's all I hope it is."

Dell trotted after him, not sure she'd heard him over the horses' hooves. "What?"

He shrugged and cast her a sideways glance. "What are you proving, Dell? And to whom? Me? You'd be a lot better off thinking about Becky and the girls."

"I'm not sure I know what you're saying," Dell retorted. Their knees brushed as the horses sidled closer together to go around an overhanging branch. Jovi batted the branch away from their faces, and when he let go of the limb, his arm grazed her shoulder so lightly she wondered if the touch was deliberate or accidental.

He sighed heavily, and the sound seemed loud even among the river sounds of birds and rustling lizards. "Coming down here is stupid," he said finally, repeating the warning he'd given over and over. "You're not afraid, Dell, and maybe there's nothing to be afraid of. But how can you take chances with Becky? How much would your bravery mean to that little girl if something happened to you?"

She gaped. She'd only fleetingly thought of that, and she didn't like him telling her she should worry. Her ranch should be safe, for God's sake—was safe. He was just—just—she couldn't figure out his concern. But she didn't want to listen to his warnings. He had no right to bring Becky into this. She thought of the tiny little girl, so full of laughter and love, and blinked away sudden tears. The toddler's life would be unaffected by her riverside rides because there were no real risks, in spite of Jovi's continued insistence. But all the same, she might very well lose the little girl someday.

Grimly, she turned Josie away from the river, trusting the mare's power to carry her up the embankment and back toward the pasture. She heard the flurry of movement as Jovi, startled by her unexpected maneuver, followed.

"What's this all about?" he demanded, catching up. "Weren't we going all the way around?"

She shook her head. "Too long and too hot," she said succinctly. He'd used Becky to worry her, and he'd succeeded. But she had no intention of admitting his logic had backfired, because she, not Becky, stood to lose everything.

CHAPTER FIFTEEN

The next day made Dell wonder about returning to work after all. She sat at a table draped with an immaculate white cloth, surrounded by business people, and wished she could be back at the ranch.

"So, how'd I do, girl?" Hal McDade's booming voice made Dell's hands clench in her lap, and she was glad the table hid her tightly knotted fingers. The oilman was impossibly rich—and impossibly boorish, though he didn't mean to be. Dell had dealt with him in the past, and knew his frequent gaffes were the products of a culture and an upbringing now frowned upon. In spite of his firm's admirable hiring policies, he regularly infuriated women and minorities of all kinds with his good-old-boy humor. He had just delivered the brief speech he intended to present in Monterrey to the governor of the Mexican state of Nuevo Leon. His Spanish, while well intended, had been mangled, and she didn't think the cosmopolitan governor and his fashionable wife would appreciate the bedroom jokes about politicians.

She sipped her tea, trying to find a polite way to tell him to send an emissary—or just not speak.

"You know," she ventured, unable to stand another swallow of tea, "most of Mexico's top leaders speak English fluently. But it's sort of traditional for them to deliver speeches in their own language—in Spanish. Maybe you should bow to that and use English in your speech."

He plopped down in the ornate chair, immune to the discreet elegance around him, and frowned at her from under his bushy, graying eyebrows. "You think?" A huge paw swiped across his mustache and mouth, not wiping his frown away.

"Is my Spanish that bad?" he asked after a minute. "Still?"

Dell couldn't quite not smile, and across the table, his secretary Carmela laughed out loud.

"Your Spanish is horrible," she said, with none of Dell's discretion. "Absolutely hideous." She rolled her dark eyes at Dell.

"But dang it all, I understand the language so well!" McDade insisted. "And I like it, I truly do. Danged if I know why I can't get the hang of it.

"I thought you did a little better," Dell consoled him. "A little," she repeated firmly, as the secretary's mouth fell open. "But look, if you don't want to do it—why don't you just get an interpreter, Mr. McDade?"

The big man rubbed thoughtfully at his face again, then glanced over at his secretary.

"Oh, no." The raven-haired woman pointed a spoon at her boss. "I haven't spoken formal Spanish in years—I'm not going to go make a fool of myself in front of all those government officials in Monterrey! No way."

He sighed and looked mournfully back at Dell. "Can't pay her enough to change her mind, either," he complained. "Twenty-three years, I haven't gotten her to once. The fool woman won't even marry me, can you imagine that?"

"Secretaries shouldn't marry their bosses," Carmela retorted, but her eyes smiled at him.

Dell smiled, too. "So quit," she suggested, and they laughed.

"Don't go giving Carmela any ideas," McDade protested. "She's got too damn many of her own." They were silent a minute. Around them, the soft murmur of voices and laughter filled the room. The lunchtime crowd was gone, and the restaurant was unusually quiet. Suddenly McDade straightened, slapping the white linen cloth so hard his unused spoon rattled against his plate. Carmela jumped, and Dell flinched.

"By God, what a good idea," he boomed, and then reached out

and patted Dell heartily on the shoulder. "You're a genius—an absolute genius."

Dell's befuddlement gave way to a piercing suspicion. "Look, Mr. McDade—"

"You're perfect," he interrupted, cutting off her protests. "Isn't she, Carmela?"

The older woman smiled at Dell. "It was your idea," she said. "And yes—you'd do a great job. Who better than you?" She lifted a piece of pie to her mouth, effectively leaving Dell and her boss to hash out the issue of who the man's interpreter should be.

"You've represented me before," he pointed out quickly. "That was just a wonderful presentation you made over in Houston about the retail opportunities in northern Mexico. And we'd only be there a couple of days at the most," he added as her frown deepened.

"That isn't the point." Dell shook her head and then tapped her fingers on the table, searching for ways to explain. "Mr. McDade, until recently, I did represent several firms. I was very active in the trade situation here because it was my primary interest. But I've moved into other areas. I really can't afford the time—"

"Look, I know you're helpin' out some girls who got messed up. And I've heard rumors you're tryin' to get your horses back into a paying business. And you picked up an odd job or two in the business already."

Dell's brows arched, and McDade's bark of laughter turned several heads in their direction.

"Honey, I know people see me as somethin' of a fool." He grinned. "But I'm not on *Forbes'* list by accident. I know most everything, 'bout most everyone, to boot." His face softened, and he leaned toward her, lowering his voice and placing his big hand over hers in a fatherly gesture. "I even know about your maw and grandpa. Reason enough for anyone not to want to go."

"Then?" Dell asked, her voice remarkably composed.

He pulled his hand away and shrugged. "You'd make a lot of money for a little work—not that you mind hard work, I'm not implyin' that. You'd keep your foot in the door in case you ever want to get involved in a big way again." And then his weathered face broke into a wide grin. "And you might just knock that bastard Lionel De Cordova on his bony can."

Carmela laughed, and even Dell smiled at the vision of the stately, silver-haired millionaire falling on his backside.

"Don't you do business with him, though?" she asked curiously, wondering at McDade's apparent dislike of Lionel De Cordova.

He shrugged again. "Course I do, girl. Play golf with him now and again. Sold him his two best Angus bulls, too. But I don't like the man, and he don't like me. Still, we smile at each other like two life-long friends any ol' time we have to. That's just business."

"It doesn't bother you?"

"Nope." He drained his coffee cup in a gulp and waved off the waiter who hurried over to refill it. "Does it bother you? Me talkin' 'bout your family?"

Dell considered his question before shaking her head. "No. It does surprise me, though. I didn't know you knew."

"I've always known, girl. It's my business, knowin' things." He looked abashed. "Remember the first time I asked you to make those calls to that Monterrey firm three or four years ago?"

She nodded.

"I thought you'd play on your name, truth be told, or that folks knew who you were. But you did a good job all on your own, and since you never told me who you were, I pretty much guessed you didn't care to acknowledge old Lionel any more than he does you. Pity, that he and your mom'd give you up. Sure doesn't say much for them."

In spite of herself, Dell had to ask. "You know my mother, then?"

Beside her, Carmela breathed in sharply. Dell glanced at her and saw pain flash across her face, then disappear. Hal McDade's fingers were tight around his water glass as he emptied that, too, before answering her question.

"Yeah, I know Erika," he said. "Beautiful woman, your mom." He shook his head. "No offense, girl, but she's also the coldest, most heartless bi—woman I ever saw."

Dell thought of her father, plodding through his hopeless last years, but said nothing.

"I fell for her . . . some years ago," the oilman continued, almost in a monotone. Carmela stood up, stretching, and excused herself to go to the ladies' room.

"Poor Carmelita. She's put up with a lot," McDade said when she was out of earshot, using his pet name for her. "Your grandfather probably would have loved Erika and me to marry, even though he don't like me. We'd have owned a sizeable part of two different countries. Hell of a lot of power in that." He moved his empty water glass back and forth methodically. "I came real close to proposin', too."

"But you didn't?" Dell asked, her voice barely audible.

"No." The older man stretched, twisted his head from side to side, then massaged the back of his neck. "Thank God for that. I might have given up my pride and Carmela's love for a well-dressed, snotty little girl in a woman's body."

"I've never heard anyone refer to Erika De Cordova that way," Dell mused.

"I really don't blame her. I s'pose she grew up the way a lot of rich women do, cloistered and spoiled." He was silent for a few seconds before continuing. "I'd been growin' apart from her for some time before we officially quit 'seeing' each other. But something happened . . . One of her maid's kids came to spend his birthday with his ma at the De Cordova house. He was helpin' do dishes and cut his hand pretty badly. The boy's mom was hysterical—I don't blame her. She didn't know what to do. We were goin' out, Erika and I, both in our evenin' clothes. She was furious when I helped tie up the cut until an ambulance came for the kid. I got blood on my shirtsleeves. We didn't go out, and I told her *adios* the next mornin'. We speak if we meet, but not too warmly." He shrugged, "I woke up. I think that's when I realized Carmelita hadn't spent all those years being my secretary, confidante, and conscience for a little paycheck."

"I think I'll see if she's all right," Dell said, blotting her lips and pushing her chair out. "She can't like hearing about my mother."

Carmelita was touching up her makeup when Dell found her, and she smiled into the mirror.

"Usually I don't get like this," she said. "He caught me by surprise, I guess. It's been so long since we mentioned her."

"I can see why the memories are unpleasant." Dell patted her own hair into place. "If it helps, my memories of her aren't any better."

"I'll never understand," Carmelita sighed. "Women like me, who're never mothers . . . and women like her, who never should have been given the blessing."

"Hmmm." Dell hesitated, then decided to ask. "Carmelita, would it bother you if I do go? Would you be there, too?"

"No," the secretary replied, turning toward the door. "Hal likes me to keep things going when he's away, and it's just a short trip. Go." She smiled serenely at Dell. "Hal has a lot of faults, but one thing he is, is loyal. Piece of paper or not, he's been true to me since he decided he loved me."

"That says a lot for both of you," Dell said. Carmelita patted her on the shoulder.

"Every woman should find a good man, and that's no easy chore. So when you get one, you darn well better hang on!"

They were still smiling when they rejoined Hal at the table, but Dell kept turning the other woman's remarks over in her mind. A good man . . . no easy chore. Jovi Treviño was devastatingly handsome. He liked the arid ranch that was her home, he made a living with horses . . . all things she wanted in any potential mate. Of course, he seemed determined not to show his interest in her now. But she saw the way he watched her, knew the desire and attraction were still there. Was Jovi really intent on protecting her by not loving her? She wasn't sure why, but she didn't think he was being honest about his motives. And his apprehensions about her grandfather troubled her. She certainly didn't worry about Lionel. Why should he, unless . . .

She frowned. Unless he envisioned being able to profit, someday, from Lionel De Cordova. What kind of man was Jovi, anyway? A good man, the kind Carmela had urged her to find, or just someone else out for a fling—or a fortune?

"So, Dell . . . " Hal's voice jerked her back to the present. "You'll go give my speech, won't you?"

She sighed. Going to Monterrey was the last thing she wanted to do right now. But he'd pay well. The girls wouldn't suffer from her brief absence. Karla would jump at the chance to spend a day or two on the ranch helping watch the girls. *And she just might have an opportunity to look her family in the eye and tell them, silently at least, where they could all go.* "Call me," she said after a moment, more to Carmelita than Hal, "and we'll work out the details. I guess I can leave the girls for a day or two." She was getting up from the table when she realized, with an unpleasant pang, that she would also be leaving Becky—and Jovani Treviño.

*

Hot wind blasted against Dell's face as she bent over the thoroughbred's neck, urging her on. The mare flattened out, seemingly enjoying the unusual chance to run as much as Dell was enjoying the ride. The afternoon was still searingly hot, though, and after a few more exhilarating yards, she reluctantly stood in her stirrups, easing the mare back into a lope, and then a trot. Finally, she reined the bright chestnut to a walk and laid a hand against her neck. It had a slight sheen of sweat, but Josie was breathing easily and wasn't lathered. Relieved, Dell guided the horse onto the path leading down to the river.

Jovani wouldn't approve, she knew. She hadn't come for years, but now that she'd come home to the ranch, she couldn't stay away. At least now she was mounted and carried a rifle in the handmade scabbard hanging behind the English saddle. She didn't automatically shoot rattlesnakes and coyotes as so many ranchers did, but she was prepared to protect herself or her stock from any unexpected danger. Thanks to Pete's handiwork, the flat saddle also secured a small bag, which held her cell phone.

She smiled. People in this part of the country viewed her penchant for English saddles as treason, if not insanity. But she didn't see how people could enjoy riding if they had to sit in those bulky Western rigs, all leather and no horse. They entered the shaded part of the path, and she looked around in surprise. There had been some obvious clearing out, and the path had been reclaimed from the undergrowth.

The mare broke into a trot as they descended toward the river, then suddenly spooked and flung herself sideways. Dell found herself sprawled on the ground, still hanging on to one of her reins. She stood up gingerly, checking her arms and legs to see if everything still moved. She should get a helmet, she reminded herself sternly. Especially since she rode so seldom now. She never would have been thrown a few years ago.

Speaking gently to the nervous mare, she shortened the reins and looked around to see what had spooked the mare. Nothing moved off into the trees or slithered across the ground. She looked carefully, though, and listened, but heard no telltale dry buzzing from a rattler.

Cautiously, Dell swung back into the saddle and urged the mare toward the cabaña. She pulled the horse up by the front door, noticing at once that the padlock had been replaced and the brush had been cleared away. The wooden shutters that had protected the glass from vandalism and storms were open, allowing a blurry look into the front room from her vantage point on the mare. Except that someone had been doing some unauthorized cleaning, apparently nothing was amiss.

She listened again, cataloging the bird calls and rustlings in the trees. None of the sounds were foreign to the riverbank. She glanced over her shoulder at the wide, green waters of the Rio Grande, scanning the reeds on the Mexican side. Nothing moved there, either. No sign of people fishing, trying to cross—not even stray livestock, pushing down to drink. Chiding herself for her apprehensions, she swung off the horse and tied the mare's reins securely to the post holding up the structure's rusted tin awning.

Still a little wary, she stepped up on the porch and examined the new lock on the door. Frowning a little, she realized she no longer had a key to a building on her own property. She nibbled her lower lip thoughtfully as she fingered the padlock. Danny and Pete were pretty much confined to work with the horses. If either of them had been involved with this, it had to have been on Jovani Treviño's instructions. Yet he had tried to dissuade her from coming down here. Her eyes narrowed as she glanced over her shoulder at the river again. Why was he cleaning this long-abandoned part of her past? And what was with his determination to keep her out of the cabaña? Her face grim, Dell moved to the window and stood on tiptoes, trying to see farther back into the shadowed building.

"Would this help?" Jovi asked, and she spun around to find him just behind her, a shiny brass key dangling from one bronzed hand. He reached out without invitation, brushing a dry leaf from her sleeve. "I didn't mean to scare you."

"I'm not scared," Dell retorted crisply. "Just startled." She frowned at him. "And annoyed. Why do you have a key for a building I should be able to get into?" She waved a hand at the area surrounding the cabaña. "And what is all this about?"

"What, cleaning up a beautiful riverside campground?" His mouth quirked. "I thought I'd hear something along the lines of 'oh, what a good idea.' Go figure." He shrugged, and then his mouth tightened. "Besides, certain people insist on ignoring my warnings about staying away. With the brush cleared out, you can at least see danger coming—if you're lucky."

Dell shook her head. "You just don't get it, do you? This is *my* place, Jovani. I shouldn't have to stay away. I won't stay away." Her frown deepened, and she plucked the keys from him. "And I won't be kept out, either."

He made no argument when she slipped the key into the lock and twisted it. She pulled the lock out then hooked it back in the hasp, opening the door and stepping into the front room of the old cabin. Dust carpeted the floor. Apparently Jovi's efforts hadn't extended to housekeeping. But there were no questionable packages stacked against walls, no indication anyone had used the room for any reason. Still, she didn't think she was imagining Jovi's nervous tension as she moved through the room toward the small back bedroom. She pushed open the half-closed door, grimacing at the gritty dust that powdered her hand.

The bedroom was much as the front room, dusty and unkempt. But a frown knitted her brows when she saw the makeshift bed against one wall, a stack of blankets and old sheets folded into a rough resemblance of a cot. Two concrete blocks near the bed made a rough table, which held a book of matches, an empty, crushed pack of cigarettes . . . and a metallic hair band she knew belonged to Maribel. Sickened at the suspicions suddenly accosting her, she turned to confront Jovi.

"What is this?" she asked, her voice barely audible.

His face grim, Jovi shrugged again. "I'm not sure. But what it looks like is pretty obvious." He waved at the room's one window.

The sill was partially clean, and when she walked closer, Dell could see the faint outline of a shoe in the dust underneath it.

"I changed the lock and opened the shutters hoping to keep people who shouldn't be here away. Someone came in that window, though."

"Someone?" Dell ran a hand through her hair. "Jovi, you're the only one with a key. And don't ask me why someone would come in a window—someone apparently did. It looks a lot like it was Maribel, too. How could she even know this place was here? When could she get away from Rosa—and from me?" She jerked at her collar, walked over and stuffed the band in her pocket. "Unless she snuck down here in the middle of the night—and even then—"

"If you're implying Maribel sneaked in that window to wait for me, don't," Jovi said curtly. He indicated the window. "I've already nailed it shut. Can't be opened again. As far as the key, I'll get you a copy. But I don't think anyone else should have one, Dell."

"Why do you need this key, Jovi? Why make a copy? Just give me the key, no?"

"No." He shook his head, and moved toward the door, and after a final, disgusted look at the stack of bedding, she followed him out onto the porch. He turned and carefully closed and locked the door.

"I told you—this place is an invitation to all the wrong people." He rattled the door again, leaned for a moment against the wall then jerked upright and swatted at something crawling up his arm.

"Dell, I won't be a party to drug smuggling, and you know what the situation is right now. I also think you better be real careful about who Maribel can see and where she can go."

Dell's mouth pursed. "Just what are you saying, Jovani? That something illegal's going on here? That I know about it if it is?" Her voice echoed the anger in her eyes. Jovi turned toward the river, and Dell reached out, catching his arm. Her fingers dug into his forearm. "Don't you dare walk away without answering me, Jovani Treviño! How could you possibly think—"

Jovi didn't answer her immediately. Gently freeing his arm, he walked over to the edge of the porch, looking off toward the river. The mare snorted nervously and threw her head up, watching them alertly.

Dell, her concentration broken by the mare's sudden edginess, drew in her breath. "*You* spooked Josie, didn't you?" she demanded, and that question, at least, he seemed able to handle.

"Not intentionally." He turned back to her, and concern replaced some of the grimness. "How do you feel? I saw you get up and get back on, so I assumed you weren't too seriously injured."

"My pride was dented," she admitted, smiling a little in spite of herself. "I used to boast that I couldn't be thrown."

"Older and wiser," he said, nodding. Then something of the grimness returned as he added, "But aren't we all." She didn't think he was still talking about being thrown. "Look, Dell," he said finally, "I don't know that anything's going on, or that you know anything. If Maribel sneaked down here somehow—well, that's pretty serious. She's no less at risk than anyone else is, if smugglers *should* come by. You probably better call whoever's in charge of her case, because there's a chance she wasn't alone. But you're blinding yourself if you don't realize how inviting this place could be to traffickers. You know what Ortega said. It would be a miracle if this place wasn't targeted, at least before we started coming down fairly often to look it over."

"I suppose," Dell said, massaging the back of her neck. Jovi hadn't answered her questions, she realized, but why was he dodging them? Frowning a little, she admitted to herself she wasn't eager to press the issue. She didn't want the vague, nagging uneasiness she felt about Jovi's interest in the cabaña to color her feelings about him. There was something fascinating, something very intriguing about the man. She had admitted that to herself, too, some time ago. She didn't want to give up—to have to give up—the tiny flickers of awareness that darted through her when she walked into a room and found him there. "So what do we do?" she asked eventually.

He looked around again. "Not much more than I have, I guess. Keep the brush down so anything has to happen in the open. Keep the locks on. I'd prefer you not come down here alone— for your safety." He shrugged and shook his head. "Of course, I haven't gotten through to you yet." Then he rubbed a hand across his face, hesitating, as if debating whether to continue. "And you should fire Danny."

Dell gaped at him. Danny Brewer had been on the ranch for years—not as long as Pete, but her father had hired him shortly after his divorce. The man fed horses and cleaned stalls and never said a cross word, as far as she knew. True, she had seen some recent signs of complacency, like unfinished work and those tools left around carelessly. But he could be given another chance. Finding qualified help was hard. Her brow furrowed, and she shook her head in consternation.

"Fire Danny?" she repeated. "Why?"

Jovi's jaw set. "Because," he said.

"Because?" She plucked at the front of her blouse in agitation. "You need more than 'because.' What has he done?"

"Who had keys to the cabaña?" Jovi asked. "Have you ever asked Pete about Danny? If he does his job, if he's around when he should be? If he's the kind of man you want on a ranch with girls who have troubled pasts already?"

"Pete's never complained," Dell said stubbornly.

"But you never asked, did you?" Jovi persisted. "Look, I'll be honest, Dell. I was going to fire him without asking." A tiny flicker of amusement came and went in the depths of his eyes. "Then I remembered your control-freak alter ego and changed my mind."

"Control freak." She snorted. "Still, you don't really think . . ." She just couldn't see Danny as a villain. And while the man never spoke of supporting family or having any place in particular to go, she hated the idea of taking his paycheck away on Jovani's suspicions. She slanted a glance at him. Or was there more?

"He had a key to the old lock," Jovi pointed out quietly. "He smokes—that brand." He waved at the cabin behind him. "And I suspect he knows you're Erika De Cordova's daughter."

"I suppose he could," Dell confirmed. "Has to, really, because he worked for my father. But—"

"Someone told Maribel," Jovi pointed out. "And it wasn't me."

Dell's startled eyes met his. "You really think—but then he was here? With Maribel?" She swayed, sickened by the unwelcome thought. "No. I couldn't have put Maribel in a position like that." She covered her face, pressing her hands tightly over her throbbing temples.

"You didn't put Maribel in any position," Jovi said shortly. He reached out, pulling her hands away. His strong fingers cradled her face, surprisingly comforting. "Maribel may only be sixteen, but she's been making her own decisions for a long time. You had no idea. And I'm not even sure about it. But I still think Danny should go." He tilted her chin up, peering into her eyes. "Are you all right?"

"I'm fine." She shivered, though, still unnerved by Jovi's accusations. Then she took a step back, breathing deeply. "All right. You're the foreman. You fire him."

He smiled without mirth. "Delegating, Ms. Rosales?"

She nodded in agreement. "You'll have to be the hatchet man. After all, they're your suspicions." Silently, she stepped off the porch and untied the mare's reins.

Jovi could feel her pain and confusion as she swung up into the saddle. But he couldn't reach out to her, not when he, too, had questions.

Danny Brewer, he had discovered through old tax and bank records, had been employed about the time Sam Rosales received the first of several large sums of money from one of De Cordova's businesses. The first transaction was supposedly payment for a shipment of three Appaloosa broodmares to the man's Nuevo Leon ranch. But he had checked the Appaloosa registry, as well as the ranch books, and he'd gone through the scores of photo albums Rosales had kept of his prized horses. None of the horses Rosales sold ever existed.

Did Dell know? How could she not? During his brief stint as a cop, Jovi realized that where drug smuggling was involved, there were seldom innocent parties. If nothing else, Dell had to know her father's sizable inheritance was suspect—didn't she? Watching her ride away, he realized with sudden, shocking intensity that he didn't want her to know. Because if she did, he'd have to bring her down. And he didn't know if he could.

CHAPTER SIXTEEN

Dell stepped out of the armored, chauffeured limousine and smiled her thanks at the driver. Hal McDade certainly hadn't spared any expense in arranging her visit to Monterrey. She smoothed the crisp, aqua skirt she was wearing, and looked around Gran Plaza with a slight frown. The plaza was sleek, attractive and modern, but she no longer felt as comfortable here as she once had. Too long away, probably. She glanced over at the high-rise Hotel Emperador and forced herself to relax. The speech to the governor and a group of businessmen earlier this afternoon had been a complete success. Hal beamed at her when she finished and flashed her a silly thumbs up, unconcerned with all the conservative men in their dark suits and starched shirts.

Smiling a little at the memory, she headed over to the towering fountain of water in the center of the plaza. Hal might not be a social prize, but he was genuine and generous. She hoped Carmela would reconsider before too long and marry the man. There was a marriage that had a chance.

Her smile faded though, as she thought about marriage. She had seen Lionel De Cordova in one of the front seats, staring at her with his contemptuous gray eyes. When she first saw him, a tiny spear of fear stabbed through her, and she deliberately addressed herself to the other occupants of the room. McDade's ideas for a closer union of Monterrey and Texas businesses were sound ones, and she concentrated on explaining his ideas, eventually forgetting her grandfather's presence altogether.

After the speech, the governor, accompanied by Lionel De Cordova, insisted they come to his home for dinner. She wasn't surprised when the politician began introducing members of his inner circle to Hal McDade and herself. Nor was she surprised that the first of the wealthy men to step forward was her grandfather. When the governor presented him, her grandfather had taken her hand and smiled coldly.

"We know each other," he had said, matter-of-factly. "*Como estas, hijita?*" Calling a young woman "*hijita*," or "daughter," wasn't out of the ordinary, and Dell didn't know how many of the men around her knew who she was. She nodded, formally and with detachment, then turned her back on the man. Hal McDade immediately stepped between them, easing her away to introduce her to a friend's wife who had just joined the group. Dell knew she hadn't fooled McDade at all—he must have sensed the overwhelming anger and bitterness she struggled to conceal.

Hal McDade helped extricate her from the group lingering with the governor, reassuring her he'd be close by at the dinner later on. He leaned close to her as they waited for his car. "Don't mind me stayin' a bit? My driver can take you back to the hotel."

She shot him a quick smile. "Am I being dismissed? Most of the women I know wouldn't stand for that."

He chuckled. "Tell me. I'm always settin' off one of my gir— umm, employees. But—" He shrugged. "Times are changin' here, but not too fast."

"I know." She saw his car approaching and stepped away. "Think I'll go shopping, though. The bargains are huge right now."

Hal looked alarmed. "Monterrey's not safe like it was—not even here."

She shook her head. "I'll let myself be excused from your dealing, but I'm not sitting around in a hotel room. I'm not afraid, Mr. McDade."

He looked chagrined but bit back his concern. "See you later then," he muttered. "But be careful, girl, won't you?"

Dell ducked into the car as the driver held the door open. "I will," she promised, with conviction.

She revisited some of the old sites, many of them much-changed, and marveled again at the occasional glimpses of the old Monterrey—the vendors with their *raspas*, or snow cones, and the lone horse and wagon trotting down a side street. Not too long ago, she'd even seen similar horses pulling their carts on Monterrey's fastest highways. This one was apparently a solitary relic, heading back out toward the hills on the lower reaches of the mountain that jutted up above the city. Eventually, though, she headed back to the hotel. Enough of the old memories. Now, just one more night here—one last ordeal to get through. Then she could go back to the ranch. Back to Becky. And, a sneaky little voice whispered, back to Jovani.

She frowned at the insistent clamor of the tiny voice. She hardly knew the man. She didn't trust him—or at the very least, didn't think she should. How could his presence have intruded upon her solitary life? Because in spite of Rosa's loyal companionship, in spite of the friends who called with invitations to movies, the theater, trips to San Antonio—in spite even of the teenage girls, whom she genuinely cared about, she was alone. Becky she held fast, clutched to her very heart and soul, but the others were always farther away, not an intimate part of who she was. Yet, increasingly, Jovi's flashing white smile or daring, dancing eyes would tease her memory. His voice, low and husky, would whisper in the still darkness of her room when she hovered between wakefulness and dream. When her engagement to Jeremy ended in betrayal and then his suicide, she had sworn never to care again. She sighed and smoothed her hair absently. Only she knew the hurt, knew why she'd given up on love. That word, loud though unspoken, brought her to an abrupt stop just outside the hotel's polished glass doors. *Love?* Where had that come from? She'd come close to saying it to Jovi, and here it was, intruding on even her private thoughts. Shaking her head in disgust, she fled into the cool, dark lobby and retired to the empty safety of her suite.

*

Hal McDade looked genuinely dismayed as he stood in the sitting room of the suite hours later. He turned his white Stetson in small, anxious circles while he waited for her to absorb what he had just said.

"It's a difficult position the governor put us in," he said, after a moment. "I understand that. If you want, we just won't go. I can't lose anything much by not goin' over to old Lionel's place."

Dell put a hand up to massage her throbbing temples. The silver lamé halter gown she wore sparkled with every movement, every breath. She had gone all out tonight, aware of the importance social gatherings could play among McDade's Monterrey associates. She had been prepared for her grandfather's presence in the governor's luxurious home. She hadn't been prepared for another violent incident to call the governor away to deal with the fallout. The governor sent word that his old friend, Don Lionel De Cordova, had graciously stepped in and that both Hal McDade and his lovely escort must attend the event at the De Cordova estate.

Dell shivered, remembering her grandfather's mansion. The imported pink marble floors. Gold-plated bathroom fixtures. Expensive furniture arranged impeccably beneath expensive prints. And yet, though she didn't really want to attend, she wanted even less to seem afraid of attending. A part of her demanded she confront her grandfather in that lifeless palace which had never welcomed her father, and which had never really been a home to her.

"You should go," she said finally. "I'll go with you."

"Atta girl." He beamed. "You're a fighter, pure and simple. Whenever you wanna leave, just say the word. We won't stay late. I want to get back to Houston."

"And Carmela?" Dell grinned, and he laughed.

"Yeah, and Carmela, too. No secret there." He watched as Dell draped a lacy, embroidered black shawl around her shoulders and picked up the tiny, silver clutch that matched the gown. "Too bad she didn't come," he said. "She'd love seeing you like this. She likes all this fancy, glitzy stuff. But she hardly ever gets to go anywhere this spiffy."

"Marry her," Dell prodded again, moving toward the door. "She could go everywhere as your wife."

"You think?" McDade asked, pulling the door behind them.

Dell smiled. "Yes, I do think. I also think she deserves the chance to be seen in places like this." She stepped into the elevator ahead of Hal and fell silent. The small, mirrored chamber reflected their images, the silver shimmering and shooting sparkles of light back and forth through the cage, cloning her impression, fragmenting it. She stared silently into the gold-veined, silver elevator panels and tried not to think of herself that way—thousands of shattering, silvered shards of pain and apprehension.

*

The black-coated orchestra members were playing the traditional Mexican love song *Solamente una vez* softly in the elegant ballroom of the De Cordova house when Dell pushed open the door of her grandfather's study. It was empty, but a small, crystal lamp cast a golden glow across his massive, antique desk.

A few moments ago, she'd whispered an apology to Hal and explained she needed to get away from the crowded room for a few minutes. He'd suggested leaving, but she hadn't missed the cluster of Monterrey's power brokers pulling him aside for conversation, waving others over to join them. He was wheeling and dealing, undoubtedly, and she didn't have the heart to ask him to go. It was early, not ten yet, and parties in Monterrey started late. She'd been able to endure the dinner, seated among elegant, jeweled women and their well-dressed husbands. She'd even been poised and polite when Lionel De Cordova asked her to dance after dinner. They'd hardly spoken, but she sensed he was assessing her, judging her potential, possibly, and deciding if she was a Rosales or a De Cordova.

Luckily, Hal McDade cut in after a few minutes, and though she suspected there were whispers about what their relationship was, she didn't care. Now she slipped into the room with its dark wall paneling and soft lighting and sank into the well-padded chair behind the desk. She doubted her grandfather would approve; she'd never been encouraged to come here as a youngster. Now, hopefully, no one would look for her here.

She sighed and leaned her head back for a few precious seconds. The distant music was barely audible, and the shallow, self-centered clamor of voices couldn't be heard at all. Smiling contentedly, she closed her eyes and drummed her fingers quietly on the polished wood desk. Unexpectedly, some stale smell— old smoke, an unidentifiable mustiness—made her sneeze. She opened her eyes and searched for a Kleenex. Her grandfather never would have a box of tissues on his desk, though, and she pulled open the top desk drawer, not really expecting to find anything there, but hoping. Her fingers moved aside an envelope and touched something soft and cottony. Thinking it might be a clean handkerchief, she peered inside. There was a folded hankie, but she didn't pick it up, staring instead at the small, glossy photo she had uncovered.

Silent, dark, and unsmiling, Jovani Treviño stared back at her.

Her heart pounding, Dell pushed the desk shut. She propped her elbows on the desk and cupped her head, her lips trembling. Jovani Treviño wasn't a rich man. He wasn't powerful or political. There was not one reason in the world Lionel De Cordova should have his picture in that desk drawer. Unless . . .

Dell drew herself up straight, staring at the wall. She'd heard the rumors about the De Cordovas and drugs. She'd dismissed them, thinking her grandfather didn't need drug money. But

Jovani Treviño had shown up at her place, looking for work when she could least afford to wait. He'd developed an interest in the old riverfront property and had fired a long-time employee. Nothing made sense—except that Jovani worked for Lionel De Cordova. For some reason, the rich old man must have wanted someone he trusted on her father's ranch—her ranch. Grimly, Dell stood. She walked to the door, then stopped, walked back, and took the photo out of the desk, stuffing it remorselessly into the tiny clutch. Then she forced her unwilling legs to carry her back in the direction of the noise and Hal McDade.

Nothing had changed in her absence. Men still huddled in a corner, talking with the animation of several drinks and inflated egos. She didn't realize she was frowning at them and turned, startled, when a soft, cold voice behind her said, "Well!" in slightly accented English.

Erika De Cordova stood in front of her, imposingly tall, slender, and blonde. The dark, almost black fabric of her designer gown called attention to the paleness of her skin, and she hadn't aged noticeably since Dell had last seen her.

"Aren't you going to kiss your mother?" she asked, and Dell turned her head away as the woman bussed the air in the way of the social elite.

"I didn't intend to, no," Dell returned, amazed at the absence of emotion her mother engendered. She didn't regret the distance between them, didn't feel fondness, didn't even feel hate.

"You are incredibly beautiful, my dear," Erika said, with little expression. Her green eyes swept over Dell appraisingly. "Quite beautiful. You're much more like your father than me, of course—in color, at least."

"In everything." They eyed each other silently for a moment. Finally, Erika's full lips twisted. "You're here with a man who once courted me. Strange, isn't it? Almost perverse, I would say."

Dell regarded her mother aloofly. "Perverse? No. We're only

business acquaintances. He loves Carmela—you remember her, I suppose?" A small dart of pleasure speared through Dell when her mother flushed angrily, and she allowed herself a small smile. "But believe what you choose, *Mother*." The word dripped from her lips with undisguised poison, and the older woman looked discomfited. Her expression changed back to one of arrogance as Dell's grandfather crossed the room toward them, lean and elegantly dressed, one well-groomed hand clutching a drink.

"Well, my darling," he said to Erika, kissing her cheek, "you look stunning tonight, as always. But your daughter"—he slanted a glance at Dell—"could fast become the talk of the town, if she'd stay."

"But I won't," Dell said quietly. "Why would I?"

"Why, indeed?" Her grandfather regarded her with his imperious, gray gaze. "Perhaps because you are a De Cordova. The Rosales part of you is virtually nonexistent." He held up a hand, silencing his daughter's protests.

"Your mother is going to tell me that you have the Rosales darkness. Colorwise, you don't resemble your mother much. But you're a determined, competent woman, I hear." He smiled, but the gesture had no warmth. "Someone told me they call you '*inalcanzable*.'" The glance he directed at Erika was still full of old bitterness. "Your mother could have done well to be a little choosier in her youth." When Erika would have spoken, he silenced her again. "She's done well, now, though. She is engaged to Carlos Del Huerta—the Mexican banking family. Perhaps you remember."

"I lost a family, not the ability to read Spanish," Dell retorted. She still read the Mexico City and Monterrey dailies as often as she could. When she had served as a liaison between Texas businesses and Mexican interests, she had learned a lot about who the power mongers really were. "Congratulations," she added, more coldly, to her mother. "The Del Huertos and De Cordovas suit perfectly. Much better than Rosales and De Cordova, I suspect."

Her mother didn't answer, although Dell doubted it was from remorse or any twinge of conscience. Her grandfather frowned.

"You are rude, Dell," he said matter-of-factly. "It would behoove you—us—to consider mending our fences. You have no one, and while I have family, you are a De Cordova. Losing you would be a pity."

"Losing me?" Dell's derisive snort was full of contempt. "You don't have me to lose. You never had that right."

"Possibly not." The man was silent for a moment, then shrugged. "You should learn from your mother's mistakes, my proud little one. What do you intend to do with your life? Your father's money—money that really was De Cordova money, as you must know—won't support you and your teenage prostitutes and drug addicts forever, child. And sleeping with horse handlers loses its glory eventually." He turned sneering eyes on his daughter. "Doesn't it, Erika?"

"Damn you, Father," she whispered, adding in soft Spanish, to Dell, "*Ten cuidado*. Be careful. It just never ends." Blinking away tears and pasting a smile on her face, she waved at someone across the room and left them.

Her grandfather's annoyance was evident in the tight slash of his eyes, the brief look of contempt as Erika left. But he turned back to Dell.

"She's right, Adela. But it can end. You can choose to be a De Cordova, you know. You can choose the top instead of being a glorified maid tied to someone who shovels out stalls."

"I'll honor the name Rosales every day of my life. Tell me where the honor is in being a De Cordova?" Dell shook her head and walked away, but she felt her grandfather's gray stare follow her across the room. Hal came across to meet her, and she forced a smile and allowed herself to be introduced to a new group of elegant strangers. One of them, Hal mentioned, was a recently hired executive in his entertainment conglomerate, and was working on putting together a water park proposal for Laredo. Similar measures had failed, but Hal felt the time was ripe for a new venture.

The man seemed out of place and uncomfortable, and Dell spent the rest of the evening talking to him, sharing a dance or two, and wishing the whole time that Hal McDade would call it a night and rescue her. They wound up staying until three, to be driven back through the deserted streets in the comfortable silence of De Cordova's own armor-plated limousine, escorted by two unmarked police cars. Kidnapping and armed robbery were less common in Monterrey than in the capital, but those with money were reluctant to take chances.

Just before they reached the hotel, Dell, mulling over the evening's events, realized Brock Hampton, the man Hal McDade had introduced her to, must have known who she was. Some of his questions about horses and social concerns made no sense unless he did. Troubled and tired, she said a rather curt good night to Hal McDade, went into the suite, and bolted the door carefully. Then she sat down on the sofa, fished the picture of Jovani Treviño out of her clutch, and stared at it with a devastating sense of loss.

CHAPTER SEVENTEEN

Dell picked up the phone reluctantly. She had been back from Monterrey for two days now, and it seemed her brief absence had cost her far more than she had earned, even given Hal McDade's generous terms. They had made the three-hour drive without incident. They talked about various business and political issues the trip raised, but neither broached the subject of Lionel and Erika De Cordova.

Dell fought back the grimness she felt every time she thought of the picture, transferred from her evening bag to her handbag. Although she toyed with the idea of dismissing Jovani immediately, the trip had given her time to think things through. There was no point in firing Jovi yet, in spite of his obvious betrayal. Now that she knew her grandfather had sent him, she could deal with him. Having him close at hand was probably safer than having him out of her sight. There was still time to find the resolution to the problem of Jovani Treviño.

Back at the ranch, though, she had been received with the surprising and disheartening news that Selina was leaving. Her ex-husband and his parents had convinced Judge Ovalle-Martinez that the young couple should be given another opportunity to work out their problems. Selina, who had been arrested twice for public intoxication after marital problems, had been sober since coming to the ranch. She insisted, to both the judge and Dell, that she had grown up enough to cope.

Dell hoped she wouldn't suffer. The girl and her teenage husband were both so young. The path ahead would be hard. But Dell put on her best face and said a painful good-bye to Selina, then tried to deal with the anguish Amy and Michelle felt. Maribel was her usual resentful self, telling anyone who would listen that the marriage would once again fail, and Selina would come back in disgrace within days.

Maribel. Dell had called the caseworker before the trip to Monterrey, but the woman only made vague promises about talking to supervisors. The girl was a prostitute, she clucked into the phone, and Dell shouldn't be surprised. She couldn't move her, anyway, until a spot opened, she'd insisted. In fact, she'd seemed a little surprised that Maribel hadn't run away again. Dell thought about raising a little hell with social services, but held back. Clearly, in spite of the girl's baggage, she wasn't leaving anytime soon, and she'd keep a closer watch on the girl until there was some other place for her.

Jovi greeted her politely on her return, but there was something in his eyes—a wariness?—that had not been there before she left. To her surprise, she found he'd sold another of the surplus mares to a breeder for an excellent price. He offered her the check, explaining he hadn't wanted to deposit it until she returned. The same buyer had offered to take the last two mares up for sale, but only if he could have Red Sugar Cash. Jovi declined the offer, but felt she should have the final say. That was an easy decision, and Jovi promised to call the man back and tell him her father's favorite was not for sale under any terms.

The last item among the notes on her desk ordered her to call Judge Ovalle-Martinez. Karla had underlined the word "urgent" three times, so Dell picked up the phone. She smiled grimly as she held the receiver to her ear. It hardly seemed possible that in a few days, the world could have turned itself so totally inside out.

"We have a problem, Dell," Patricia Ovalle-Martinez said in her ear, and Dell knew at once it must be serious.

"Worse than what just happened with Selina?" Dell dragged a hand through her hair and braced herself. "What?"

"Becky's mother wants her back. And the agent with Child Protective Services has been told the child is endangered. That . . ."

Her high school friend paused, and Dell could picture the frown pulling at the corners of her mouth and etching worried lines into her forehead. "Someone said you're involved in illegal activity. That the child's welfare has been compromised. When the caseworker tried to call you, you weren't in. I talked her into waiting to talk to you, and I vouched for you personally. But, Dell, I'm worried. Who in the world can be out to hurt you?"

Dell closed her eyes. A tear dripped from her eye and splattered on the desk. Who it was didn't make much difference. Could she live without Becky? And why had the mother suddenly decided to fight for custody of her abandoned child? Clutching the phone with trembling fingers, she fought back the overwhelming grief.

"I don't know who's behind this," she muttered. "Patricia, I don't want to lose Becky."

"I know. And I'll do what I can. But, Dell, you knew this could happen. You took this risk when you agreed to keep her there." Patricia's voice was gentle, but the words tore at her heart. "The law's almost always on the side of the mother. If she can prove she's responsible now . . ."

"When do I have the meeting with the caseworker?"

"She'll call you. It won't be for a day or two, though. There wasn't enough evidence of imminent danger that she thought Becky should be removed immediately. Meanwhile, I've asked some friends in various departments to check out the mother's behavior very carefully. I don't want the child placed back in an abusive situation. I'd love her to stay with you, if she can."

"Thanks for letting me know," Dell managed, and disconnected. She picked up the heavy, silver-framed picture of Becky in her last Easter dress, then put it back down and stood, walking over to the window. She didn't even try to stop the tears. Nothing she'd lost over the years hurt like the thought of giving up Becky's love and happiness. Suddenly, strong, warm hands closed on her shoulders.

Gently, Jovani turned her around, his face concerned as he saw the tears streaming down her cheeks.

"I knocked, but you didn't answer," he said, trying to wipe her tears away. The gentleness in his touch just brought new tears, and he tilted her face up. "What in the world is this all about?"

"They're going to take Becky away," she choked, refusing to acknowledge that this man could be behind the rumors threatening to crush her. "I can't lose Becky. I thought I could, but I can't."

Strong arms closed around her shaking shoulders, drawing her close into strength and comforting warmth. "Ssssh. Don't cry, *querida*." The Spanish term of endearment barely registered, but she felt the tenderness in the fingers lightly stroking her shoulders. "That can't happen. They have no reason, no right. How could they take your daughter away? You're a wonderful mother."

The words didn't penetrate her misery at first. When they did, she stiffened and drew away a little, looking up at him in confusion. "My daughter?" she whispered brokenly. "Then, you don't know—you thought?" She shook her head. "Becky isn't mine," she said. "She isn't my daughter. She's here because her mother abandoned her."

Surprise filled Jovi's dark eyes. Surprise, and Dell thought, in spite of her anguish, a brief flicker of something like relief. "So— she's a foster child? You never said—"

"I guess I just didn't think to mention it," she explained. "Rosa and the girls knew, and I . . . I never liked talking about it. Made having her seem—I don't know. Temporary." She took a deep breath. "I didn't talk about it," she admitted.

"Still, I'm surprised you thought that Becky was mine. "Just seems . . . most of the men I've known would have asked. If not about her, about her father."

"I just assumed . . . There are so many single mothers these days. And you obviously love her. Nothing else seemed important." He closed the distance between them again, took her into his arms, and hugged her. It was a gentle, reassuring gesture with none of the hungry demand he had demonstrated on other occasions. "But don't cry, Dell. There has to be a way. Have faith."

Bracing herself, Dell nodded and stepped reluctantly out of the sheltering arms. In spite of the genuine concern in his eyes at the moment, she had to remember she couldn't trust this man. This man could hurt her. But she simply couldn't believe he was behind the rumors endangering Becky's custody. His surprise and sympathy were too real. Mustering her courage, she walked over to her desk and picked up a Kleenex, blotting her face. The simple act reminded her of the chasm separating them. She faced Jovi from behind the protection of her desk. "Did you need something?"

"Nothing that can't wait. You seem to have other problems to deal with."

"There's nothing I can do at the moment. I have to meet with the caseworker before things go any further." Disgusted with the sensation of weakness seeping into her limbs, she sat down in her chair and waved a hand at the chairs in front of the desk. "Have a seat. Tell me what you need."

Instead, he walked over to the window and looked out for a time, much as he had when they first met. Finally he came back over to sit down. Without the hat to turn, he reached over and picked up a pen, flipping it absently in one large, bronzed hand while he studied her thoughtfully.

"You've changed," he said suddenly.

His words surprised her. She arched her brows and leaned back in her chair. "Changed?"

"Yeah." He smiled, and humor filled his eyes again, replacing the unreadable expression of moments before. "When I came, you were so—so cold. So uncaring." The tantalizing grin widened. "You decided not to like me," he added. "But I think you slowly warmed up to the idea of having me around. It certainly seemed that way at South Padre. And on a couple of other occasions."

"Does this have a point?" she asked, determined he'd never know just how thoroughly she *had* warmed up to him. Literally and figuratively. Just the thought of him had been able to generate small shock waves of heat. He knew she wanted him. But hopefully he didn't know she loved him.

She watched as the grin faded and the humor left his face. Remembered how Carmela's words had encouraged her to toy with the idea of Jovani Treviño as a man. As, possibly, *the* man in her life. Until a photo hidden in her grandfather's desk had shattered her dreams and killed the warmth.

"It's funny. While you were in Monterrey, I'd get these . . . sudden urges. Just to see you. To know how you were. And yet, you weren't gone for even forty-eight hours." He stretched in the chair, apparently trying to relieve tense muscles. She saw indecision in his eyes and a sudden tightness in his jaw. She wasn't surprised when he abruptly stood up and paced back to the window; avoiding head-on confrontation seemed to be a habit with him. So she waited silently again, and again he finally came back to sit across from her. This time, though, she blinked in surprise when he reached across the desk, curling fingers gently against her cheek in an unexpected caress.

"It was good, having you back from Monterrey, Dell. At least I thought it was. Until . . . " He paused, and there was a huskiness in his voice when he continued, so slight she almost believed she wanted to hear it. "You're different now than you were before," he said. "Remote again, just when I thought . . . " He shrugged and pulled his hand back. "Some of it might be my fault. I know I said we should wait. Maybe I shouldn't have pulled back that night you came over to see me.

"This isn't the same kind of distance, though. I don't know what happened in Monterrey. But I'm not sure I can continue working for you, Dell."

His quiet announcement stunned her. She'd decided that she would dismiss him soon—but not yet. This man's easy betrayal and probable allegiance to Lionel De Cordova were inexcusable. Unforgivable. Even if he merely worked for her grandfather and had no particular loyalty to his employer, he had come here under false pretences. De Cordoba thought they were lovers, clearly, but that error didn't change the facts—he knew Jovi was on the ranch. Knew about the girls. Probably even that they'd gone to South Padre together. She thought back to the day he'd come about the job. He'd been intense, clearly wanted the position badly.

Jovi was here at Lionel De Cordoba's bidding. And if his reasons for wanting Danny gone were what she suspected . . . Still, she forced herself to mask her surprise as well as she could. She could appear surprised, but not concerned. Not shocked. And certainly not hurt.

"Well," she said, after a moment. Then she shook her head. "I have to admit this is unexpected." Her fingers drummed the desk as she turned over a multitude of questions and discarded them. "I'm not sure I understand," she finally said, honestly, and he shrugged.

"I don't want to leave. And I'll stay for the moment. But . . ." Something in his eyes seemed dark and pained as he gazed at her. "Monterrey was a bad idea," he said. She didn't know exactly what he meant, but she knew with chilling certainty that he was right. Whatever could have been between them had ended with her visit to Lionel De Cordova's house. The strangest part of it all, she admitted to herself, was that she understood exactly what Karla Gonzalez meant when she'd offered her unsolicited advice. The man sitting in front of her was at least a liar and a spy, and at worst a criminal. But she didn't care. She loved him. Only she couldn't. So she wouldn't. She ignored the irritating voice that had come to dwell in her head since Jovani's arrival at *Nueva Brisa*. The one whispering, "Yeah, right," as she stood up with her customary detachment and nodded simply at him.

"Please let me know if you decide to go," she said quietly, and walked out of her own office to escape him.

CHAPTER EIGHTEEN

Her meeting with Becky's caseworker, along with Patricia Ovalle-Martinez, was scheduled for Friday morning at eleven. Wednesday night, Dell stood pressed against her bedroom window, watching rain slash down and lightning blaze across the dark night sky again. Webb County with its dry summers usually escaped this kind of onslaught, and the violence of the storm surprised her. This storm, coming after other, recent rains, was sure to cause flooding, locally and downstream.

She turned and glanced at her bed. Becky had been terrified and had come to Dell for comfort. Now she slept peacefully in the middle of Dell's bed, clutching a plaid pillow against her tummy, unmindful of the unending rain and wind. Smiling in spite of herself, Dell walked over and brushed a light kiss against the girl's forehead, careful not to wake her. She felt her eyes sting with the ever-present fear of losing the child, and quickly went back to her vantage point by the window.

The yard was dark, and from her window, she couldn't see very much. Still, she stiffened with surprise and flattened her face against the glass when she thought she saw a shape moving across the yard, heading in the general direction of the stables, but going furtively. A sudden bolt of lightning flared, turning the outside world an electric blue, and Dell gasped in stunned amazement. The light briefly illuminated the bent, running figure, and she realized in shock that it was Maribel.

Almost unable to believe her own eyes, she turned and hurried through the hall to the girl's room, throwing open the door. The room was empty—her eyes had not deceived her. Incredulous, Dell stood for a minute, staring into the room. She went next door and looked in at Amy and Michelle. Amy mumbled a sleepy greeting, barely awake and clearly not worried by the weather, and Michelle was sound asleep.

"Go back to sleep," Dell said gently, and went back to her own room. She rummaged in her closet for seldom-used galoshes and a slicker. While not particularly afraid of storms, she didn't relish going out in one. The ranch country was flat and dry. Lightning strikes often claimed livestock out in the open and could kill anyone caught without shelter. Additionally, the hard-packed soil didn't absorb water, and flooding occurred quickly. The land was so flat water didn't run over most of it, just sat, creating danger as it covered holes, cactus, and other obstacles. To worsen the situation, arroyos and washes filled quickly with water that raced down toward the Rio Grande, already swollen by heavy rains up river in Del Rio.

Grimly, she pulled on the boots and slicker. She couldn't leave Becky alone, though, and on her way out, she stopped in the kitchen. Rosa, humming some old tune under her breath, looked up, startled and then shocked by Dell's rain gear.

"You can't possibly be going out—"

"There's a problem, Rosa," Dell said. "I don't know what she's up to, but Maribel's out there. Even if she's alone, it's dangerous. She's certainly not prepared to be caught out in this."

"But—"

"I'll be fine," Dell assured her. "Listen, the thing is, Becky's asleep in my room. I don't want her to wake up alone."

Rosa nodded and tossed a cloth over the cookies she'd been rolling out. "I'm on my way up," she said without hesitation. "But I still wish you wouldn't go."

"I don't have a choice." Dell forced a brief smile. "I can guarantee, though, Maribel is going to wish she'd have to face another storm, and not me, when I find her! Take good care of the girls, Rosa. I saw her heading toward the barn. If she's inside there,

I'll be back in a couple of minutes, or I'll call if we decide to wait the storm out there."

"Okay." Rosa came over and gave her a brief, hard hug. "Be careful, though. I bet the yard and path are knee-deep in water already."

"Well, ankle deep. Go on up with Becky, okay?" She waited until Rosa disappeared up the stairs before resolutely going to the door and jerking it open. Rain slashed at her, hard and relentless, and the lightning sputtered too near for comfort. Trusting herself not to step into some unseen depression or hit her toe on a rock, she sprinted for the barn, hoping Maribel had the good sense to have headed there.

The barn was silent and dark, although at the far end, light glowed from the office. At her entrance, heads appeared over the stall doors. One of the Arabians, already edgy from the storm, reared in her stall and flailed the air, then dropped back and kicked the wooden walls in a frenzy.

"Calm down, Night," Dell whispered, but stayed back, aware her flapping clothes were likely to cause more panic. She thought about turning on the main lights, but decided against it. The less disturbed the horses were, the better. Trying not to rush, she continued to the end of the hall and pushed the office door open. No one was in the small room, and the dim light seemed to have been left on only for security reasons. Stymied, she paused just outside the office, collecting her thoughts and wondering what to do next.

Could anyone be stupid enough to be out in this? she asked herself once again. But if Maribel hadn't taken shelter here, then where had she gone? She walked back toward the partially open barn door and stood, squinting out into the downpour that all but blinded her.

Suddenly she thought of her father's workshop, used now by Pete to store cleaning tools and extra feed. The old shed was likely unlocked, since nothing in it was of special value. The building was probably thirty yards away, and she braced herself for another sprint across flooded ground. Lightning struck nearby, exploding into fire followed immediately by deafening thunder. She gasped and ran faster, lunging under the awning and stumbling to a stop. She hadn't bothered coming quietly, but the storm's fury effectively drowned out the sounds of her labored breathing and sloshing strides. She paused a moment, a hand on the door of the shed. Then Maribel's loud, angry voice made her draw her hand away and flatten herself against the wall, listening.

"You promised!" the girl raged. "You promised to get me out of here. I did everything you wanted. You can't just walk away from me—"

A low, masculine voice said something in Spanish that she couldn't hear. She couldn't even recognize the voice, muffled as it was by the storm's noise, but fear pounded through her. Who could it be except Jovi? She didn't believe for a moment that it could be the loyal, elderly Pete. *He* would never betray her. But there was no one else on the ranch . . . except Jovani. She slumped miserably against the wet wood, trying to hear.

"—could get me sent away, damn it. Don't you care about that?" Maribel's furious hiss apparently had no effect at all on her companion, whose short bark of laughter was masculine and filled with derision. It didn't sound like Jovi, Dell told herself. His laughter was . . . warm. And human. Not this beastly bark in the storm-filled darkness. Still, there was only one sure way to know. Confront Maribel and find out what was going on.

Gritting her teeth, she straightened up slowly and pushed off the wall. Moving to the door, she took a deep breath, then shoved the door back and stepped into the room. Maribel screamed. There was a blur of movement and an explosion of sharp, sudden pain in her head. Then Maribel's screams faded into the blackness that washed over Dell, easing her away into darkness.

*

When light returned gradually, she blinked it away and tried to turn away from it. The light was insistent though, and gradually the sounds around her penetrated, too, making her wince but calling her back. Maribel's sobs. Rosa's angry mutterings about ungrateful, stupid delinquents. And Jovi's strong, skilled fingers, pressing a cold, damp cloth against her forehead. Her eyes snapped open, and she tried to sit up, but he held her down with one gentle hand. Anyway, her head hurt. Frowning at him, she let herself be restrained. Then she closed her eyes again. Someone had hit her on the head—whoever had been there with Maribel. And now Jovi was standing here, dripping wet, trying to ease the violent pain throbbing in every part of her head. She tried to bite back a small moan as the throbbing intensified, but a muffled sound escaped her thick, dry lips.

"Stay still," he ordered, his voice both firm and gentle. "We tried to get a doctor out, but there's no way in this storm. It isn't safe to try to drive you in to Laredo right now, either—they've actually closed part of I35 from the flooding."

"I'm fine anyway," Dell forced herself to say. Her eyes snapped open, and again she tried to sit up. "Becky—"

"Becky's sound asleep with Michelle and Amy," Rosa said reassuringly. "You just stay where you are, miss. You had us all worried sick." She cast a venomous glare at Maribel, huddled in a corner, still sobbing. Dell looked around her and realized she'd been carried into the house and was on the couch.

"What in the world happened to me?" she asked. "Maribel—"

"You got hit in the head," Jovani said grimly. "Hard. You can deal with Maribel later." There was no sympathy in the glance he cast in the girl's direction. "She almost got you killed. I hope she's aware of what she's done."

Dell sighed and closed her eyes again. Nothing made sense. Forcing her head to turn, she looked at Rosa. "Could you bring me something to drink?" she asked, and the housekeeper immediately hurried toward the kitchen. With difficulty, she focused her gaze on Jovi's face.

"Who hit me, Jovani? And why? Was it you?"

He looked startled, then angered, by her question, as he saw her eyes take in his sopping clothes before returning to meet his eyes levelly.

"Maybe you should ask Maribel," he suggested grimly, and waved at the girl, indifferent to her obvious agitation. "Tell Dell who hit you," he ordered tersely. "And tell her why."

Tears still flowed from the teenager's eyes, and she ducked her head, not meeting Dell's eyes. But after a moment, and after a brief, apprehensive look at Jovi, she answered.

"It was Danny," she said in a monotone. "He didn't want you to see him. He knew he'd be in trouble for coming back on the ranch."

"Danny?" Dell repeated in disbelief. She tried to lift her head, but again Jovi's hand pressed her back gently. "Why were you there with Danny, Maribel?" A snatch of their conversation came back, and she pushed Jovi's hand away and sat up, swaying and closing her eyes until the spinning stars dissolved and her vision cleared. Oblivious to his wet clothes, Jovi sat down beside her, steadying her with an arm around her shoulders. "What did Danny promise you? And what did you give him . . . for whatever you thought he owed you?"

Maribel's old rebelliousness didn't surface as she refused to look up, her face still contorted with fear and shame. "He . . . would bring me cigarettes. I couldn't just quit smoking, you know." She ventured a glance at Dell, trying not to look at Jovi at the same time. She sniffed and wiped a hand across her face. "He called a . . . friend of mine. I was going to run away. Leave here . . . leave Laredo. Until I got things together."

"And for that, you did what?" Dell demanded, remembering the pallet of blankets in the cabaña sickly.

"I . . . I'd really rather not talk about it," she said brokenly, looking down again. Then she looked back up at Dell. "But he knew all this stuff . . . about you. About your mother . . . He made me think it would be okay . . . doing things."

Dell sighed and leaned back against the tweedy fabric of the sofa, letting her eyes drift shut. Rosa came bustling back, carrying a cup of steaming tea. Dell glanced at her and wrinkled her nose. "I can't drink that," she protested. "I need something cold!"

Rosa clucked. "No, *señorita*. You're gonna die from your death of pneumonia, anyway. You're drinking this tea, like it or not. And I've got water on for the next cup."

"But tea . . . " Dell protested, hunching against new pain. She blinked, turned her head. "Maribel—and it's late, we need to get things straightened out and get some sleep—"

Jovi and Rosa exchanged glances.

"You're not going to sleep," Jovi said, after a moment. "Not for a few hours, at least."

Dell tried to turn her head around enough to see him, but her head, neck, and shoulders had stiffened as if set in cement. Annoyed at the petulance in her voice but unable to disguise it, she looked instead at Rosa, who was still within sight. "Why?"

"Concussion," Jovi said, his voice gentle and reassuring. "We have to be sure you don't slip into unconsciousness."

Dell tried to sniff in disdain, but managed only a shaky moan as the world wobbled around her again. Sighing, she refocused her attention on Maribel. "So . . . what things did you do?" she asked, her lips pursing as she took in the tear-ravaged face.

Maribel fidgeted. She didn't look up as she mumbled, "I . . . made some calls. I didn't tell my name. I told the welfare people Becky wasn't being taken care of. That there were drugs here." Her voice trailed off.

Dell leaned into the cushions silently, motionlessly, unable to digest the girl's words. She was hardly aware Jovi leaned over, picked up the cup of tea, and raised it to her lips.

"Take a sip," he ordered, and held the cup until she managed to follow his instructions. He put the cup back on its saucer and sat silently. Maribel sat, head down, fingers interlocked. Dell lifted a hand carefully and wiped away a tear that trickled down her cheek.

"Go to bed, Maribel," she said quietly. "We'll talk tomorrow."

The girl stood without comment and started toward the door. She stopped there and turned back, as if to speak.

"Don't," Dell said flatly. "If you're going to say you're sorry, just don't. Not tonight. Just go." The girl burst into new sobs and fled from the room.

"Good riddance to bad rubbish!" Rosa muttered. "Little—"

"Rosa, never mind," Dell interrupted. "Go to bed. It's late, and I may need extra help with the girls tomorrow, especially Becky. Get some sleep."

Rosa glowered at Jovi and shifted uncomfortably. "I really should stay up with you two," she protested. "You might need me."

Jovi shook his head. "No. I'll watch her." He shifted, moving his arm, but being careful not to jolt Dell, then added, with humor lightening his tone, "Don't worry, though. I've kept many a woman up nights. We'll have a great time!"

Rosa snorted, her displeasure and distrust clear. "*Mira*, Jovi—"

"Really, go," Dell insisted. She managed a small smile. "I don't need a chaperone, Rosa. Neither does Jovi." Her grin widened in spite of the night's events. "If he tries anything, I'll just tell him I have a headache." There was a moment of startled silence, broken by Jovi's low laugh. Rosa's frown deepened, and she shrugged as she turned away.

"Stubborn woman," she muttered, and stalked out of the room, leaving them alone.

Jovi drew his supporting arm away and propped up the throw pillows that had been dropped from the sofa to the floor, making a mound in a corner. "Let me sit you up here," he suggested, lifting her and settling her against the pillows before she could protest. "It'll be easier to stay awake if you're not lying down." He stood up, stretching. "I'll be right back. I'm going to go change." He stood looking down at her with concern. "Should I call Rosa back meanwhile?"

"No." Dell leaned her head back carefully. "In fact, you really needn't bother, Jovi. I'm fine. I can take care of myself."

"Sure you can," he agreed easily. "But I'm coming back anyway. Just to find out if you've ever really used that line about headaches before." He walked over to the bank of windows that formed one wall of the living room.

"Can you believe it's still pouring? The flooding this time is going to be bad—real bad." He swiped a hand through his hair and headed for the door, snagging his slicker from the coat tree. "I'll be back in less than ten minutes." He stopped, came back into the room, and handed her the cordless phone from the end table. "Use the intercom button if you need Rosa before I get here." He half turned, then turned back and placed a light kiss on the top of her head. "—*que te mejoras*," he murmured, and left.

CHAPTER NINETEEN

Water sloshed up around his legs, soaking the already-wet denim, but Jovi rushed toward the foreman's house, unable to shake the night's horrifying events. He'd been checking on the water level in the stable, then planned on walking over to talk to Pete, when a dark shadow had stumbled off toward the ornamental shrubs lining part of the drive. When lightning flared, he thought he recognized Danny, but wasn't sure.

He'd looked around and seen only the tool shed as a place the intruder might have come from. In a momentary lull between sheets of rain, he saw the door banging and raced over.

Maribel was in a corner, hands over her face, sobbing. He could remember the sudden tightness in his chest, the stab of terror when he saw Dell on the floor, unmoving. Lack of light and the violence darkened the scene, and for a moment, he felt as angry and as helpless as when he'd busted into drug parlors in south Florida, aware of the danger but unable to beat it back.

"Get to the house," he hissed at Maribel. "Before me, or I swear to God I'll lock you out in this damn storm!"

He knelt over Dell, lifted her gently, and started toward the house, relieved that she moaned a little, though she didn't come to.

The heart that almost stopped when he saw her unconscious on the floor thudded as he finally managed the steps up onto the porch and threw his own door open. He raced up the stairs, grabbed the first shirt and jeans he saw, and jerked his clothes on.

"That stupid little—" He clamped his mouth shut. He'd take the girl up with Dell later. He needed to call Ortega or Hampton, have them check Danny out. Or the sheriff. As soon as he reached for his cell, he cast that idea aside. With the waters rushing over the banks of the Rio Grande, all the first responders would be out trying to save lives.

For the moment, Dell was safe.

Safe. The irony of it stopped him for a half a second as he headed toward the door. The investigation was pushing on, and Dell would never truly be safe until his buddies at DEA cleared her. *And if they can't?* He hurtled off the front porch and headed back to the house, making it in record time in spite of his dark thoughts.

*

Dell rested a hand on her forehead, shielding her eyes from the dim floor lamp in the corner. Jovi's worry over her was sincere and apparent, even in her muddled state. But why had he been out in the storm? He must have carried her—she realized suddenly that someone had helped her change, too. She stroked the velvety sweater, and fought to focus. Rosa, of course. Still, Jovi's picture had been in her grandfather's desk. The fact Danny had attacked her didn't lessen Jovi's betrayal at all.

Unbidden, the feel of his hand soothing away her pain came back to her, and another solitary tear slipped from an eye before she could blink it away. For a few brief moments, she thought about calling Rosa to keep her company and sending Jovi back into the storm—back to his own, deceitful world. Then the door opened, with rain blasting more loudly until the panel swung shut, cutting it out. Jovi shrugged out of his rain gear and came toward her, his eyes still troubled. Soon enough, she thought. Soon enough, she would send him away. But not tonight.

Light caught and glinted in his hair, and his teeth flashed whitely as he gave her a brief smile, then he touched her forehead and trailed a finger across her cheek. "So how do you feel?"

"Like I got hit up the side of the head with a shovel. A very heavy shovel," she retorted, relaxing under the soothing caress of his fingers.

"Are you sure you're okay? You really should see a doctor, but this weather—"

"I'm fine. A little shocked," she answered truthfully, thinking of Maribel. "But fine." She glanced at Jovi, rocked back on his heels, and shook her head. This time, the slight movement didn't bring sharp darts of pain and nauseating dizziness. Reassured, she smiled. "Get a chair before you fall," she suggested.

He stood up wordlessly and pulled the recliner close, but perched on the edge.

"Are you going to stare at me like that for the rest of the night?" she demanded, not entirely comfortable with his closeness now that her throbbing head didn't buffer the awareness of his presence.

He nodded. "Pretty much."

"But—"

"Do you have any idea how dangerous a blow to the head can be?" he challenged. "There's no way I'm going to leave you alone and find you in a coma—or worse—tomorrow morning." The tenderness in his eyes took most of the sting out of the sharpness of his reply, and she found herself watching him intently. How could this man—this agent of Lionel de Cordova—care? He did, though, and she pressed her hand over her eyes and held the comfort close.

*

At some point, Jovi must have let her drift off. Dell woke in an empty living room with the smells of *guisado* and beans scenting the air. She checked in with Rosa, busy over the stove, who assured her Michelle and Amy were watching Becky. Rosa insisted she didn't need help, so Dell went up to her room, worry eating at her. She walked over to the window, casting a glance up at the sky. The leaden gray color hadn't changed, except that a darker band of clouds was forming already. Dell frowned as she pulled on jeans and a lightweight turtleneck.

Would this unexpected, unusual rain never stop? The fact it was barely drizzling at the moment had very little to do with the fact that rain from a tropical depression was expected to continue through the afternoon and night. Upriver, in Del Rio, alarm was spreading with the river, which had already covered the flood plains. And now the Rio Grande would bring not only Del Rio's water rushing down to the Gulf of Mexico, but all the rain water still falling on south Texas.

Shaking her head, she took a jacket from the closet and left the room. Becky came out of her own room, smiling sunnily and pulling a bright, floral umbrella behind her. Dell laughed and swept her up in her arms, kissing her cheek.

"Hi, princess. Whatcha doing?"

"Play," Becky said seriously, and Dell laughed again and shook her head.

"I'm afraid not, sweetheart," she said. "The water in the yard's already deeper than you are tall. Maybe you can get Amy or Michelle to read you a story?"

"Okay," Becky agreed without argument, and wiggled out of Dell's arms. "Amy! Mitchell!" she called, trundling through their open door.

Dell smiled through the pain of thinking about what tomorrow's meeting might bring. That she could lose this precious little person was simply unimaginable. She stuck her head in to check on the girls, who were giggling over some sitcom on the television. Becky made herself at home between the two girls, propping her head on little hands and gazing at the television. Dell's grin faded as she reached Maribel's door. She knocked briskly, then swung the door open and stepped in.

The room, for once, was neat; everything had been picked up since she had paid a visit to the girl earlier this morning. Maribel sat in a corner of the bay window, staring blindly out at the gray sky and rain-soaked yard. In spite of her anger and resentment over Maribel's behavior, Dell couldn't help feeling a twinge of pity over the girl's desolate expression.

"Your room looks nice," Dell ventured, and Maribel turned her head reluctantly.

"Yeah. I figured I'd better clean it up. Before I leave and all."

Dell tapped her leg idly with her fingers, considering the girl. "You surely can understand why it would be hard for me—wrong for me, really—to let you stay?"

Maribel nodded without speaking.

"Patricia—Judge Ovalle-Martinez—and I are meeting tomorrow. Over Becky." Dell saw color sweep through the girl's face, and the teenager looked away again. She sighed. "Maribel, if I lose Becky . . ." She shook her head. "You have to know, I wouldn't want you here if you could do that much harm."

The teenager didn't turn, drawing into herself and making a slight gesture akin to a shrug. "Yeah."

Dell hesitated, common sense and anger warring with a flicker of compassion. Strangely, she thought fleetingly of her mother— elegant and aloof. Unable to care. "No one's going to understand this—I'm not even sure I do. But I thought I'd talk to the Judge about you staying until school starts—if they don't place you out first."

Maribel turned back, clearly confused. "Why? I almost got you killed—not that I knew he'd hit you, but still—"

"You endangered all of us, Maribel. Most of all yourself. What kind of a man forces a sixteen year old into the position Danny put you in? You're lucky he didn't use the shovel on you when you confronted him." She shook her head. "This is your very last chance with me, girl—and it's not up to me, really. Don't waste it.

I won't fight to keep you here. And—well, never mind. I suppose I can't threaten you with the outcome of tomorrow's hearing."

"Would it help if I told the Judge what I did?" the girl asked slowly, her eyes full of fear, but her face resolute. "Because if it will . . ."

Dell regarded her soberly. "Thanks, Maribel. Hopefully I don't need to involve anyone in this. Surely the agency needs proof of wrongdoing to remove her. Anyway, part of the problem is that her mother may want her back. I'll have to face that possibility sooner or later." She started toward the door, then paused and turned back.

"Maribel, there's something I don't understand. This morning, when we talked—I didn't think about it then. But how did you call the agency? They should have been able to trace the calls back here, and someone should have asked about them."

She shook her head. "I didn't call from one of your phones," she explained guiltily. "Danny had a cell phone he loaned me. He didn't want Rosa to catch me on the phone."

"Hmmm." Dell nodded and pulled the door open. She was almost out in the hall when Maribel added, "Or the drug guy."

Puzzled, Dell hesitated, then pulled the door firmly shut behind her. Undoubtedly Maribel was referring to one of Danny's contacts. She thought about asking, but realized there would be time for that later. She had gotten almost all the way to the kitchen door before she remembered the photo of Jovi Treviño in her purse. And the rumors about the newest of the De Cordova businesses. Pushing aside her suspicions, she headed for the barn, slogging through water that rose to her ankles.

In spite of the early hour, the lights in the barn were all on. She could hear the sounds of nervous horses, banging stall doors, snorting, anxious whinnying. Pete greeted her with a nod as she came in, shaking his head as he looked out the door.

"Rain ain't nearly over," he said. "Horses don't like it a bit, either."

"It has gotten a bit old," she agreed. "Even as badly as we ranchers usually need rain." She stopped to pet Red Sugar Cash, murmuring to the mare. Sugar didn't seem overly upset, and Dell was glad all over again that she hadn't been sold. How could she ever sell this mare, her father's favorite? She thought of the deal that had fallen through because of her refusal to include Sugar. It didn't bother her, though—she wouldn't part with Sugar, and that was final.

"Have you seen Jovani?" she asked Pete, and he paused, leaning on the rake he was holding.

"Well, yeah, sure. He was here not too long ago, checkin' on the horses." He waved a hand at the far wall of the barn, and she noticed a line of neatly stacked sand bags piled up against the back door. "Water was already getting' through. He don't figure it will out and out flood, but the horses don't like water coming in. They may be standing in some by nightfall if we can't pump and fan it out."

"And Jovi did that?"

"Him and me. And he hooked up a pump, just in case, and has the big fan we used to use in the old stallion barn working. He said he could dry out some of the moisture if he had to."

"And where is he now?" she asked, glancing around.

Pete shrugged. "Might have gone to lie down. He looked really tired." Dell nodded. She could easily understand that, since he'd spent the night sitting in a chair, talking to keep her awake. Then he had apparently come straight to the barn to work on protecting the horses.

"Shall I go get him?" Pete offered, and Dell quickly shook her head.

"No. It really isn't anything important." She walked back over to the door and looked up at the gray sky consideringly. "How long do you think the rain will hold off?" she asked.

Pete joined her, turning his own weathered face up to study the dark, oppressive ceiling. "A while, I guess. I don't think we'll get any more hard rain. The problem is gonna be the river."

"It won't come up this far, will it?" she asked. Pete had been around when the flood of '54 had washed out Laredo's first international bridge and damaged much of the city.

"Could," he said shortly. "But most likely it won't."

Dell nodded thoughtfully, then went back and pulled open the stall door, leading Sugar out and tying her to the ring on the door.

"*¿Que haces?*" Pete asked, startled, as she retrieved a saddlecloth and threw it over the mare's back.

"I'm riding down toward the river," Dell said matter-of-factly, and went to the tack room, coming back with the mare's saddle and bridle. Pete was watching her in befuddlement, clearly questioning her sanity as well as her actions.

"Don't worry," she told him reassuringly. "I just want to see the water level and be sure the cabaña's closed up tightly. They said on the news the level's rising pretty quickly. I'll be safe on a horse."

"I could drive you down," Pete offered.

"No. I think a horse is safer. The truck can get into mud and get stuck. Sugar's as steady as they come. If the weather gets any worse again, we'll just turn around. Don't worry about us."

He watched her balefully, concerned anyway. "Does Rosa know?" he asked finally, and she shook her head.

"Heavens, no! You know she'd be out of her head with worry if I told her. She knows I'm down here. I'll be back before she has any reason to check." She tugged at the girth then patted the mare's neck. "Don't you worry, Pete. And don't you dare tell Rosa I left. I don't want her sending a search party." She swung up in the saddle and guided the mare toward the door. Sugar threw her head and pranced a little when cold water sloshed up over her fetlocks, but obediently headed toward the paddock gate when Dell insisted. Pete watched them, frowning, then, grumbling in Spanish, went back to his work.

*

Jovi started, waking from sleep abruptly, then lay quietly for a minute, listening to the silence around. Nothing moved in the small, two-bedroom foreman's house. But something felt . . . strange. Wrong. He rolled out of bed, still fully dressed except for his boots, and walked over to the window that looked down toward the barn. Nothing seemed out of place . . . but then, farther off, a flash of red snared his gaze. Stunned, he watched as Dell and Red Sugar Cash disappeared down the trail that led toward the river and the cabaña.

Cursing under his breath, he pulled on his boots and a jacket. Cold anger lanced through him, settling heavily in his stomach. The woman was riding out into an oncoming storm, oblivious to the threatening clouds overhead. Headed, apparently, to the riverside cabaña, which might already be flooded. There was no logical explanation. Grimly, he thought about Brock Hampton's call from Monterrey. Both she and De Cordova, Hampton said, had disappeared from the ballroom for some time. He had seen them talking, later, from across the room. And although Hampton said they appeared to have argued, if Dell and her grandfather were truly estranged, why had she been in that house at all?

He shoved his hat down and went out, hurrying toward the barn. He went in quietly, looking around, but he could hear Pete at the far end, yelling at one of the nervy Arabians as he tried to muck the stall. He considered calling the groom over and inventing some excuse for his unusual ride, but decided against it. Working alone, Pete might not miss a horse he'd already fed. And if he did . . . well, explanations could wait.

Quickly and quietly, he pulled a bridle from its peg and led the Appaloosa out of its stall. The spotted horse shied and fidgeted as he led it outside, but he swung up on the horse's bare back and dug his heels into its sides, forcing it to follow the same water-soaked path Dell had taken moments before.

*

Dell kept glancing apprehensively at the sky as she rode, but the weather seemed to have broken for the moment. Except for a momentary spatter of cold, wet drops and the unbroken gray clouds, the rain had stopped. Unwilling to gallop because of the wet, slippery ground, she still urged the steady-footed mare on at a rapid trot.

As she neared the descent in the path leading down to the cabaña, the water ran off, allowing a clear view of the path. Still, the heavy, clay-based soil was slick, and Sugar slid a couple of times, throwing up her head in concern and slowing even more. The trees, still obscuring some of the path, were rain-soaked. Wet branches splattered Dell and slapped heavily at her face and arms when she couldn't avoid them.

Coming out into the clearing by the cabaña, Dell reined up in shock, gasping. The river had already flowed over its banks and was pushing up near the front porch of the building. In the river, debris floated by—trees, torn up by the water, unidentifiable pieces of flotsam and, incredibly, some rancher's water tank, bobbing and turning crazy circles as the currents rushed it along. Dell closed her eyes in a brief prayer as she thought of the damage and grief this flood was going to cause. Just that heavy tank, born along like a surfacing torpedo, could collide with the struts of any of the international bridges downstream and cause serious damage.

Seeing the tank also made her think of the few surrounding neighbors, people on the adjacent properties, whose houses were situated closer to the river. Getting into Laredo was impossible, yet staying in their own homes might prove deadly.

Grimly, Dell turned the mare around. She would shelter her neighbors in the house, if they could get over. It was high enough and far enough to be safe. Rosa would understand, and the girls could help. And Jovi. Surely he wouldn't mind. The mare was eager to head home, and snorted in disgust when Dell reined her to a stop beside the cabin. But in the face of the imminent flooding, chances were good this old remnant of her past would be swept away. She could say goodbye.

She climbed off and looped the reins around the nearest post, then walked to the front window and peered inside. Nothing moved in the shadows of the cabin, but if she closed her eyes, she could remember her father's bulky figure moving around, calling her to come out and join him in some adventure on the river banks. Her mother, when she came at all, would pull on a hat and spray herself from head to foot with insect repellent then shut herself inside the cabin, waiting irritably for her husband and child to tire of their games. Dell shook her head and swiped at her hair in frustration. Samuel Rosales had deserved a simple life and the happiness it could have given him. He certainly should never have married cold, rich, and spoiled Erika De Cordova. What fools people in love were.

She untied Sugar's reins and patted the broad red head absently, casting a last, forlorn look around. What had her grandfather said? That she should know better than to sleep with a horse-handler? She frowned. How strange that her grandfather should care whether or not she was involved with Jovani Treviño if he'd sent him here to begin with. In fact, it was strange he'd bothered to send someone to watch her at all. She gave her head a slight shake. Nothing really made sense. Unless, she thought, it wasn't really about her.

She looked around the clearing again, her frown deepening. Maybe Jovi's main concern, his main job, was to be sure that only the right people had access to this long-forgotten part of the ranch. Before she could spend much time thinking through that possibility, Sugar tensed, throwing her head up and looking around alertly.

Dell gripped the reins more tightly and stepped closer to the mare, wondering what she'd heard. She had come unarmed and without a phone, and mentally cursed herself for her carelessness. Murmuring a soft word to the horse, she stepped off the porch and edged toward the corner of the cabin. She heard nothing, but she knew from Sugar's interest that something—or someone—was nearby. Drawing a deep breath and straightening, she turned the corner of the cabin.

She almost walked into Jovani Treviño, flattened against the cabaña wall, pistol drawn.

CHAPTER TWENTY

For long, silent seconds, neither of them moved.

"Are you alone?" Jovi hissed, and then, before she could answer, he moved past her, still keeping against the sheltering wall, and peered around the corner to where Sugar still stood, waiting, and down to the river below.

"What in the name of God is this all about?" Dell asked, still shocked, staring incredulously at the stubby black pistol and the hard, angry stranger holding it.

He didn't answer at first, and although he lowered the gun, he didn't immediately put it away. When he finally put the gun away and turned back to face her, the cold fury gripping his face was frightening.

"So." The word was somewhere between a threat and a sneer, a low, snarled word that spoke volumes. Dell could only gape at him, unsure what was she was supposed to do or think.

Suddenly, another possibility for his presence on the ranch occurred, and she shuddered. Her mother and grandfather wanted the ranch, and both she and Samuel Rosales had refused to sell it. Her grandfather could pay for virtually anything, from river front property to murder. If she were out of the picture, the ranch would probably belong to her mother.

Immediately, she made herself discard that idea. Lionel De Cordova couldn't want this piece of underused property enough to kill for it. Jovi was simply pursuing some criminal intent of his own. Straightening, she took a single, deep breath.

"So, what?" she asked, challenging him. "How funny—and how convenient for you, I'm guessing—that we always seem to wind up here together—alone."

"Convenient?" His tone was laced with quiet menace. "I doubt you're really finding it convenient. It's a little hard to conduct business when outsiders keep showing up, isn't it, Ms. Rosales?" His mouth twisted. "Or should I say Ms. De Cordova?"

The sarcasm in his question was unmistakable, but nothing he said made sense.

"I don't know what your problem is, Jovani. But I think it's pretty obvious that you have your own designs on my property. Illegal designs." Unexpectedly, she remembered something Maribel had said when the girl had complained that Rosa wouldn't want her to stay. And someone else—"the drug guy." She swallowed, aware of the danger confronting her, but unable to bite back the sudden revelation. "It wasn't just Danny, was it? It wasn't about him at all. Maribel was right when she said 'the drug guy' wouldn't want her to stay. Rosa told me you encouraged her to get Maribel sent away, Jovi. But it didn't click at first. Maybe because I didn't want it to! *You're* 'the drug guy'—not some trafficker I thought must have been calling Danny!"

The expression in Jovi's face didn't change. The grimness didn't ease. But his mouth twisted. "That's right, Dell. I *am* the 'drug guy.'" He raked a hand through his rain-darkened hair. "DEA. And I was here to find out if this ranch was still being used to funnel drugs north." He was silent for a moment, then shook his head. "When I said I'd come, I pretty much figured it was. Didn't mind a bit, trying to close the gate." He stopped again, then continued flatly. "But then I met you. And I almost—almost—let you make a fool of me. Because I wanted to, I guess."

Dell stared at him blankly, struggling to sift through the information he'd just provided. She, too, shook her head. "DEA? I don't believe you still work for them. I don't believe you're still a cop. Do you have a badge? Proof?"

"I'm not an agent, Dell. And if I were, I wouldn't be carrying a badge around with me out here on a flooded riverbank. Not where

I might run into people who wouldn't much respect a badge." He regarded her steadily, and the accusations were still there in the dark depths of his eyes.

"If you're not an agent—"

"I'm a paid informant. Sort of," he explained. "You knew I used to work for the DEA—it was on my resume. And I told you." He shrugged minutely. "They called me in because I was from the area, and they knew I'd help them out."

"No." Dell said the word slowly, definitely. "No. I don't buy that. Because there's one little item that contradicts that. I found your picture in my grandfather's desk, Jovi. I don't know why, but he must have paid you. To watch me—check up on me—I don't know." She paused again, noticing that a new look—of caution, or of masked surprise—flitted across Jovi's face.

"So if you link my picture in your grandfather's desk with me, and with drugs—you're aware the De Cordovas have moved into—at least—money laundering?" he asked sharply.

"No. I don't know anything about the De Cordovas," Dell retorted furiously. "But it stands to reason—"

"Give me a break," Jovi muttered grimly. "It stands to reason that a woman as intelligent as you are would know the money in Sam Rosales' account isn't legit." He held up a hand, forestalling her protests. "I know you were much younger, and some of the money was deposited after you left for college. I did a lot of checking into your father's financial records and into your whereabouts and activities at the time. But even so . . . " He shook his head with finality. "A quarter of a million dollars, almost. Before the insurance settlement you received after his death. Where the hell did you think your father got that money?" Sarcasm crept back into his voice. "Selling quarter horses in south Texas?"

Sudden, heavy drops of rain splattered them.

"My father was not a drug dealer," Dell whispered, hardly aware the small, separate drops were becoming an insistent shower.

"No." Jovi sighed heavily, glanced up at the sky, then quickly at the river before turning his attention back to her. "I don't think he was. I think he allowed the De Cordovas—whatever part of them may be involved—to pay for his silence. And to use this cabin and this ranch as a staging area. Danny was an emissary. Pete was too busy with the horses and too unaware of the threat to know. I'm convinced it was only Danny. And I think he was placed here on purpose."

Dell wiped rain, mingling with a few escaped tears, from her face. "This is all insane. I don't know who you are. Why you're here." She turned away from him, tugging on Sugar's reins, gathering them and swinging up into the saddle. "I don't know why your picture was in my grandfather's desk," she said again.

"If it's what I suspect, he knows I used to work for DEA," Jovi said matter-of-factly. "I hope his sources have also told him I don't any longer, but that's something I can't worry about right now." He shrugged. "Maybe he was just checking to see if you were involved with someone. Let's hope so." He reached out, catching Sugar's bridle before Dell could escape.

"Dell, I don't want to believe any of the things I think I see here." His tone was soft, urgent. "Tell me why you came here today. In the rain. The flood."

"I had to." Dell looked down at him, his face blurring in the rain. Through her tears. "I love this place, but it's not going to make it through this one." She glanced over her shoulder, squinting as the rain blinded her momentarily, unable really to see the river, but knowing it was there, then turned back to Jovi. "I had to say goodbye," she said, her tone as soft as his.

"All right." He took a step closer to the mare, laying a hand on her shoulder to quiet her; the driving rain was making her nervous. "Tell me just one more thing." He paused, sorting out what he wanted to ask. What he needed to know. "We had a man down in Monterrey. Brock Hampton."

"Brock Hampton?" Dell's echo was shocked. "Hal McDade's friend—the one trying to fund the water park?"

"That was his cover," Jovi said dismissively. "That doesn't matter. What I need to know is—why did you meet with your grandfather? What did you talk about? I thought you two weren't even on speaking terms."

Dell looked at him blankly. "We didn't talk—unless you could call a five minute conversation with my mother and him a meeting."

"But you weren't in the ballroom for nearly an hour, Hampton said. Neither was he. He left right after you did. Hampton knows you went into your grandfather's office—someone saw you. She didn't see him, true, but—"

"I spent an hour in my grandfather's office trying to get away from the pain of being in that house again. I neither know nor care where Lionel De Cordova was." She pulled the reins slightly, and Jovi's hand slipped off as the mare tossed her head and took a tentative step backwards. "I'm going back to the ranch. This flood's going to be devastating. I'm going to call the Wilsons and some of the other ranch families in the area and let them know they can stay at the house if they need to. Their property's lower than mine."

"I'll ride back with you," Jovi agreed, holding up a hand when she started to speak. "We'll finish this later," he said. "I know it's not done. But you're right about the river—let's do what we can to help now. Our problems will have to wait."

What he said made sense. Still, Dell frowned at him. "Sugar doesn't ride double."

For the briefest of seconds, his mouth relaxed in a slight smile. "Too bad," he said, then shrugged and turned toward a thicket of bushes. "Luckily, I brought my own transportation."

Realizing she could hardly boot her horse into a gallop and outrun him in this drenching downpour, Dell nudged the mare after him and waited while he swung up onto the bare, wet back of his own horse. Together they headed back toward the stable, their horses slogging together through the water and mud, the Appaloosa stumbling as they crossed one of the new arroyos snaking across the path.

Without thinking, Dell reached out, grasping Jovi's wet arm, holding horse and rider up through sheer will.

"This is going to be bad," she breathed, shrinking a little from the intensifying rain. He looked across at her, nodded, and grasped her hand, giving it a quick, hard squeeze.

"*Que dios nos bendiga,*" he said, the prayer almost washed away by the storm.

Dell heard, though, and sucked in a deep breath. "God bless us," she echoed into the never-ending wetness.

*

Thank God for generators. Dell tucked a pillow under Mrs. Simmons' head and smiled reassuringly at the elderly widow. "Don't worry, Doña Alicia," she soothed, using the Spanish term of respect for the woman. "You're not any trouble at all. The river should crest tomorrow by noon, they said. And the rain is supposed to stop. Everything will be fine."

The eighty-year-old woman nodded her frail, white head and reached up to touch Dell's face with a trembling hand. "You're a good girl," she said. "And that young man who carried me out . . . " She glanced across the room. Jovi was asleep on the sofa, Becky curled in his arms, with one of the Vasquez children, a book clasped in chubby arms, leaning against him, also soundly asleep. "What's his name again, *niña?*"

"Jovi," she answered, her heart twisting painfully at the sight of Jovi surrounded by children. For almost sixteen hours, she, Rosa, and Jovi had worked non-stop, calling neighbors in and providing for them. The girls, too, had helped with entertaining frightened children, serving food, and clearing and straightening up after the twenty-odd people who sought shelter here. Jovi made a harrowing drive over to the neighboring Simmons' ranch, carrying the woman out through water reaching in places to his knees—and the water was still building in the river. The elderly couple who cared for her came as well, along with the two men who took care of the Simmons cattle. Jovi had tried to drive the cattle to the highest end of the property but, drenched and on foot, had not been very hopeful about their welfare. His concern for the neighbors touched Dell, much the way seeing him with Becky and the neighbors' children did. But the accusations and suspicions hovered unspoken between them when their eyes met in unguarded moments.

"That poor man must be just exhausted," Alicia Simmons clucked sympathetically. "He sure has been a godsend to us, girl. You got a good man to help you out."

Dell nodded noncommittally, excused herself, and stepped away. She wouldn't listen to anyone sing the praises of Jovani Treviño. Not too long ago, she had been whispering them to herself. Well, she wouldn't think about that now. She was untouchable. Unattainable. *Inalcanzable*. Surely she could keep herself from feeling the pain of Jovi's betrayal all over again. Briskly, she headed back to the kitchen.

Rosa was humming a song softly, her fingers patting a small ball of *masa* into a tortilla.

"Good heavens, Rosa!" Dell exclaimed. "Are you still working? We've got close to thirty people here, for heaven's sake—you can't make flour tortillas for all of them."

"*Sí puedo*." She put the smooth white circle down, reached for the rolling pin, and began rolling it out. When she glanced up at Dell, tears glinted in her eyes. "Some of these people might have lost their homes, or at least the belongings in them," she reminded

Dell. "Making tortillas is the least I can do for them. Besides, the girls helped me until they were just ready to drop."

Dell nodded and reached for one of the *masa* balls. Rosa was right. "I'll pat, you roll," she said simply.

The tortillas were spread out to cool when Jovi appeared abruptly in the kitchen door, his face only slightly less fatigued after his brief nap.

"I carried Becky up to her room," he said, stretching wearily. "Hope you don't mind."

"Of course not. She didn't wake up?"

"Not for a second. I told Amy and Michelle to keep an eye open in case she did, though. They looked pretty tired, too, though." He wandered into the kitchen, looking out of place.

"Can I help do anything else?"

"No. I think we're finished." Dell wiped her hands on a towel and hung it up, glancing around the kitchen. "I'm glad they've re-opened I35 into Laredo. We may have to make a grocery run."

"No good yet. Most of the stores will have bare shelves," he noted, glancing at the tortillas.

Wordlessly, Rosa picked one up and handed it to him. "Didn't see you eat."

He took a bite of tortilla and waved off her worry. "I'm fine. Call me if you need me. I'm going down to check on the horses and make sure Pete has everything under control. The water was still managing to seep in under the door at the far end of the barn." Nodding, he headed for the back door, pulling his still-wet jacket from its hook.

Rosa watched him go, then shook her head. "Now that's one man I just flat misjudged," she said apologetically, and Dell flashed her a startled glance.

"What?"

"Yes, ma'am. I thought he was an arrogant, no-good—I don't know what. But I'll tell you right now, *chiquilla*—not many are as compassionate and straight-headed as that man is."

Dell frowned. "Rosa, I think you're putting a lot of stock on what you've seen in a few hours in an emergency situation," she protested. Rosa was the one person she didn't want on Jovi's side. Now more than ever.

Rosa snorted. "What better way to judge someone than in an emergency?" she demanded. "A man who helps someone who can't help himself—who's lost everything like the Simmons—or someone alone and scared like the Vasquez kids, with their folks trying to save things at their home—now that's a real man." She turned to pull the whistling teakettle off its burner and filled two cups with hot water, then plopped tea bags into them and pushed one across the counter toward Dell. Rosa spooned sugar into her tea and stirred it methodically. Finally she looked up from the swirling liquid in her cup. "I thought you'd be glad to hear I realized my mistake," she offered, lifting her cup to blow into it. "Don't you want me to like the man you're in love with?"

Dell's eyebrows arched, and she barely stifled a gasp of disbelief. Or surprise. Or revelation. "What?"

"You heard me," Rosa retorted, turning back to the stove. "Drink your tea. And after—you go get some sleep. They'll reschedule Becky's custody hearing as soon as they can, I'm guessing." And ignoring Dell's consternation, Rosa began adding seasonings to the soup simmering on the stove.

*

It took almost another forty-eight hours for the last of the storm's refugees to leave the shelter of the spacious ranch house at *Nueva Brisa*. Mrs. Simmons and her caretakers were the last to go, hugging Rosa, the girls, and Dell, and expressing their gratitude over and over. Jovi helped load them into the SUV and drove them back to survey the damages from the receding water. Dell had planned on going with them, but one of Alicia's daughters had managed to fly in from Dallas and was already at the ranch. Dell was sure the young woman could manage. And she couldn't face the trip back alone with Jovi yet.

Dejected, Dell considered helping rearrange the living room and launder the towels and linens piled up in the laundry room. The girls were scuttling around busily, though, apparently glad to be occupied, and Dell decided to make the trek down to the barn instead.

Pete was nowhere in sight. He undoubtedly was taking a couple of hours off to rest. Like the others, he had worked through the worst of the weather, keeping the horses safe and calm. Stall by stall, Dell wandered down the aisle, looking in on each inhabitant, murmuring reassurance to those startled by her sudden appearance. Then she walked slowly back to the office, going in, sitting down and absently running her hands over the smooth, polished wood.

Tired. She was so tired. She tried to focus her thoughts on Becky's upcoming custody hearing, but she could only think of Jovi. Of his smile, the dark eyes with the *chispitas*, the tiny, dancing sparks of flame in their depths. Of his passion that night he had kissed her, and his tenderness when he had held her. Of his betrayal. Sighing, she pushed herself off and forced herself across the small room on legs that didn't want to work. She stared out the large window into the empty arena and fought off tears of exhaustion. She wouldn't cry.

Could Jovi really be who he said he was? An informant trying to stop drugs? She bit her lip, not sure it mattered. Whoever he was, whatever—he wasn't who he had said. He wasn't the man she had secretly, foolishly believed might want to share a life here—a life surrounded by the horses. With Becky. With the girls, or others like them, who needed help.

Karla had warned her, hadn't she? That when the right man came, nothing else would matter. But Karla had been wrong, really. She'd said nothing could come between a woman and the right man, yet their mutual recriminations, the suspicions, the accusations were an impossible wall to climb now.

And Karla had been wrong about one other thing, too. "Wouldn't it be funny," the woman had asked, "if Jovani Treviño were the man?" Well, he *was* the man . . . and there was nothing remotely funny about that unwelcome truth.

CHAPTER TWENTY-ONE

A slight noise startled Dell into wakefulness. She jerked upright, wiping a hand across her face and blinking in surprise as she realized she had fallen asleep behind Jovi's desk. Strange—she remembered being at the window, not the desk. Remembered thinking of Jovi . . . nothing but Jovi. She ran a hand through her hair and yawned, then stretched. She wasn't sure what she had heard, but a glance at the wall clock showed her she'd been dozing for some time.

"Finally," Jovi said from the door, and Dell started again. He came into the room, tall and imposing, and Dell's fingers curled into the soft warmth of the warm-ups she was wearing. He had changed and shaved, and stopped close enough to the desk that his aftershave teased her senses.

"I came in a little earlier," he added, by way of explanation, "but you were dead to the world. I didn't see any reason to wake you—you have to be drained."

Wordlessly, she stared at him. How he could speak so blithely? Her own throat was constricted, squeezed tightly shut from the pain of seeing him so near when so much kept them apart. When he had lied to her. When he had accused her father—her—of being involved in something as sickening as the drug trade.

The silence stretched, cruel and unbreakable. Then he stepped closer, reaching out and touching her face. "Don't," he said. "Don't look at me like that. I can't stand what I see in your eyes." He turned, walking over to the window, his shoulders hunched. "I have to leave now," he said, not looking back at her.

"Yes," she said tonelessly. She wanted to stand, to force him to confront her face to face, but she couldn't push herself from the chair. Finally, he did turn back.

"Dell, I had a job to do." He walked back across the short distance, crouching in front of the desk, making himself her height. "When I met you—as I got to know you—it wasn't a job I wanted to do. But I had to."

She managed a small, indifferent shrug. "I understand."

"No." He shook his head. "You don't. There was reason to believe that you could be involved. If not evidence, certainly circumstance. I . . . I know you're not. But the doubts I had—that I allowed myself to have—I can't take those back. And I know how they hurt you." He took a deep breath. "And my conclusions about your father—I can't change those, either. Investigations stemming from what we believe about that have to go on. I just won't be involved."

"So what will you be after you leave here?"

"The same thing I am now . . . I hope. Someone who loves horses. A trainer, foreman for a stable. That's what I am. The rest is . . . " He paused, groping for words. "A matter of conviction. Something I only do if no one else will, or can." Sighing, he pushed himself back to his feet. "Good luck with Becky—she should be here, with you." He leaned over and brushed a feather-light kiss across her cheek. "*La inalcanzable*," he murmured. "It fits . . . so well. But how I wanted them to be wrong. How I wanted to touch you." With a final, desolate shake of his head, he turned and left the room.

*

With Becky's custody hearing rescheduled for yet another Friday, Dell found herself concentrating on each day's small trials and chores to get her through until then. She took Michelle to visit her mother, as the court ordered, and she spent hours with Becky, knowing the pain would be worse if she lost, but that the memories would be precious. She also spent hours in the stable, going over the records, considering her options with the horses. A man called from California asking to speak to Jovani about the stallion he had inquired about. Hiding her pain, Dell said Jovi had moved on and took the information herself. Apparently Jovani had planned on purchasing an Arabian stallion to reestablish the *Nueva Brisa* breeding program.

In spite of herself, she got out old bank records, old ledgers, and financial papers she'd never really looked at. Could her father have really taken De Cordova money for the reasons Jovi thought? She couldn't imagine Samuel Rosales doing anything that wasn't strictly ethical. And yet she, too, had known the money wasn't entirely innocent. But she had considered it blood money— money Lionel De Cordova had paid to reclaim his daughter and be sure a granddaughter of embarrassing lineage stayed far away from the De Cordovas' riches.

Late Thursday, as Dell puttered in the kitchen, Michelle wandered into the room. She nibbled a freshly baked cookie and offered to help.

"I'm almost finished with these," Dell assured her, holding out a tray of chocolate chip cookies. "Here, have some more."

The girl declined the cookies but lingered, clearly wanting to talk but unsure she could.

"So what's up?" Dell prompted gently. "Just say it."

Still, it took Michelle a few moments, and she seemed to be visibly bracing herself. "Jovi's gone," she said at last, in her small, childish voice.

"Yes," Dell said, forcing herself to keep her tone level and her expression indifferent.

Fidgeting, Michelle took a cookie, bit it, and then put it back on the counter. "Why?"

"There were . . . several reasons. We both thought it was best if he went."

"Maribel said it was her fault," Michelle pressed. "That she'd messed things up for you."

"No." Dell put the last tray of cookies in the oven. "Maribel did some awful things. But she had nothing to do with Jovi going."

"But you . . . miss him?" Michelle blushed, but she seemed insistent on finding out as much as she could. "You . . . you liked him."

"Yes." Dell picked up a sponge and wiped the counter absently. "I cared a great deal about him." She looked across at Michelle. "Sometimes, though, if you know someone just isn't right— sometimes it's better to move on. For everyone."

"But . . . you're so old—" She blushed furiously, shaking her head. "No, that's not what I meant. Not so old. Just—just old enough. Like, to marry and stuff. Don't you want that?"

Dell closed her eyes for a brief second, closing out Michelle's confusion. Her concern and embarrassment. Married and stuff— to Jovani Treviño. Yes, she would have liked that. But how little it mattered right now.

Sighing, she faced the girl honestly. "Michelle, I wish Jovi and I could have had more time together. Things might have worked out differently. But don't ever think . . . A woman doesn't have to have a man to be something, Michelle. Really."

Michelle picked up the uneaten cookie, considering it with concentration. "*Mi mamá*—my mother said no. That a woman without a man *daba pena*—was nothing but a pity." She frowned, breaking a bit off the cookie. "She couldn't see herself alone. That's how the trouble started with her boyfriends. And when I stayed with Beto, because I couldn't go home . . ." Her voice trailed off for a minute. "It doesn't matter now. But I used to think I wanted to get married. Now I see it doesn't make sense."

"No. Not for you—not yet. But maybe it will someday."

"And for you?" Michelle tilted her head, studying Dell's reaction. "Will marriage make sense for you someday?"

The image of Jovi's face—smiling, eyes laughing—forced her to suppress a shiver of longing. *Could* she marry? she asked herself. "Maybe," she told Michelle hesitantly. "I don't see it now—but maybe, someday." The teenager nodded somberly, finished the cookie, and gathered a handful to take upstairs to Amy. If Michelle knew she had just been lied to, she didn't say so.

*

Becky's caseworker averted her eyes and fiddled with the thick file on her desk. "So, you see, Ms. Rosales, I really do have to apologize. But I'm sure you understand my position." She finally looked up, meeting Dell's eyes. "I have to take care of the children first and foremost. Would you want anything less for Becky?"

"Of course not," Dell said. Beside her, Judge Patricia Ovalle-Martinez straightened her shoulders.

"Still, you made some serious accusations—or at least raised some serious questions about Ms. Rosales," she said severely, in the courtroom voice that was really so unlike her. "Perhaps you should have checked those rumors and their sources more carefully before you forced Ms. Rosales to go through all this."

The woman sniffed and dabbed at her nose with a tissue. "Look, Judge, I do the best I could. I was told the child might be in danger—"

"Ms. Rios, you know I routinely send young ladies there to work out their problems, don't you? Would you expect me to do that if I were not absolutely sure of their safety?"

"No." The woman sniffed again. "This sinus is killing me," she muttered plaintively. "Anyway, Ms. Rosales," she said appeasingly, "our investigation has convinced us Becky should remain with you."

Dell leaned across the desk, lacing her fingers together. "But for how long?" she asked insistently. "I'm not sure I can keep her now and then lose her later." She drew back. "I ask myself," she went on quietly, "if I'm more concerned with helping Becky or helping myself. If it hurts me this way—what is this doing to Becky's real mother?"

The caseworker and judge exchanged glances.

"I think you should tell Dell the whole story," Patricia said after a moment, darting a meaningful glance at her friend before turning implacably back to face the other woman. "The *whole* story," she repeated firmly.

Dell arched an eyebrow at the judge, who merely settled back in her chair, crossing her arms and waiting.

"What should I know, then?" she asked the caseworker, who discarded her well-used tissue and plucked another from the box with its ornate floral covering.

"Well . . . we found out Becky's mother was given a sizeable sum of money to tell us she wanted her back." The caseworker paused, risking a glance at Patricia, then decided to continue. "The money was from a small but well-known drug dealer. What his interest was, we're not sure, but we know he paid for her to come to us. And we also know," the woman went on, her tone becoming contemptuous, "that she used that money for drugs. Drugs! And she expected us to consider her a fit mother? Really."

Dell shook her head. Although she couldn't deny the relief she felt—she wasn't losing Becky, at least not now—it was colored with sadness. How could anyone trade a child's love for the momentary pleasure of drugs? She just couldn't conceive of the desperation the woman must face, or the sadness she would know if she ever realized what she had lost.

"There's more," the caseworker said. "We've already spoken to your attorney and to the judge. We're planning on filing a motion to terminate the woman's parental rights. We don't believe the child can ever be safely returned to her mother. She is literally a puppet of drug dealers and drug users, not to mention being an addict herself. Given your financial situation and your reputation—the help you've provided to Becky already—it's very likely you can adopt her."

Dell closed her eyes, breathing a silent prayer of thanks. Then she looked back at the caseworker. "So what do I do now?" she asked.

"Well, really, not much. Your attorney can take care of the paperwork." She smiled, a tired smile, but sincere. "I truly am sorry I doubted you, Ms. Rosales. I see a lot in my line of work, but I should have checked things out more carefully, as the judge has said."

"I know you were thinking of Becky," Dell said, adding honestly, "I couldn't do what you do. Sometimes just providing some shelter and attention to teenagers takes more than I think I have in me. I can't imagine having to decide . . . whether or not a child should be taken from its mother." She held out a hand, and the caseworker stood and shook it briefly. "So—everything's done? Becky stays?" Dell repeated again.

"Yes," the caseworker agreed. "Becky stays."

Dell thanked her, and Patricia softened enough to shake the woman's hand and give her a slight smile. "Take care," she told the woman pleasantly as she accompanied Dell to the door.

"What was that all about?" Dell asked as they stepped into the hall. "Why were you picking on the poor woman? If anyone should have been angry, I should have. You positively intimidated her just for doing her job."

"No," Patricia said with conviction. "Believing rumors without checking them out—damaging rumors like the ones someone spoon-fed her—that's *not* her job. Her job is protecting children from real harm, not harming children's protectors."

"You should be a politician," Dell teased, and they laughed.

"I may run for the Senate someday." The judge grinned. They walked together out of the building and into the morning sun.

"You'd never know it rained for most of a week, would you?" she groused. "Same old, same old."

Dell shrugged. "I don't mind the heat," she said absently.

"You don't sound like a woman who just got what she wanted," Patricia said bluntly, eyeing her shrewdly, and Dell shrugged.

"I can't celebrate. I keep thinking what a devastating loss it is to give up someone you love forever."

"Dell, don't hold yourself responsible for another woman's stupidity," Patricia warned. "There are women who can't—or who shouldn't be mothers. We both know that."

"Yes," Dell agreed, thinking of her own mother rather than Becky's. She managed a slight smile. "Don't worry about me, 'Tricia. And I'm delighted—happier than I've ever been, really. Becky means the world to me. I just wish . . . " She shrugged. "Everything will be fine."

"Yeah." They had reached the parking lot, and Patricia fished keys out of her jacket pocket and deactivated the alarm. "Aren't you at all curious about how the caseworker got her information?" she asked, pulling the door open but not climbing in.

"I hadn't been," Dell retorted. "I assume there are ways. I'm an interpreter and a negotiator, not a detective." She smiled. "But since you want me to ask—what strings did you pull, *amiguita*?"

"Me?" The judge's dark eyebrows rose in mock consternation. "Dear friend or not, I did nothing. No, the information was well-documented and delivered just in time."

Curiosity stirred. "So?" she prodded, and Patricia gave a half shrug and lowered herself into the car. "An investigator—federal, I guess. Some guy named Brock Hampton." The judge's lips twitched. "But the word is, it wasn't his idea to provide the caseworker with the goods on Becky's mother." She paused for dramatic effect. "If you want to thank Jovani Treviño," she said, "his mother's address is in the phonebook. Aurora Treviño, on Davis Street." She waved a hand and pulled the door shut.

Dell just stared after the car until it had merged with the late-morning traffic on the busy street. Eventually, she made herself walk over to her own vehicle, unlock the door, and climb in.

*

The house on Davis was like many of Laredo's older homes—a small wooden structure set back from the street behind a chain-link fence. Roses bloomed in spite of the recent bad weather, and bright yellow trumpet vines climbed over the fence on one side.

Dell glanced around. There were no signs advising her of a vicious dog, and Jovani's pickup wasn't anywhere to be seen. She hesitated, trying to decide whether to rattle the gate, call out a greeting, or go up the short walk and just knock on the door.

"*Pase, pase,*" a voice called suddenly in Spanish, inviting her in, and so she lifted the latch and went in.

An elderly woman in a faded housedress opened the door, urging her into the room with a gnarled hand. Many of Laredo's long-time residents seemed unaware of the city's rapid growth and the danger of inviting a stranger into their homes so freely, Dell thought regretfully. How sad that this trusting woman could unwittingly endanger herself.

"Hello, Mrs. Treviño," she introduced herself, "I'm Dell Rosales."

"Yes, yes," the woman replied, beaming. "I know. You're Jovi's friend."

Dell managed not to show her surprise, but the woman's reaction caught her off guard. Jovi had come back to Laredo—maybe—to be with his mother. So she supposed it was logical that he had visited her frequently, even though she had seldom noticed his absence at the ranch. Yet why—how—had he discussed her with his mother?

The woman ushered her insistently to what Dell guessed was

the place of honor on the comfortably worn sofa, smiling and talking contentedly, her voice still holding a huskiness that spoke of congestion and illness.

"Jovi's not here. But he won't be long. I'll just bring you something to eat. I have some *sopa*—ah, *y un guisado de pollo*."

Dell protested feebly—she really didn't want lunch, although the smell of chicken simmering in a spicy sauce was appetizing. Still, she knew feeding guests was part of the culture she and Mrs. Treviño shared, and she couldn't bring herself to actually refuse the woman's hospitality.

Within moments she had been moved again, seated at the small dining table with a plate full of food in front of her.

"You're way too thin," Jovi's mother clucked, placing a basket of steaming tortillas near her and then setting a glass of freshly made lemonade on the table. "Jovi never noticed, of course. He thinks you're perfect." She brought a small dish to the table. "I usually don't eat this early," she confided. "But I'll keep you company. Go ahead, eat! *¡Con confianza!*"

Dell obediently took a spoonful of food, but she wasn't sure how much at home she felt. Any minute she expected to hear the sound of Jovi's truck outside and to hear him come through the door. *Well*, she scolded herself, *you came here to talk to him*. To thank him. Still, she was nervous. Surprisingly so—confrontation didn't bother her much these days.

She blew on a spoonful of food too hot to eat and glanced at the wall. Pictures of Jovi as a baby, as a laughing toddler, punctuated the worn paneling. His graduation picture, pictures of him in his uniform—pictures of a child growing up loved.

Always loved. She forced herself to swallow the *guisado* and set her spoon aside.

"I was sorry when I heard Jovani wasn't working for you anymore," Mrs. Treviño was saying, her expressive face drawing itself into a perplexed frown. "But he said—I don't know.

Something about you not really needing him." The thin shoulders shrugged. "*La economia*—"

Dell considered the woman thoughtfully. Did she know what Jovi was? Who he was? Even if she did, he was probably still just her son. Would the older woman understand why what he had done had been so wrong? How hurtful his deceit had been? She herself didn't know yet if his suspicions had been allayed. Jovani's apparent role in proving Becky's mother unfit erased Dell's doubts, at least as far as his work with law agencies went. Obviously, he had access to information that one of Lionel De Cordova's watchdogs wouldn't. But even though he hadn't been her grandfather's pawn, he clearly wasn't someone she could trust. Someone she should love.

Jovi's mother paused, peering across the table, her forehead pinched with worry and her eyes full of questions. Dell swallowed another spoonful of food. What could she possibly say? She wasn't entirely sure she knew what she'd come here to say to Jovi. After a moment, she put her spoon down.

"I really should go," she said. "I'll come by another time, or call."

"No! Don't go!" Mrs. Treviño stood up and reached for the dishes. "He'll be here any minute. I'd hate you not to see him." She cocked her head, listening, and then smiled broadly. "See? I hear his truck coming now."

Dell didn't hear anything, but she still tagged after the woman into the living room. Sure enough, Jovi's tall frame was arriving on the porch just as his mother pulled the door open.

"*Hola, mamá*," he said, bending to kiss her. "Hello," he said to Dell, coolly and in English.

Dell nodded. "Hi." Then she just stood and returned his stare, unable to say any of the million things she had come to say.

"Why don't you two sit down?" Jovani's mother suggested, beaming. She obviously was delighted to see them together under any circumstances. "I can bring you some tea, or *limonada*—"

"No, thanks," Jovi said immediately. He reached out to caress his mother's cheek. "You should be resting. And I owe Dell dinner."

He held up a hand, smiling faintly, when both women started to protest.

"Yes, I know you have undoubtedly fed Dell. And the food smells delicious. But I have to meet a friend for some business, and I think Dell would like to go." He patted the pocket of the shirt he was wearing. "But I need to pick up my address book . . . "

"Let me get it," Mrs. Treviño said immediately, and bustled out of the room, leaving them alone.

"We can't talk here," Jovi said quietly. "She doesn't know . . . anything. I don't want her to."

Dell shrugged imperceptibly. "Fine. Where? I'll meet you."

"No. We'll go together. I'll bring you back for your car. You're safe with me, Dell. And my mother wouldn't understand otherwise." His tone softened. "She worries too much about me already. Please."

Biting back a sigh, Dell nodded. "All right."

Jovi's mother reappeared, her face knitted in a frown. "I couldn't find it," she told him breathlessly.

"You know, I bet I left it in the truck. I'm sorry."

She clucked and shook her head at him. "You're hopeless," she scolded, but her scowl was pretend, and their love for each other was obvious. For a tiny second, Dell thought of her own mother—cold, uncaring Erika De Cordova. This was what a mother should be, she thought with a faint twinge of envy. She smiled at the older woman.

"Thank you, Mrs. Treviño. It was a pleasure to meet you." She offered her hand, but the older woman hugged her warmly.

"You come again," she offered, sincerely, "to see me if you don't want to see this *chiflado*."

"You're too hard on me," Jovi complained. "I'm not the least bit spoiled!" Smiling at his mother a final time, he opened the door for Dell.

"We won't be too long," he assured her. "Lock the door after us—you can't be too careful."

They walked the short distance to the drive, and Jovi opened the gate and then the door of his truck for her. She cast a regretful glance at her own vehicle. No way to escape him this way. Annoyed, she frowned as he settled in the seat beside her.

"I would have preferred to drive myself," she noted curtly. "Just where are we going?"

"Do you like water?"

She arched an eyebrow. "Water? To drink?"

He shook his head impatiently, pulling out. "No. Mom probably stuffed you. Let's drive out to the lake." He didn't talk again as they drove, and she was quiet too, watching the busy commercial buildings on Saunders flash by as they headed for the popular recreational site. He concentrated on the traffic, swerving to avoid frequent potholes and slowing when lines of orange barrels signaled yet another highway project.

"Your mother seems very loving," she ventured finally, unable to bear the silence separating them.

"Hmmm." His noncommittal response was followed by a muttered expletive as a car pulled out in front of them, forcing him to brake hard and swerve to avoid a collision.

"Sometimes I forget I'm back in Laredo," he gritted, and she smiled.

"You sound like someone's who been away for a while," she noted. "I remember having to readjust when I came back."

Although neither spoke again, the silence wasn't as heavy or strained as it had been, and Dell did a quick review of the things she wanted to say. Thank you, first and foremost. Why? And finally, painfully, goodbye. She licked her lips and breathed deeply. *Inalcanzable*, she told herself sternly. Unreachable. Untouchable.

Beyond pain. Being a Rosales had taught her how to suffer silently, she thought grimly, if nothing else. And perhaps it was the De Cordova coldness that kept her spine so straight and unbending, but it was the Rosales ability to love that she had to deny now.

Jovi followed the road that skirted the lake until he came to an isolated spot with a picnic table huddled under a protective awning. Nearby, flat, dark rocks jutted out into the man-made lake, providing a natural perch for fishers or sunbathers. He turned off the truck, stretching, then climbed out. Dell unbuckled her seatbelt and opened the door before he could come around and do it. She didn't need to step down into a virtual embrace from Jovani Treviño. Aimlessly, she walked down the graveled slope toward the water. He followed her, his boots crunching on the small rocks.

She stopped at the water's edge. Far off, someone in a small boat braved the midday heat to fish. A Jet Ski churned past, turning noisy circles and darting back and forth from the shore where a group of young people were partying, oblivious to Jovi and her. Girding herself, she finally turned, looking up at Jovani.

"You probably know I want to thank you," she said quietly. "For Becky. I don't know how I would manage without her." At the thought of how barren her life could have been without the child, a single tear traced down her cheek.

He shrugged. "I did what I thought was best for Becky," he answered. "She needs you."

"Sometimes I wonder if it's right—applying for adoption." Dell dug a sandaled toe into the moist, sandy soil at the water's edge, indifferent to the dark stain that colored her hose as a result. "Taking a child away from her mother—forever."

Jovi shook his head. "If you'd seen children in the circumstances I have, you wouldn't wonder at all. Becky's mother will be lucky if she does go back to prison. Her situation is . . . " He stopped, grasping for words. "Hopeless," he finished finally. "Believe me, the woman had chances, and she blew them all." He hesitated.

"You must know as well as anyone that not everyone can be a mother. Not everyone should have that right."

"I suppose so. And I do love Becky. I didn't want to give her up. So again—thank you." She fell silent for a moment, marshalling her thoughts. Remembering the carefully planned list of questions, of scathing accusations. Somehow, the need to say them had paled in his presence. In the knowledge Becky likely would be hers forever. Because of this man. Still, he had deceived her. Lied to her.

She moistened her lips. "But I have to ask myself . . . were you sure about me? Convinced I'm not involved in drugs?"

He sighed and looked out across the lake before facing her. "Yes. I'm not sure I ever really suspected you were, and that worried me. Trusting a suspect can be deadly, Dell. I didn't want to overlook something obvious because of how I felt about you." He stopped again, glancing around. "Let's walk over to the rocks," he suggested, and after a moment she nodded without answering.

They climbed up onto the rocks. He turned once, reaching out a hand to steady her when one of her sandals slipped on the smooth, weathered surface. The brief touch of his fingers on her wrist was electric. Briefly, their gazes locked. Then he released her and turned back toward the lake. "Making myself doubt you was one of the hardest things I've ever done," he said eventually.

"I don't understand why you had to," Dell argued, her voice tinged with hurt. "Where did this come from? I don't understand any of it. Why would anyone have thought . . . " She shook her head. "There was no reason to doubt me," she said again.

"Maybe not." He turned finally, looking down into her face. "I hate hurting you, Dell. But the investigation grew out of suspicions over your father." He raked a hand through his hair. "I agreed to help the agency—to see what I could find out about you—because I was coming to Laredo anyway. Because I've seen what drugs are doing to people in every part of this country. It sickens me." His fingers tilted her chin up gently. "But I never would have done this, never would have agreed to be part of the operation if I'd known you—before it was too late." He was silent a moment, then sighed. "Before I couldn't say no, because men I'd worked with were putting their lives on the line."

"Lives on the line—" She jerked away from him as if his fingers burned.

He kicked idly at the rock under them. "They always do, Dell. You might not see it, but you hear the news. There are bastards cutting heads off over drug money, for God's sake. I couldn't walk out once I started."

"I still don't understand any of this! My father died years ago. I made a good living in the lobbying business, in imports. Even after taking some time off, I stepped back in without any problem at all. I'm perfectly capable of making money honestly and on my own. So why the suspicion? This just doesn't make sense, Jovi." She stared up at him, agitated. "How did an investigation even begin?"

He shrugged. "I really don't know. I've been away from the field for years. I got tired of the chase, I guess. The ugliness. Death, especially of young people with no chance to live. When I was asked to initiate contact with you, I apparently wasn't filled in very completely. I didn't know about the girls, and Becky." He stopped, and drew a deep, steadying breath. "The best I can guess is that someone was told to look at you. But I don't know who or why."

"But my father?" she prodded, her voice little more than a whisper. "I don't believe—"

"Dell, you can't be that naïve." Jovi's words stung, but his tone was gentle, his expression concerned. "How do you think a man who offended Lionel De Cordova came up with over a quarter million dollars? You can't believe he was that shrewd a businessman."

Dell didn't answer for a long time. She turned away, letting the slight breeze drifting in from the lake slap at her, squeezing her eyes shut to block out the harsh sun glare.

"I thought maybe it was a payoff," she admitted finally, her voice barely audible. "But not for drugs. See, they never said as much, but I think Erika—my mother—was already pregnant when they married. My father was very devout—he'd never have let her do anything. And my grandfather wouldn't have wanted my mother to have an abortion—not if people would find out about it, anyway. I doubt he'd care about a baby's life otherwise. But my dad would have. He probably insisted they get married and threatened a scandal otherwise. I'm sure my grandfather never wanted my mother to keep me. I'm surprised she waited as long as she did to divorce my father. But I guess I always told myself the money was for me. Sort of a way to make it up to my father and me for ruining his life." Tears trickled down her cheeks, cooler than the searing summer air. "You're right. It sounds pretty naïve," she added, wiping the wetness away angrily. "But I just never let myself see that until now."

"I'm sorry, Dell. Like I said, this was never about hurting you. If it helps, both Hampton and I made it clear there's no reason to continue the investigation. Not at this end, at any rate. Not of you." He rubbed a hand across his face then stroked his mustache into place. "They've got some pretty strong evidence pointing to some of your cousins in Monterrey, though." He held up a hand, silencing her. "I know. You probably don't even know them. But they're going after De Cordova, Dell." He paused, searching for an explanation. "Whether or not he's actively involved, family members definitely are. And the obvious conclusion is that he at least knows, and he's probably done some money laundering. At the very least." He frowned. "Your grandfather's something else, though. He's very rich and very smart. I'm not sure Hampton and the others can nail him. But they're trying."

"Should I pretend I care?" she asked. "I don't care, and I haven't for years. I mean that."

"You have no reason to," he agreed reasonably. "But I have to admit I'm not too happy. About the picture you found in his desk."

The photo. Pain slashed through her again as she remembered finding it. Recognizing his betrayal, although she had misunderstood what it meant.

"I wonder why he had it, and how he got it," she mused, and Jovi grimaced.

"My best guess is Danny. And I hope his interest in me—his concern about me—was whether or not you and I were sleeping together. He must have known I was DEA at one time—traffickers find out those things. But I do hope his sources know I left them. And have no reason to suspect me now. That would be bad."

Fear twisted in her stomach. "You don't really think anything could happen to you?"

He gave a half shrug, but his expression was grim. "I'd be happier if he hadn't had a photo of me in his desk. We'll just leave it at that." He paused. "I think it was Danny that night at the pool, too," he admitted. "Nothing else makes sense. De Cordova probably had Danny watching you since he started working for your father, and then keeping really close tabs on what you and I were doing."

Dell shook her head. "This is a nightmare," she whispered. "*Una pesadilla*." She shivered in spite of the oppressive heat. "You're telling me that I—we—were spied on. And that I've been cleared from suspicions I didn't know had been raised, but you're saying it's still not over? At least not for you?"

He reached out a bronzed hand and cupped her cheek. His fingers were warm and strong, his touch reassuring.

"No. That's not what I'm trying to say at all. It's over, Dell. All of it."

"But the photo—"

"Even if he had it for the worst possible reasons, he really isn't in a position to call attention to himself. Danny's facing jail time, but he doesn't seem to know much, so I doubt he could tell De Cordova much. I'm not involved in the investigation now, even if he suspects I was. So he has no reason to do anything to me. Don't worry."

For a few precious seconds, she closed her eyes and pressed her cheek into the warmth of his hand. Then, reluctantly, she straightened. Stiffened. Drew back, reinstating the distance between them.

"Jovi . . . When you left the ranch, you still thought—"

"That you were an incredibly beautiful, giving woman," he said without hesitation. His eyes met her levelly. "And I knew you couldn't be involved with the De Cordova operations. In my heart, I knew that." He paused before adding softly, "But the part of me that used to be a cop wanted proof." Real regret darkened his eyes. "You don't know how sorry I am I didn't trust my heart."

"People should trust their hearts," Dell said, then thought of Samuel Rosales and his heartbreak. Jeremy and his betrayal. "No," she corrected grimly. "People shouldn't trust their hearts. It hurts too much. Logic is better."

"Is it?" Jovi's voice was almost as soft as hers. "Would your father have considered his life more worthwhile without you? Without Erika De Cordova, for whatever time he had her? More painless, maybe. But I doubt he would have traded what he did have for life without you, Dell. Only a very stupid man would do that." He hesitated. "You trust your heart every day, Dell. With Becky. With the girls. Even with Maribel. Your heart won't let you throw her away. If you can trust your heart with everyone else, why not with me?"

The knot in her throat kept her from speaking, and after a long, silent moment, Jovi sighed and turned away.

"I'll take you back now," he said flatly, starting toward the truck. He had taken three or four steps before Dell could loosen her constricted throat enough to speak.

"Wait!"

He glanced over his shoulder, startled, but stopped. "Yes?"

"You're right. My father wouldn't have given up the illusions he had—the memory he created—of my mother. Not for anything."

He seemed surprised, and turned completely to face her.

What she was saying surprised her, too, actually—but she realized it was what her heart had been saying all along. What she hadn't ever let herself hear.

"But memories aren't enough. Not for me. They're all I've let myself have. Memories of my mother. Of my father. Of a man I thought loved me—all the things I really didn't have." She stopped again abruptly, her throat burning and her chest tight.

"And?" he prompted cautiously.

"I don't want you to be just another one of the things I didn't have," she said slowly. "I don't need more hazy memories. Stay. Be what's real in my life."

He closed his eyes, as if in prayer. Or shock. Then he swept her up in his arms, hugging her close, whispering her name. He brushed her hair with his lips, then tilted her chin up, his lips closing over hers, first with tenderness, then with urgency.

She was breathless when he finally stepped back, looking down at her with dancing eyes.

"You probably want to set a good example for the girls," he said seriously, in spite of the laughter in his eyes.

"Of course," Dell agreed, smiling up at him. "So . . . just what are you getting at, anyway?"

"Well, we can't really carry on an affair in front of those impressionable teenagers."

"No. We can't." Dell's lips twitched, even though she meant it.

"There's obviously only one solution," he said slowly, and then his grin blossomed again. "Do you think I should ask Lionel De Cordova for your hand?"

Dell laughed and wrapped her arms around him. "Somehow I don't think he'd approve. Maybe I should just talk to your mom."

EPILOGUE

The lights faded into shadows around the edges of the yard, and the honeysuckle lingered on the slight, warm breeze. Dell yawned and leaned back more comfortably against Jovi, the porch swing creaking beneath them.

"Tired?"

"How did so many people fit into this yard?" she asked, and he chuckled.

"At times, it was a tight fit. But a beautiful reception, nonetheless."

"Yes. And having Hal and Carmela share it—they should have married so long ago. She deserves to be recognized as the woman in his life, even if we had to give them a nudge." Dell smiled and rubbed her cheek lazily against Jovi's shoulder. "Everyone seemed to have fun."

"Becky especially. She's going to love weddings."

Dell smiled wryly. "I just hope she doesn't have one for twenty or thirty years."

"Not thirty," Jovi said immediately, kissing the corner of her mouth. "That would be too late. Think how long before we'd be grandparents."

She laughed. "I sort of feel like a grandmother already, with Selina's little boy visiting so often."

He chuckled and eased her away from him to stand up.

"Everyone's gone," he pointed out, drawing her up and into his arms. "We don't leave for Florida until tomorrow—"

"Stopping to see racing stock on our way to a cruise ship." She nodded. "You're a real romantic, Jovi Treviño." She pressed into the hard contours of his body and kissed his chin.

"But you don't mind?" He kissed the corner of her mouth, and she eased away enough to look up at him.

"I don't mind meeting the Coopers," she agreed. "But, since we're married now and you should confess all your sins, tell me the truth about Griselda. Why you called her "*inalcanzable*"?

He laughed. "Expected that question ages ago," he admitted. "I never called her that, Dell. She and I worked together at DEA." He hugged her close, brushed a kiss against her hair before continuing. "When you came in and saw me with the paper, I had to come up with something." He paused, and humor laced his voice. "Can I think on my feet or what?"

"I think I'll like the Coopers," Dell murmured against his cheek. "Even Griselda." She cupped his cheek and urged him close for another, lingering kiss that left them both breathless.

"And they call you *incalcanzable* . . . " His lips touched hers again, but after a moment he drew back. "You don't know how far away I thought you were," he said. "How unreachable. Unattainable."

She eased out of his grip, then held her hand out to him. "Let's go in," she suggested huskily. "I've never been that far away," she added as he wrapped an arm around her shoulder. "No one's beyond love . . . no one really is."

"No," he agreed, and together they made their way into the darkened house, touched by love.

The End

ONE WRITER'S STORY . . .

My first published story appeared on the bulletin board of little Mt. Carmel Elementary School in Douglasville, GA when I was six. My first sale came later that year, when the short-lived children's magazine *Kids* bought a terrible poem about dolphins for an amazing $1.50.

A childhood filled with haunted pecan orchards, 4-H meetings, six siblings and a roadside amusement park would be useful for most any writer, but most of my stories and poetry so far deal with Texas, the state I once loved to hate. The Hill Country and the Rio Grande offer their own charms and stories, including *Unattainable*, my first romance for Crimson Romance.

Married with four adult children and nine (9!) precocious grandchildren, I have been a south Texas educator for 20 years, mostly in first grade, and will undoubtedly continue trying to impress six year olds with the power of words for years to come.

I would love to hear from you, either at *www.facebook.com/ LeslieP.Garcia* or by e-mail at lesliegarcia2000-author@yahoo .com.

For poetry and short fiction, please visit me at AuthorsDen, *http://www.authorsden.com/visit/author.asp?authorid=4186*.

Thanks for the opportunity to share my writing with you!

A SNEAK PEEK FROM CRIMSON ROMANCE

From In Love and War by Tara Mills
http://www.crimsonromance.com/upcoming-releases-romance-ebook/ in-love-and-war/

CHAPTER 1

Summer, 2006

Ariela Perrine's face fell and she groaned when she saw the dark blue, checked necktie hanging from the doorknob. Laying her ear against the door, she could hear the unmistakable sounds of an action movie on the television. Her eyes dropped to the necktie once more, and she bit her lip and wondered what to do.

Screw it; she was home now. They could move it into Jean's bedroom.

She knocked on the door three times—hard, so they'd hear her over the movie.

"I'm home, so zip up," she yelled, tapping her foot impatiently.

"Hang on!" Jean shot back.

You'd think they were still in college.

"Are you decent yet?" Ariela finally called again.

"All clear."

Ariela dropped the looped necktie over her head, accessorizing her smirk, and went in. Ron and Jean were still making wardrobe adjustments when she flopped into the easy chair with a dejected sigh.

Jean frowned. "Why are you home this early? I thought you were going dancing? What? You didn't like Patrick, either?"

Jean tucked her legs beneath her and settled against Ron. *He pulled her close* and kissed her on the temple.

Ariela sent her roommate a long look. "Where would I even start?" She turned to the television. "So, what are you watching anyway?"

Ron looked up. "Split Infinity,"

Ariela leaned back and *sta*red at the screen, but having missed the beginning of the movie, she couldn't catch up. "Is there anything to eat?"

Jean stared at her. "You just came from dinner."

"Like I could eat looking at that. The man never stopped talking, not even when the food came. I swear it was like watching a front-load washing machine, except with a washer, there's usually no danger you're going to get hit by something flying out of it."

Jean's face contorted in disgust. "You're kidding?"

"I wish. It was disgusting."

"So, how much did you drink?" Jean asked perceptively.

"Two glasses of wine, then I pretended I was coming down with something and that's why I didn't have any appetite. Got me out of a kiss—thank god. That tongue of his wasn't getting anywhere near me."

"There's pizza on the counter." Ron broke in with an amused smile.

Ariela popped up to go investigate. "Thanks. Anything I have to pull off of it?"

"'Shrooms," said Jean.

"You guys," she whined.

"Hey, we didn't order pineapple because you bitched so much last time," said Jean.

"I did, didn't I?" Ariela admitted.

Ron stood and stretched, letting out a low rumble with his extension. "Well, I suppose I better clear out. I have an early morning."

Ariela glanced over the open pizza box and through the kitchen doorway in time to catch Jean's pout. She smiled and tore a slice of pizza free, peeling back the cheese so she could pick off the mushrooms.

"See you later, Ron," Ariela called as the couple kissed goodnight at the door.

There was a pause before he answered back. "Be good, Ariela."

Ariela rolled her eyes. She was always good. She was boring and bored by being so good. She wanted to be bad, to be a rabble-rouser, to get into a little trouble. Too bad it didn't come naturally. She needed someone to corrupt her. Yeah, a bad influence would be good about now.

Jean wandered into the kitchen and took a glass down from the cabinet. Going into the fridge, she held up the carton. "Milk?"

"I think I'll have juice."

"I don't see any," Jean said, studying the shelves.

"Fine. I'll take milk too."

She was off to a good, rebellious start. Well, at least she was getting her calcium. Tomorrow, she'd better get to the store and pick up more of her cranberry blends.

Jean set Ariela's glass down and joined her at the table. Reaching into the box, she helped herself, wiggling her eyebrows at Ariela as she bit the mushroom on the very tip clean off.

Ariela shuddered. "Hey, I'm eating here."

"So am I. You know, I think I like cold pizza best." Jean dabbed her mouth with a napkin.

"I get into moods."

Jean leaned back in her chair and considered her roommate thoughtfully.

Wary, Ariela lowered her second slice of pizza, and her eyebrows arched up. "What?"

"Nothing."

"No no no no. Tell me."

"It's just that I figured Patrick was going to be a bust. He's just another dud in a pattern of duds for you."

"What's that supposed to mean?"

"You go out with losers, knowing they're losers and they're going to be disappointing. It's like you're setting yourself up on purpose."

Ariela snorted. "Don't be ridiculous."

"I'm just saying. You know what you want, and you refuse to go there." Jean took another bite of pizza.

"I go out with the guys who ask me."

"You turn down any guy who might be interesting."

"I haven't met any of those."

"You don't want to." Jean tossed her crust onto the table in front of her and wiped her hands. "I think you're afraid to fall in love."

"Is that right?"

"I've known you a long time and I know you better than you think. You're afraid to end up like your mom."

"I don't think this is how a psych session is supposed to work. I believe I'm supposed to be the one talking and you're supposed to take notes and nod occasionally and say things like 'hmm,' and 'I see. Very interesting.'"

"I've just made observations over the years, that's all, and you have to admit, you don't go deep with men. You keep them shallow, where they can't hurt you."

Ariela laughed. "Okay then, point me in the right direction, because I'm obviously mucking things up on my own."

"Be serious." There was an understanding look in Jean's eyes. "You can't run away forever."

*

Daylight was fading fast when Dylan Bond sat down at his computer and shot the smuggled USB driver home. As he slowly peeled back layer upon layer of evidence, the room fell dark around him. The only illumination left came from the computer screen. The unnatural glow sharpened and defined his features, the planes of his face, the clean line of his nose. Dylan's eyes, lost in shadow, flashed black, all pupil, the lapis blue of his irises completely obscured by the lack of light.

Dylan glanced at the sleeping Golden Retriever sprawled next to him. He reached out with his stockinged foot and gave the animal's stomach an affectionate rub.

"You wouldn't believe what I'm reading. This scum was already setting things up three years ago."

The dog's eyes flickered and closed. His tail flopped on the floor a couple of times as his satisfied groan rose and fell with the belly rub.

It was well over two hours since Dylan had given any thought to his aching back. All sense of time and discomfort were lost in a flurry of mental activity. He was in his zone, a maestro of political commentary, as his words flowed across the screen.

"—*and unfortunately for the American people, Senator Norton has never acted on any legislation before his financial terms have been worked out first. The Carpenter Bill is a prime example. It makes this jaded journalist pine for the days when money was passed discreetly under the table instead of brazenly and unapologetically in the open.*"

He lifted his hands from the keys dramatically, kicking back in his chair with an exhilarated smile.

"Take that you bastard—hope it stings like a bitch!"

Dylan dated his column and sent it in. Reaching for his long-neglected beer, he took a swig. His face contorted into a wicked grimace.

"Warm and flat." He shuddered and rolled back his chair, grunting stiffly to his feet. Only now did he notice the daylight streaming in the windows. "Jesus. What time is it?" He scrubbed at his tired eyes with the heels of his hands.

Max sat up and started scratching himself, his attention on his master. When Dylan grabbed the last two cheese puffs on the desk, the dog's tail pounded the floor. Dylan popped one into his mouth then grinned at the dog and tossed the second to him. Max snatched it right out of the air and swallowed it whole.

"You could at least *pretend* to taste it for my sake," Dylan said dryly.

The Golden Retriever hopped up and followed his master into the kitchen, parking himself directly behind him when he threw open the refrigerator door.

Dylan pulled out a container of forgotten lunch meat and opened the lid. Taking a cautious sniff, he jerked his head back and sent the bologna sailing across the room. It landed in the trash with a satisfying *whump*. Max gave the garbage an interested look.

"Don't even think about it," Dylan warned. *Shit, there was nothing to eat.*

He slammed the refrigerator door and straightened up, finally attuned to the stiffness he'd managed to ignore while working. Distractedly rubbing his lower back, he looked at the dog.

"I've gotta get something to eat. How does a breakfast sandwich sound to you?"

Max's tail pounded the floor in double-time.

Dylan grinned and patted his leg. "Yeah, like you know what I said."

Max leaned against Dylan's thigh while he rubbed the dog's ears.

"Come on boy." He grabbed the leash off the counter and snapped off the kitchen light.

*

Two blocks away, Jean shuffled into the kitchen and found Ariela curled over a mug of coffee, a magazine open on the table in front of her.

When Jean saw the headline, *Are you getting enough Niacin?* she gasped in alarm. "Oh my god. Put that away!"

"What? I'm not doing anything." Ariela frowned and returned to her article.

Jean snorted. "Yet." She went to get herself a bowl of cereal.

Not a minute later, Ariela glanced up. "We should really have green tea on hand."

"You don't like tea."

"I could learn. I should."

Jean groaned. "Do me a favor, stick to the makeover tips and stop reading those health updates. I don't need you imagining you've got a wheat allergy next, and I'm through, I mean it, I'm through with all those stupid fad diets."

"You make it sound like I'm a hypochondriac or something."

Jean slowly turned and gave her roommate a significant look.

Ariela rolled her eyes. "Cut that out."

"So, what time is Mrs. Corley coming in?" Jean pulled out a chair and sat down.

"Nine."

"Are you going down right away?"

"I'm going to run to the market first and pick up something for later."

"I have to bring some books over to Banks Brothers at eight."

"I'll be right back. Just go do what you have to do. I've got it covered."

"Good."

*

As Ariela dressed for work, she thought about her appointment this morning. Though it was their policy to fawn over their clients, Mrs. Corley was a woman who appreciated a bit more fuss than normal. Unfortunately, that didn't mean she made it any easier on them. Her habitual indecision was trying, but the money on the line made it worth the trouble.

Their last appointment was particularly frustrating. The knotty-pine cabinets Mrs. Corley had chosen were suddenly out. Now she wanted a radical new look for her kitchen, something sleek and modern. Maybe in oak? Ariela had crossed off the tile countertops without blinking and listened patiently while the client asked about granite, but not necessarily granite, instead. Could she do that?

"That's no problem," Ariela assured her, then brought out examples for Mrs. Corley to look over.

Then they moved on to wallpaper samples. That alone took well over an hour, even with Ariela repeatedly steering the woman in the right direction again and again.

If Mrs. Corley didn't commit to this kitchen plan today, there was no telling what Ariela would do. She could almost picture herself escorting the impossible woman out and giving her a boot in the ass as she waved her off. Ariela sighed. No way could she ever do anything of the sort. Still, it was an enjoyable fantasy. Hours of pleasure without the blowback and guilt.

Being Friday, Ariela would be on her own for lunch again. Jean had a standing date with Ron. Her roommate and business partner was already gone when Ariela slipped out the front door, locking it behind her. Heading down the front steps, she turned left at the sidewalk.

Gorgeous, the day was simply gorgeous: warm sunshine, clear, deep blue sky, and the lazy hum of bumblebees on the old-fashioned roses growing along the neighbor's fence. Ariela drew the fragrance in and sighed at the unexpected subtle finish of freshly mowed grass that came with it. It was a perfect day to play hooky, or maybe have a picnic.

Truth be told, Ariela didn't mind the Friday routine. She had an hour, one whole hour, all to herself, and she liked to stroll over to the little market at the end of the block. They usually had something good in their deli case, and a nice selection of sparkling juices and waters to go with it.

*

Pushing his way out the doors of the Spiffy Mart, Dylan

hastily chewed the last bite of his breakfast sandwich. There were two newspapers caught tight under his left arm and a second unwrapped sandwich in his right hand. Max was exactly where he'd left him, tied to the bike rack.

"Good boy."

Dylan tore the sandwich into thirds and fed it to the dog. He had to tug the animal back to untie the knot and free him. The instant Max felt the slack in the leash he took off, nearly jerking Dylan's arm out of its socket. The poor man struggled frantically to keep his newspapers from raining down on the sidewalk one section at a time.

"Max, wait! I said, wait, damn it."

If he lost anything, Max was going to pay. A newspaper was a treasure, and though Dylan could get all the information he needed off the internet, there was something intrinsically satisfying about holding a paper, having to wash the inky residue off of your fingers when you were done reading, that could never be replaced by a screen. Dylan had a habit of making notes in the margins, too. Plus, there were the daily crosswords. He'd missed those the most while he was gone.

Dylan hauled the dog back at the corner to keep him from darting into traffic. Giving up the fight for the moment, Max waited for the light, his tail happily fanning the air. When the light changed, Dylan eased up on the leash and the dog took the lead, this time striding as regally as a show dog. His owner chuckled. Right. Anyone who saw them might be fooled but he knew better. Max was a disaster waiting to happen.

He looked up from the dog as they crossed the intersection, the smile still lingering on his lips, and was just in time to see a bike messenger shoot out of a dental-office parking lot and barrel right into a woman on the sidewalk. The large hedge growing next to the lot must have blocked her from view.

The impact threw the woman backward, and Dylan winced

when he heard her head hit the concrete over the sound of the traffic. He broke into a run and reached the scene as the stunned bicyclist fought his way back to his feet. The man stared bug-eyed at the woman lying in front of his tire.

Max, always the friendliest of dogs, chose that inopportune moment to leap on the man, nearly knocking him over again. Dylan dragged Max back by his leash.

The messenger turned his horrified eyes on Dylan. "I didn't see her. I swear. She was just there." They both looked at her now. "Do you think she's okay?" the messenger asked anxiously.

The woman raised her head, a confused look on her face, and mumbled something.

Dylan dropped to one knee beside her. "Are you all right?"

Her hand went to her forehead. "I think so." She squinted to look up at him, but the sun caught her directly in the eyes. She grimaced and shut them again, turning her head away.

Despite his concern, Dylan couldn't help but notice how pretty she looked, how nice she smelled. Her delicate perfume invaded his head with his next breath. A little shaken by it, he rose and gave the bicyclist an uncertain shrug.

"She seems okay, but I'm not a doctor." One thing was certain—she was going to have one whopper of a goose egg on the back of her head.

The courier checked his wristwatch. "Man, I *really* have to fly. I'm on the clock here."

"Do you have a business card?" asked Dylan, since the woman wasn't asking for herself.

"Yes." He pulled one out of a ridiculously tight pocket and handed it over before going into an apology.

Dylan raised his hand, stopping him. "It's cool. I'll stick around."

"That's great. Thanks. I really appreciate it." He didn't waste another second in their company.

"Okay," said Dylan, turning back to the woman sprawled on the sidewalk. A sudden chill sliced right through him. She was too quiet, too still. He went back down on his knee to take a closer look.

"Hey. Still with me?"

No. Or she was doing one hell of a Sleeping Beauty impersonation. That stray thought left him wondering if a kiss *would* actually wake her.

"Better not try it," he said to Max. Dylan patted her soft cheek instead. "Miss, miss? Can you hear me?"

This is when Max decided to get involved. He nudged his way in and licked the poor woman from chin to hairline in long slobbery strokes.

"What the hell?" Dylan wrestled him back, banishing the dog to the nearby grass. If an animal could sulk, Max was certainly doing it now.

"You stay there. I mean it." Dylan pointed sternly at the animal.

"I'm bleeding!" the woman suddenly wailed.

Startled, Dylan whipped around to find her feeling her face with a look of outright panic in her eyes.

"You're not bleeding," he assured her. "That was just my dog. He licked you. Sorry about that." Who could blame the animal? Dylan was having similar thoughts himself.

"I feel wet," she said weakly.

"I know, that's because my dog—"

"What?" Then she started to fade.

"Hey! Can you focus on me?" Dylan took her head in his hands and stroked her cheeks with his thumbs.

Her eyelids fluttered open and she locked on to his deep lapis blues.

"Wow," she whispered before going limp.

In the mood for more Crimson Romance? Check out *Lost Treasure, Captive Princess* by Katherine Bone at CrimsonRomance.com.